Bizarre struggles for ... tated inhabitants of Earth, a planet whose oceans had dried into salt beds and whose densely vegetated plains had become the impregnable entity the Wildland.

The black king, John Tamerlane, black of body and of blood, was the first to claim Earth. But Sum, a powerful aggregate mind, controlled Earth through the Wildland, and sought to keep it as the base of its universe. Only a demon's price would pry the prize from Sum. And only the Blind Worm, a massive, misfit creation of a deranged mind, could satisfy Sum's demands.

Viciously they battled throughout time and the universe—pseudo-man and animal-machine. Their quest was Earth, but they were willing to ravage even that for power.

Turn this book over for
second complete novel

# Brian M. Stableford

## THE BLIND WORM

AN ACE BOOK

Ace Publishing Corporation
1120 Avenue of the Americas
New York, N.Y. 10036

## Part 1 THE QUADRILATERAL

## I

THE LONE MAN walked across the pale, uneven land, his way made difficult by jagged scars of salt-caked rock and crevices silted up with fine grit and salt. Once there had been ocean here. Where he walked had been deep under dark water. He bit his cracked lips and thought about that.

He was short and lightly built, pale of skin, with dark eyes and long muddy blond hair. He wore dull-colored clothes of supple cellulose fibers—unimaginative, as standardized as a uniform. He carried a bow of polished wood strung with plant fiber. Only his short sword was hard, cold metal. In the bag on his back was a bottle containing very little water. He thought about that, as well.

He looked back. In the far distance he could see the horizon, bearing a thin strip of green. That strip was very, very high. It was the edge of the Wildland. *There* was water in plenty—all the water which had once filled the ocean bowls that spanned the world. The Wildland had not yet invaded the dead seas to any extent. It had advanced to the edges of the continental shelves, but not much further. A few sparse cacti, pebble plants, some lichens, had descended into the salt beds, but nothing else. Perhaps all the Wildland lacked was time; perhaps it had some reason of its own for avoiding the desert seas.

Some of the animals which the Wildland had allowed to survive had come out here. Some said that they had followed the cacti and the lichens, others claimed that the Wildland had sent a few small plants to feed the animals. The molochs were here, and the diomes still glided high in the sky for hundreds of miles, as though they did not realize that the sea was no more. There were far fewer diomes now, but they did not die out, and would not. They were creatures of the Wildland despite their heritage, and the Wildland preserved its own.

The man continued his trek. Ahead of him was a deep cleft in the sea bed. It was nearly a mile wide and inestimably long. Its floor swept away, until it was lost in the black shadow cast by the afternoon sun. Down into the cleft he went, wishing for water.

His name was Silver Reander, and he was a wild man—a wanderer, a man who accepted the Wildland and would not live in the cities which the Wildland, almost courteously, left for the human race. Nevertheless, it was for a city man that he had come down into the corpse of the ocean— for John Tamerlane. Tamerlane retained both his curiosity and his ambition, which were strange traits in any man, most of all a city man. He maintained his city because it represented dignity, panache and a certain defiant vanity. The wild men respected Tamerlane, and they told him their tales, and would occasionally wander where he wished them to.

As Reander walked, he felt the salty sand beneath his feet crackling and shifting. Behind him, he left a long, lonely trail in the salt. The sun was soon cut off from view as he walked deeper into the cleft, and it was a good deal cooler. He was glad of that, at least.

The cleft curled to the right ahead of him, which would bring him back into line with the sun and so rob him of his temporary comfort. He took advantage of the excuse to stop and rest. He sat on a rock and closed his eyes. He compared the distance he had come with the quantity of water in his bag and disliked the comparison.

"A mile more," he said aloud. "It's not worth it." He was surprised and a little worried at the hoarseness and faintness of his voice. He coughed, but did not bother to speak again in order to reassure himself.

There was a temptation to sleep, or at least to relax, but he forced himself to rise and go on.

Around the curve he came, and stopped, recoiling a little as the hot light struck him again. Then, as his eyes adjusted,

6

he unwound. He licked his lips, but could not moisten them.

"Perhaps it was worth it," he whispered.

A long way off, but outlined with startling clarity by the clean sunlight, was a city. It was so clear that he could see a moloch in the street, ambling slowly along it. The city was no mirage.

It was old. All the cities of Earth were old now, but there was nothing akin to this. He had seen a number of the decrepit wrecks in the Wildland, smashed by the plants hundreds of years ago and then left, skeletal, to serve as the shells of fearful city men who needed the protection of stone and the ever-nearness of others. The cities, and their inhabitants, were the echoes and relics of civilization, permitted by the Wildland to die in their own time and in their own fashion.

But this city was not one of those. It was incomparably older than that. The Wildland had never been here. The spine of this city had been broken by Ocean, or perhaps it had been long dead even before Ocean came.

Reander had no concept of the age of the Earth, nor of the history and prehistory of his own race. But he knew the age of the city in the Gulf. He could *feel* it at a distance of three or four miles; he could feel its alienation from the world as the last millennia had shaped it. *This* city knew nothing of that. Its origin was to be measured in millions of years, or in billions.

The city in the Gulf was longer dead by far than the cities Reander knew, and yet it had the identity that they lacked. Its bones were as different from their bones as the bones of a man were from those of a plant.

Slowly, with admiration and awe, he let his dark eyes roam over the salted spires, the empty roofs, the rutted streets. He compared the jagged spurs of fallen edifices with the gnarled, scarred walls which still stood high. He identified the market place, the palace, the auditorium, the cemetery. He saw statues, so deeply eroded and encrusted that it was no longer possible even to see if their subjects were human. Reander deliberated the possibility of their not being human.

"Out of the past," said Reander in a soft voice. He mentally cursed his lack of water. He wanted to go on, to walk through the city, but it was impossible. He had found what he wanted to find, and could not reach it. There was no point to his trying—not even any point to his standing still and watching.

Nevertheless, he stayed for a long time before turning his back on the city to begin the long walk back to the Wildland. He made himself a promise to come back and walk through the streets of the city, at some indeterminate time in the future.

In actual fact, he did return to the city a long time afterward.

But for the time being the moloch was left in sole possession, while Silver Reander went to tell John Tamerlane that the stories were true.


## II


THE CITY OF Ylle was a drowned city—drowned in oily brown vapors, long pulpy fronds of alga and many layers of filth and fungus and cobweb. It had been buried so long that those who passed by or through it, or sought some kind of sanctuary from the Wildland in its darkest cellars, doubted that it had ever been intact and inhabited.

Its buildings were farstone, marble, concrete and plastic, or hewed out of the rock stratum itself, and they had therefore endured rather than crumbling to dust. But the Wildland had moved in to some extent, possessing without destroying, in the fashion it had with cities. The city had been built as a lunatic gesture, many years ago, on what was then the very fringe of the Wildland. Its proximity had made no difference in the long run, for the Wildland had come to the fringes of all the cities, in time. There were no cities now that were not engulfed by the Wildland, except for the legendary city in the Great Gulf.

When the race of Man had passed from its sovereign position, the city of Ylle had died, and passed to the Wildland with the remnants of that race. The Wildland had inherited the Earth, and used its legacy for its own purposes, and yet it left Man the cities, invading to some small extent, and obliterating only when the inhabitants died or deserted.

Ylle was one such city—deserted by the descendants of its builders. Given time, the Wildland might erase Ylle from the face of the Earth. Or perhaps not—the Wildland did not always follow precedent. It was possible that Ylle would remain as it was, a part of the Wildland, but not wholly gathered into its body. It was a home for the wild men, a place where they could meet and confer without crossing the path of the city men. There was much friction between city men and wild men, and both preferred to keep apart whenever possible.

For these reasons, it was to Ylle that the Blind Worm came to see such men as ever saw him. It was in the city of Ylle that the Blind Worm met John Tamerlane, the black king.

The black king was a king in truth, although a king among men was of no real significance. His subjects were few, and in the face of the Wildland he was as weak as they. Among his fellows, though, he was master. It was not merely a consequence of physical size and fighting ability, but a matter of drive and forcefulness. Leaders of the city men were rare, because few city men cared enough to lead. The black king was not a typical city man.

He was tall, with huge shoulders and braided black hair that hung to his waist. His face was wedge-shaped and his eyes were big and round. All the pigment in his body was black. He had black skin, black eyes, black lips and black blood. As befitted a king, he was attired in more clothing than the usual city man—or wild man, for that matter. He wore a breastplate of brilliant green leaves carefully sewn to a comfortable fit. A network of coarser, tougher fiber covered the leaves and also added extra protection to the loose garment around his waist and loins. He wore high boots of supple black material. On his head was a crown of thorns.

The thorns were undeniably real and sharp. At several points they bit deep into his flesh, and the scarred skin had grown around them until the crown was inextricably embedded in his temples. There were a good many stories telling how and why the king of the City of Sorrows had obtained his weird crown. He invented a lot of them himself.

He came to the city of Ylle looking for the Blind Worm. People had come to Ylle before in search of the Blind Worm and had gone away disappointed, because no one knew the ways of the Blind Worm, and it was usually a matter for his own consideration as to who would be fortunate enough to find him. John Tamerlane was not, as a rule, a man to deal too adventurously in fortune, but even he knew nothing of the Blind Worm's aims and motivations. He was sure that he hoped that rumors of the proposals which he had to make would bring the Blind Worm to meet him.

Tamerlane did not know what the Blind Worm was. There were men who said that the Worm was a man reared by the Wildland at its very heart, and had never known his own kind for many of their generations. But who were men to know that? Certainly the Wildland loved and protected him. Others said that when the Wildland had fought and defeated Ocean, the last sea creatures had fled to the human race for sanctuary, and that the Blind Worm was the progeny of a cross-mating. But men were ever in the habit of equating two unknowns, and the identification of the Blind Worm with the cracked Ocean deserts, whose salt-burned abysses were yet to be reclaimed, was the confusion of old memories.

The black king believed none of the stories, because he knew his race's liking for myths and romances. But even he cherished his own guess—that the Blind Worm was a natural creature of the Wildland, especially created to be better than a man in every way, in case the Wildland ever needed to go to war against mankind for possession of the Earth, in the same way that it had fought Ocean. But when the Wildland had taken the Earth without conquest, the Blind Worm had become purposeless—a lonely wanderer.

The Blind Worm undeniably had a great deal of empathy with the Wildland and had almost certainly talked to the hive mind of the plant complex, the entity called Sum. And therefore he was at least in touch with the desires of the Wildland. What the black king wanted to discuss was a matter for Sum to decide, and so he had some reason for thinking that the Blind Worm would appear at Ylle, if only to see what he wanted.

# THE BLIND WORM

Tamerlane had set out from the city which he ruled—the City of Sorrows—several days before. He brought with him four people. One of these was the boy called Swallow. Swallow was, in substance, the key to his quest. Like the Blind Worm, Swallow had an extraordinary empathy with the Wildland. By some means he knew what the Wildland was, and could understand it. He knew what the Wildland wanted, and could understand that. And in his mind, he knew, was the mechanism which could give the Wildland what it wanted. Swallow had the secret, and John Tamerlane had Swallow. The boy was no city man, but the son of a wild woman who had been killed in a skirmish with the city men.

Tamerlane's other companions were Vanice Concuma the hero, Silver Reander, and a girl called Zea, who was Tamerlane's mistress.

Concuma, like Reander, was a wild man. He was tall and blond. Like Reander, whom he addressed always as Shadow, he was a friend of the black king, and had adopted Tamerlane's ambitions for his own ends. He styled himself the greatest warrior in the world, as did the black king, but probably had more justification for his claim. His strength was in his hatred, which enabled him to draw on his greatest capacity for the defeat of every enemy.

Zea whispered her name to sound like sea. She took that name from her appearance. She had long, deep blue hair which faded and shone as the sun rose and set, and eyes which were circles of disturbed darkness. Her vitality seemed to ebb and flow in rhythms reminiscent of the long-forgotten tidal pendulations of Ocean. The black king was attracted to her exotic qualities rather than her beauty, for she could hardly have been called beautiful by the standards of city men or wild men. Even so, it was obvious that Concuma was also attracted to her. The black king privately wondered when the girl would switch her affections to the blond man. He had no illusions about the type of hold which he exerted over her.

It was dark when the five reached the drowned city. The bronze vapors hung like the depths of the long dead Ocean, and the algal blisters and lorate streamers seemed grotesque-

11

ly like the seaweeds of long ago. It was probably the closest Earth now approached to a marine suggestion, for the Wildland, while it could not erase the scars of the Ocean depths from the face of the Earth, had done its best to bury all other memories of its erstwhile rival where they could not reflect its enemy's former glory.

Zea seemed as happy here as she had ever been, for it was like her in nature: a kindred echo of the deep past. The black king watched her somberly as she responded to surroundings, and darted glances at Concuma. Tamerlane was depressed and somewhat impatient. He had calculated to arrive earlier, while it was still daylight, but the journey had been slow, through waist-high forests of Sordaria and similar root fungi which fouled the floor of the Wildland and filled the dim tunnels with choking spores. The prospect of spending a night in the drowned city before the Blind Worm could reasonably be expected to appear was not very pleasant. He contemplated taking the group back into the Wildland, to spend the night in a higher and cleaner place, but decided that it was not worth the trouble.

Vanice Concuma was wary, as touchy as nettlehair. He moved restlessly, fingering the hilt of his sword incessantly. Shadow, on the other hand, seemed as completely at home here as in any other environment. His long supple arms twined about each other as he leaned casually on a wall thickly encrusted with lichens.

"What now?" asked Concuma.

The black king stard at the blond man. "We sleep. What's the matter?"

"I don't like it here. I detest cities."

"You loathe too many things." Tamerlane smiled—a weird smile that was invisible in the darkness, for his teeth were as black as his skin. "You kill what you loathe. That is why you are still alive; other men have not hated enough, and have not had such a deeply rooted need to win. Go and hate somewhere else if you feel the need. But not too far."

Concuma retired to the shadow of a wall which was not too deep in vegetation. Shadow was already there, stretched out and, as far as could be ascertained, asleep. Swallow sat down near them and rested his head on his knees. He murmured something, half to himself, half to the two in the shadow of the wall.

"Quiet!" ordered Tamerlane. Zea had already curled herself into a fetal position and was sleeping with her head pillowed on a sponge-like growth of fungus at the feet of the black king. He looked at her still form pensively, suppressing the urge to lay down beside her. She was obviously tired.

They slept, with the exception of Tamerlane, who stared into the narrow chimney which the Wildland left above Ylle. High in the vapors, he could see the thin, wan light of the moon, and watched it flicker and dim as long streamers of brown mist clothed and unclothed the tunnel in the sky.

He sat still for a long time, neither drowsing nor feeling tired. He was not watching, merely waiting. Abruptly, he became conscious that someone or something was standing watching him from the darkness to his right. The image was confused by the vapors and the distant winking lights of bioluminescent flowers on the edge of the Wildland, and he could not see it when he looked directly at it. Trying to keep the shape in the corner of his eye, the black king turned slowly, carefully avoiding the still form which lay at his feet.

"You know me?" asked the silhouette.

"No," replied the black king, "but I think I can guess your name. I think you know me well enough."

"Well enough," agreed the Blind Worm, speaking in a soft, toneless whisper. "You are John Tamerlane, the black king. A strong man and a cunning figher. A king by the strength of his body and his mind. An arrogant man, but a self-sufficient one. I know your companions, too. Vanice Concuma—a strange man whose strength lies in his hatred, because his hatred is so great that it dominates his will. Reander—quick of mind and foot, difficult to kill. Swallow—a unique mind, a talented mind, a valuable mind to its owner. . . ." The Blind Worm stressed the word *owner* very slightly. "And Zea, who is more than you can know, and yet nothing."

"Nothing?"

"To you. To me, perhaps," added the Blind Worm. "To Concuma, I think, she is something. A symbol. She is something more than that, in her own right."

The black king nodded, although he did not understand, and the Blind Worm moved from the camouflaging background of the medusal coils of alga. He, or it perhaps—for the Blind Worm could not be judged by human standards —was almost as tall as the black king. He was stark naked and was sexless. He was not sexless in the sense that a hermaphrodite is sexless, in terms of definition, but absolutely sexless—he possessed only a single excretory pore. His skin was hard and jointed like an exoskeleton, and he breathed through gill-like slits which were concealed beneath opercula hung on his torso except when he inhaled. The opercula resembled, by virtue of their position, breasts. He was a cyclops—his single large eye was situated centrally in his head, and was a hand-span and more in diameter. It bulged, with a vast pupil which covered a far larger angle than a pair of human eyes. The cornea was hard and inflexible, defending the vulnerable eye from hurt.

Tamerlane knew from the stories that the Blind Worm was faster than a human, stronger, better armored, that the eye—though single—could resolve in three dimensions, that the sensory pores beneath the breast opercula were far more various and sensitive than the poor human receptors of taste and smell, that the lipless, many-toothed mouth beneath the eye had a more powerful jaw mechanism and a more versatile larynx than a human's. The Blind Worm, in truth, was far more than human. And perhaps there was yet a further advantage, a psychological one, in that the Blind Worm still resembled, in the broadest aspect of his shape, a human being.

"Concuma will not like you," said Tamerlane. "He will nurse a deep hatred of you."

"Do not underestimate Vanice Concuma's hatred," said the Blind Worm. "It is a valuable weapon. It would be far easier to fight you or me than Concuma, because as you begin to force Concuma backward, his hatred, and thus his strength, increases greatly. Concuma will never be killed by one he hates, unless his enemy is already dead."

14

"You may be right. I agree that it is unlikely that anything Concuma hates will ever find an opportunity to kill him. But I worry about the extent of his hatred. Shadow will trust nobody, with a single-minded stubbornness I admire. If only I could be as sure of Concuma's strength of will."

"You may underestimate the man. Don't ever fight him while you think that."

John Tamerlane smiled with bitter arrogance. "No one will kill me. Not Concuma, nor even the Blind Worm. Only the black king has the power to decide the destiny of the black king."

"That is a bold statement to make when the Wildland has such power over all our destinies," commented the Blind Worm. The black king smiled again, without humor.

"The Wildland is not a god."

"Sum is the closest thing to a god you will encounter in your lifetime."

"Perhaps."

"Why do you want to speak to me?" asked the Blind Worm, abruptly changing the subject.

"I would rather wait until morning."

"I would rather not."

"All right," conceded the black king. "If the darkness suits you better, we will talk in the night. I have a proposition for the Wildland. Are you of the Wildland?"

The Blind Worm did not reply for a moment. "I am not a part of the Wildland. I acknowledge no guiding principles save those that are a part of me. But yes, I am bound to the Wildland in more ways than you. I have an affinity with the Wildland; to some extent I understand Sum. Is that sufficient?"

Tamerlane sighed. "I do not think that such precise definition helps. What I am concerned with is whether you can actually speak to Sum. Can you take me to Sum?"

"I can talk to Sum. I could take you there, but first I would have to ask Sum. And I disagree that definition does not help. You should not think of me as something I am not, nor I of you."

"Then tell Sum I want to see him. I will wait here until you have done so."

"You must tell me what you want to say to Sum. He will want to know."

"If he wants to know, then he will hear it from me. Why should I tell you?"

"When half a city knows what you want and what you claim to have for bargaining, it seems ridiculous to be unnecessarily secretive."

"Very well. I shall explain my position, and what I want. You know me, I think—John Tamerlane of the City of Sorrows. They call me the black king. I *am* a king, but what do I rule? One city. A handful of people. All around the City of Sorrows is the Wildland, which feeds us, and clothes us, *and owns us!* I am king in name, but king by the sufferance of the Wildland. I cannot expand, I cannot conquer. Communication is so difficult as to make any unifying move impossible.

"I want more room. I want my independence from the Wildland. I want my people to grow their own food and clothing. I want an area of land which is *mine.* Land we can use ourselves. I want the seed of certain selected plants, to develop as we wish. And above all, I want freedom from the Wildland. I want no wall around me.

"I want the Great Gulf."

The Blind Worm was silent for a moment. "Is it true that there is a city in the Gulf?" he asked.

"Yes. Shadow has seen it. Primarily, I want that city. But more than that, I want my freedom to use it as I want. I want the Wildland to maintain its present boundaries."

"And you offer."

"I offer Swallow, and what he has to give. I know that the Wildland fought hard to win the Ocean beds, and will not be ready to give them away. But I believe that I have what the Wildland wants far more than the sea deserts. I have the key which will complete the Quadrilateral."

The Blind Worm had no human features, and so could not have expressed surprise in a fashion the black king could have understood, but even so, Tamerlane found the cyclops's

16

perfect equanimity annoying. "What does Swallow know about the Quadrilateral?" asked the Blind Worm calmly.

"Swallow is unique, as you have said. He has a strange mind. He knows Sum—can feel him, understand him. It is not a matter of speech, but some flux of *need*. Swallow *knows* Sum. I cannot explain very well. He can do it a little better. In any case, he knows about other beings than Sum —three of them. Who they are and where they are he cannot tell me. But he knows they exist, and he can feel their mutal quest: the blind *need* to become a single organism, a united group of minds. And more than that, he believes that he can join them, by using his own mind as a bridge between them. Swallow claims that he can seal the Quadrilateral."

The Blind Worm nodded slowly. "The Wildland is only one small part of a vast complex, a thing whose magnitude you cannot imagine. Sum is a mere part of mind which spans hives on four worlds in four universes. There are an infinity of universes. When you look into the sky of the Earth, you can see no end. There is no end to be seen. But beyond the sky there are countless more universes, worlds without end over and over again. They are linked physically. They are as near to each other as the fingers on your hand. With the right power, it is as easy to walk from one to another as it is to walk from here to where Concuma is sleeping. But something keeps them apart, something keeps the four fractions of the Quadrilateral bound to their own local environments."

"Swallow can break the boundary. Swallow can carry the links across the barriers separating the fractions."

"Are you sure of that?"

"I am as sure as I can be. That is my condition. I will complete the Quadrilateral if the Wildland will acknowledge my sovereignty in the Great Gulf."

"*You? You* will?"

"I and what is mine. I own the mechanism—not within myself, but it is mine. The Quadrilateral needs Swallow. Without me, it will get nothing."

"I will tell this story to Sum."

"Explain it carefully. Only you can deliver the message."

"I will do that," said the Blind Worm carefully. "But I cannot make promises on behalf of the Wildland. If Sum is not interested, there is nothing I can do. Sleep now, if you want. I will try to return as early as possible tomorrow morning. Then I will give you the answer." The Blind Worm drew back into the shadows and was gone, lost in the dark mists of the drowned city.

Tamerlane remained staring morosely at the place where the cyclops had stood, seeming to see the weird outline still cut from the brown fog. He did not sleep, but rested in a sitting position for the time that remained of the night. The dawn was not long in coming, but the darkness and twilight lingered a long time beneath the clouds of vapor which haloed Ylle.

Suddenly and soundlessly, before the sun had grown strong enough to penetrate the vapors, Shadow unfolded in a single fluid motion.

"Someone is coming."

"Someone has already been here," said the black king, in a soft voice which sounded completely unperturbed.

"The Blind Worm. I know—I watched and listened. But this isn't. The cyclops came openly and honestly. This one creeps, and tries to remain hidden."

"Is he alone?"

Reander shrugged.

"Where is he?"

The slim man pointed to the right, to the nearest edge of the Wildland, where the lightblooms could dimly be seen moving over the tangled wood of the Wildland's skeleton.

Vanice Concuma awakened more slowly, but as soon as he saw the other two standing he was alert, and rose quickly to his feet. He stood with his back to the wall, anxiously watching the direction Shadow was silently indicating. There was, for the moment, no sound except for a slight stirring of the wind. Swallow stirred and sat up, exposing his position.

"Look out!" howled Reander, and Concuma shot out a boot to hook Swallow's small body away. The boy sprawled, and an arrow split as it hit the rock he had slept next to.

Shadow was already in a crouch, bow in hand. With astonishing speed he released an arrow, but it was obvious from the rattling sound as it disappeared into the Wildland that he had hit nothing. He turned to the black king and shrugged helplessly.

Swallow was now safely under cover, and Reander hung back in the shadow of a half-fallen wall. Concuma and the black king stood their ground, the latter protecting Zea with his body.

"There will be no more arrows, King," called a deep voice with controlled volume.

"I think I'll kill you anyway," yelled back Tamerlane.

Concuma had drawn his sword, and stood running his finger slowly up and down the blade. Carefully he spat on it, and dropped gradually into his half-crouch as the pause lengthened.

"You're surrounded," said the deep voice.

Tamerlane flashed a glance at Reander, who shook his head.

"We give in then. Come and get us."

"Just send out the boy."

"Come and get him."

There was a pause, then the sound of someone approaching. Concuma's eyes gleamed. A tall man with scaly yellow skin and long, webbed fingers stepped into sight between two of the ancient buildings. He walked forward along what had once been a road.

"Who are you?" demanded the black king.

"I know him!" said Concuma in a high-pitched semi-whisper. "Dragon! That's what he's called."

"Jose Dragon," said Reander quietly and reflectively. "What would you hope to gain by starting trouble with us?"

"I want to talk," said the yellow man.

"A moment ago you wanted to fight."

Dragon grinned. "I missed," he pointed out.

"I think I'd still rather fight," said Tamerlane, returning an equally nasty smile.

Zea, roused at last, crawled away from the black king as he stood belligerently facing Dragon.

"Last night you talked to the Blind Worm," said the yellow man. He was sweating, although the morning was not warm. He looked tired and far from relaxed. Whether he was simply afraid, or was agitated for some other reason, was hard to judge.

"What is that to you? How do you know?" demanded the black king, deciding against killing the yellow man for the time being.

"The Wildland knows. The Blind Worm talked to Sum a short time ago. I know because the Wildland knows. King, you must not give the Wildland the key to the Quadrilateral."

"You are prepared to go to extreme lengths to stop me, it seems," said the black king complacently. "It would have cost your life if you had killed him. It might cost your life in any case. Had you succeeded—or if you try again—I will tear the Wildland apart to find and destroy you. Nothing will prevent me from sealing the Quadrilateral if Sum agrees to my terms. *Nothing.*"

"It is far more important than you seem to imagine. The Quadrilateral must *never* be completed. Sum is powerful now, but it is a helpless cripple. Imagine its power when healed!"

"Go home, Dragon," murmured Reander, with mock kindness and insulting condescension.

"There is no reason why the Quadrilateral should not be completed," said the black king brusquely.

"It is against the interest of every man on Earth."

The black king shifted his weight from one foot to the other and frowned. "Dragon," he said evenly, "*I* decide what is in my interest and what is against it. I am not ignorant. I am not a child to be led by you or the Wildland. I hold the stakes, and I will do what I want with them. I do not want to hear your arrogant preaching. I do not even want to hear your reasons. Whatever they are, I will continue on the path I have chosen as the best means of getting what I want. You can take nothing from me by force, and gain nothing by argument. I advise you to go quickly, Dragon, and go a long way."

The yellow man stood still and folded his arms. The black king watched him steadily.

"I apologize, King," said Jose Dragon, "but I must tell

you what I know and what I think. You are a ruler of men. You live among men, by the tolerance of the Wildland. You know nothing of the Wildland itself, nor do the wild men. You must see that your view of the Wildland is necessarily one-sided. You live in the Wildland; it is your environment as well as your boundary, your barrier. You cannot rule that world, or the men who live in it, no matter whether they will obey you or not, without the toleration of the Wildland. What you are trying to do is force the hand of something you do not understand. You do not know the bargain which you are offering or its consequences. You do not know what you are doing.

"Tamerlane, I know the Wildland. I have known Sum for hundreds of years. I knew the world before there was a Wildland. I know Sum and I know that he is not to be trusted. He has too much power to be worried by honesty and fair dealing. He will take everything he wants from you and give you nothing in return. You will achieve nothing, and you will do a great deal of harm."

"What will *you* give me for the key?" asked Tamerlane, still very calm and not in the least disturbed by Dragon's accusations against Sum.

"I have nothing to offer. I do not *want* the key. But I do not want the Wildland to have the key. I believe that the Wildland must not be united with the rest of the Quadrilateral, because if it is, there will never be any chance for any of us to achieve our independence. If the human race wants its world back then it had to take it. If the Quadrilateral is complete, it will be too powerful for anything ever to dislodge it. Destroy the key. Don't even risk it falling into the hands of Sum, or even the Blind Worm."

"No."

"You must."

"You are a madman, Dragon. If you will give me nothing for the key when you want it so badly, then there is no conceivable reason for withholding it from the Wildlands, for even if it does give nothing in return, I cannot be worse off."

"You're wrong, Tamerlane. You can't buy the Earth by offering its owner more power. You can only strengthen his hold upon it. The Earth once belonged to men, before Sum took it. We didn't fight then, when we could have won. But there will be another time, in the future, when we will again be able to destroy Sum. If you complete the Quadrilateral, that time will never come."

"The Wildland is too strong to fight *now*. You must know that to fight the Wildland would mean total annihilation. There is absolutely no possibility of winning."

"Not now, no, but in time . . ."

"Time! The hell with time. It is for me, John Tamerlane, I that am living, not for my descendants. *I*—do you understand that, Dragon?— *I* want the Great Gulf, and I want it now. The Wildland is my most powerful ally, not my enemy. If I fought I would lose everything. While I try to make bargains I have everything to gain."

"You will lose everything. Not only for now, but forever. Our position will be hopeless if the Quadrilateral is joined. It's useless, isn't it?"

"Go away, yellow man. You're lucky. If I ever see you again, I'll kill you."

"We'll meet again," Dragon said as he turned to leave. "When you've seen more, perhaps you'll realize the truth."

The black king watched the retreating figure until it was lost. "I don't understand him. He can't mean all that idiocy about fighting the Wildland. Why should he not want the Quadrilateral joined? Or is it that he does not want me to have the city in the Gulf?"

"You should have killed him," said Concuma. Tamerlane shrugged.

"He's a dangerous man," said Reander. "If he was speaking honestly, then he's an idealist and a fanatic. If he was lying, then there are things we don't know. Either way, Dragon is a threat. Vanice is right—you shouldn't have let him go."

"Save your advice," growled the black king. "There was no point. I hold the key and I am the king. He can do nothing."

"He tried to kill me," said Swallow.

"Agh, there's nothing to be afraid of. I need you—don't think I'd let anything happen to you."

"But—"

"Shut up!"

There was a long pause while the black king stared at each of his companions in turn. Concuma did not care. Shadow was slightly amused. Swallow was petulant. Zea, as always, was totally unfathomable.

Finally the black king smiled, his shining black teeth glinting in the pale daylight which filtered down the narrow chimney of clear air above the city. Concuma, sword once again sheathed, climbed up a sprawling algal holdfast to a point some ten feet from the ground, where he could get a fairly wide view of Ylle, although visibility was bad in the dull mist. Even though Concuma was alert and on edge, the Blind Worm came unnoticed and unheralded.

## III

EVEN SHADOW had not sensed the cyclops's presence until he was actually among them. He was less disturbed than Zea and Swallow at the sight of the weird figure, having listened to the conversation of the previous night. Concuma leaped down, clearly angry that he had not observed the Blind Worm's approach. It was obvious that, as Tamerlane had predicted, the tall wild man took an instant and strong dislike to the Blind Worm.

"I will take you to Sum," said the cyclops, as he moved toward the black king. There was something sinuous in his movements—there was no sensation of his stepping from one spot to another, merely a smooth transition. Shadow moved around so that he was positioned at Tamerlane's shoulder. Zea rose and went to stand beside Concuma. Swallow still lay where Concuma had kicked him.

"What did Sum say about the bargain?" demanded Tamerlane.

"He will agree to it. I will take you to the nerve center of the Wildland—the mind of Sum. From there, he will project us in turn into each of the universes of the other members of the Quadrilateral, where they will be joined in the mind of your . . . property. Then the Great Gulf is yours."

"Mine under the conditions I laid down?"

"Yes. You cannot totally divorce yourself from the Wild-land. The crops which you will grow will still be a part of it, because the Wildland is a hive organization. Every plant on Earth is a unit of the hive—simply by transplanting them, you cannot destroy their identity. But the Wildland will not interfere with you in any way. There will be no attempt to colonize the Gulf, and you will be allowed to develop the city and the sea bed in whatever way you please."

"I am satisfied."

"The Dragon will not like it," murmured Shadow.

"Dragon?" said the Blind Worm. "Has Dragon been here? What did he say to you?"

"He was here. He told me I must not complete the Quadrilateral. He tried to kill Swallow."

"Why didn't you kill him?"

"I saw no need."

"Jose Dragon is a very dangerous man," warned the Blind Worm. "He is incalculably old, extremely clever and absolutely mad. I wish he were not involved in this, but I suppose it was to be expected. He has an insatiable desire to cause trouble."

"There is no trouble that he can cause."

"Dragon knows the Wildland well enough to cause trouble for anyone in it. He knows his way everywhere."

"But the Wildland is on our side. You have just said that Sum is in agreement."

"You don't understand," said the Blind Worm. "Sum is merely the mind of a vast hive organization. The plants of the Wildland perform their functions by reflex—they are what they are and Sum is the sum of all of them. But Sum can no more instruct individual plants than you can instruct the cells of your stomach. They are stomach cells, and will behave like stomach cells, whether you want them to or not. And yet they are still a part of *you*. We are within the body of the Wildland, but always remember that we cannot look to the mind for direct help. The Wildland will not tell us where Dragon is, nor what he is doing. We shall have to protect ourselves."

"I can protect what is mine," stated the black king.

The Blind Worm nodded what might have been approval, and half-turned, inviting the black king and his companions to follow. Tamerlane stepped forward to join him. The Blind Worm did not pause once he had begun walking. Tamerlane followed quickly, with Shadow at his shoulder. Swallow rose rapidly and hurried after them. Concuma and Zea hung behind. "How long will it be?" asked Concuma.

The black king looked back and frowned when he saw Zea standing so close to the blond man.

"Not long," he replied.

"Sum must be deep in the heart of the Wildland," guessed Concuma. But even as he said it, the wild man was falling into a comfortable stride.

"You've traveled the Wildland before," muttered Tamerlane impatiently, half to himself, because only Shadow heard.

"Be grateful that Concuma is scared," said Shadow. "When he fears, his hate is thriving."

"He's not afraid," said the black king.

The bitterness in his voice betrayed what he was thinking.

"What does it matter?" purred the slender man. "She is nothing to you but property, and she remains that."

"But to Concuma!"

"Concuma is your friend," reminded Shadow, with a slight accent on the last word. "Your jealousy can only hurt you."

The black king acknowledged the truth of what Reander said. "You are a clever man, Shadow."

"One has to be," said the wild man, with a strange kind of sigh. "It's only experience and staying alive. Wild men are either clever, cunning or indestructible—or dead."

"Which is Concuma?"

"Indestructible."

The black king nodded sourly. The Blind Worm laughed. He had an oddly musical laugh.

They passed from the vapored deadness of abandoned Ylle to the naked and splendid Wildland. Their path took them above the musty ground via a mass of matted vines. These formed many-layered carpets intricately woven into a series of nets which bore them high into the plant hive. The way was springy and often steep, but not particularly difficult to negotiate. Between the tightly wound vines were smaller climbers and the everpresent lightblooms which provided a supply of photosynthetic energy for local emergencies, when translocation from the canopy would be too slow. It was these which lit—albeit dimly—the eerie roads through the Wildland. Fat worm-flowers—damp motile bags of plant flesh—scavenged dead tissue and cellulose debris from the vines.

They had to cope with the defensive elements of the Wildland, too. The thorns of the net-nettle and the stinging hairs of a multitude of threadstalks and hyphae hurt their feet, but the race of man had long ago become immune to the poisons they used. Once, those alkaloids had wiped out most of the animal life on Earth. Now the structures which bore them were more or less vestigial. A more serious inconvenience to the travelers were the vast anthers of some of the vine flowers—often the size of their heads—which dropped clouds of choking pollen. The pollen never reached the ground, but germinated and knit itself into the web, repairing damage and perpetuating the strucutre.

Higher up, they passed from the carpet to the less dense skeletal region of stouter branches and more varied incidental flora. The seeds of geumgiants became stuck to their flesh and clothing more than once, but no one incurred serious wounds. They were forced to stop and rest often, sprawled on the stout branchwork. The Blind Worm seemed able to go on forever without tiring, and Concuma was determined to show no weakness. But Swallow and Zea tired easily, and Reander was not too proud to show his own fatigue. The black king was too impatient to even think of rest. He swore and clenched his fists every time Swallow demanded a stay in their journey.

Often now they crossed the giant green-mottled palmate leaves that were the lowest light-traps of the Wildland canopy. High above them, they could see the first glimmerings of sunlight filtering through to them. Water glands wept as they walked near the fern sori which covered many of the leaves.

# THE BLIND WORM

The Blind Worm led them unerringly. Time after time he avoided the concealed pits of the pitcher plants and the gluey mats of syrup fungi, either of which would have held them fast and permanently injured them. The traps were primarily designed to catch cactoblasters, the ghost-like moths which were all that remained of the insect kingdom, but if humans were unlucky enough to fall foul of them, they suffered the consequences. The euphoric amaranth plants were also hereabout, but all they saw had their golden blossoms closed, and so there was no need to fear breathing the perfume. Amaranth perfume was a trap for humans—the hallucinogen would lose them instantly in the avenues of their own minds, unconsciously dreaming while the tap roots of the plants dug into their flesh and drank their blood.

At times Tamerlane might have believed himself in an amaranthine trauma, for they were entering a part of the Wildland he had barely glimpsed before. Although he was a city man, he was no stranger to the Wildland, but he had always kept close to the ground. It was a fault of his imagination rather than his courage, for it had never really been clear to him that the higher reaches of the plant complex were a totally different world from the one he knew. Even the wild men habitually conducted their wanderings in near-surreptitious fashion, hugging the ground and the perpetual dimness. The gaudy crest of the Wildland was avoided by careful men because there seemed no need to risk the regions where amaranth grew and blood red tendrils of octopetalloid snakeflowers reached for them.

The functional elements of the Wildland were clearer here. The black king saw and identified the thick conducting cables which carried water and organic materials from one site to another within the hive. He saw, too, the gigantic balloon-like reservoirs which held water. He often wondered whether all the water the Wildland had taken from Ocean was held in the plants themselves, or cached away in some subterranean hollow accessible only to the roots of the system. He believed the first, because it was conceptually impossible for him to think of "free" water. He had never seen more than a few liters of it, and that extracted from roots. In actual fact, the roots of the Wildland were now primarily miners—although that did not preclude their being water miners as well—excavating with biological finesse the essential elements, isolating and converting them into usable substances by myriad intricate processes.

Swallow liked it here. He had always known the Wildland intimately and had been at home there, although he had seen so very little of it. Perhaps he alone of the city men knew the tremendous diversity of the Wildland, how it varied from crown to base, and from latitude to latitude, and yet he had seen less of it than most. Swallow *knew* the Wildland, he *sensed* its perfect ecological balance. He understood its hive nature.

He understood far better than the black king, or any of the wild men, how the Wildland was not a mass of vegetation consisting of separate species mindlessly vying for the substance of existence, but a single integrated whole. There were many types of plant involved, many castes, but they were united in one mind, one sentient intelligence called Sum. In a way, the plants were more suited to hive mind than the social insects that had first developed the phenomenon. The insects were perennially limited by their clumsy devices of sexual reproduction. The single functional female —the queen—was always vulnerable, and the caste system was weakened by the methods for caste selection. The Wildland, being vegetative, did not need sexual reproduction. It had abandoned it. Genetically it was a lone, immortal individual.

Its component parts played their individual roles of support, transport, storage, protection. There was hyperspecialization. It was no longer necessary for each unit to photosynthesize, transpire, anabolize and excrete. Each could link up to the common good, and live in symbiosis.

Swallow could put none of this into words. The ideas were unclear and only half-formed. But when he looked at the bright green drapery of the upper canopy, the bulky skeleton which supported them, the arrowstalks which altered their orientation to suit the position of the sun, the tubestems which were the blood vessels of the Wildland, and all the smaller motile reclaimers of waste, he felt the strange sense of dispersed unity which was the identity of Sum. That was Swallow's power—his empathy.

Every ecological niche was filled abundantly, for as the physical elements of the environment changed, so did the flora. Two thousand miles north, the Wildland would look totally different in detail. But essentially it was the same. It would be Sum, even though its anatomy was not the same. It would be doing different things, coping with different problems, as though it were an arm as opposed to a leg.

What Swallow did not understand was the position of man. He had no empathy with his own species, but that probably would not have helped. The wild men and the city men were by no means stupid, but they simply were in no position to evaluate the anomalies of their situation. Man did not fit into the pattern. He served no function, yet the Wildland tolerated his continued existence, as it tolerated the ernes, the diomes, the leeches, the cactoblasters and the molochs. Man had never fought the Wildland, and the Wildland had never tried to exterminate man. The diomes and the leeches were allied to the Wildland—had been used by it. The cactoblasters and the ernes survived in spite of all the Wildland could do. All the other species of animal which had endured seemed to fit into one or other of these categories, save man. The relationship between Sum and the human race was unclear, even to Swallow. The Blind Worm did not know either. Jose Dragon thought he did, but only Sum was in a position to know.

It was a new experience for Concuma to walk through the roof of the Wildland on what seemed to him to be terms of truce, if not equality. He had been here before, several times, but had felt like a thief in the night, invading where he had no right to be. But in the wake of the confident Blind Worm and the bombastic Tamerlane, he reached new heights of self-assuredness. There was also the girl by his side. He knew that there might well be a reckoning with the black king over Zea's change of allegiance, but simply because of the burst of identity it gave him, he was prepared to defend his claim.

The black king looked back at Zea several times, but

the girl avoided his glare. In other circumstances, Tamerlane would not have tolerated her desertion but, at the moment, major ambitions overrode everything else in his mind, and for the time being he was prepared to accept the situation.

## IV

IT WAS CLOSE to dusk when they saw the pinnacle. It was very near before it was visible in the abundant greenery which surrounded them. Behind it was the darkening eastern sky, but it stood out because of an odd sharpness of outline. The body of the pinnacle was made of some bluish wood which had some slight luminescent properties. It did not quite shine, but its presence could not be overlooked.

"That is it?" asked the black king.

"Sum, or at least the mind and voice of Sum, are within the mountain," confirmed the Blind Worm.

The gate of the peak was a tightly knit barrier of thorned wood which looked absolutely impenetrable. Around the gate, the smooth, sheer walls of the mountain swept away. It had a diameter of nearly a mile, and a depth as great as the depth of the Wildland at this place, plus the extra height of the peak above the canopy.

The gate, on closer inspection, was a cage with an oblique entrance which led by a tortuous maze into the heart of the mountain. The tunnels were guarded, impossible to pass without the knowledge and approval of Sum. But these guards, at least, were under voluntary control, and not the reflex-bound machines that were the rest of the Wildland's unit.

The guards might have been the Wildland's substitute for men. They were smaller than men, softer and white. They bore six limbs, which were differentiated into arms and legs to varying degrees on the individuals they saw. There were also long pulpy limbs which were motile without the need of joints, and which bore a ring of seven digits surrounding a suction pad.

Their heads were small and narrow and brainless, mounted on short, thick necks and bearing flat black photoreceptors which were not like eyes. They had no ears, but a lateral line system ran down the sides of their bodies. They were unique in the Wildland, and grotesquely unlike men in that they wore protective clothing—loose strips like plate-mail armor.

They saw the guards as soon as they were within the gate. The boneless things gathered about them, wielding long thorn spears and blowguns with suggestive malice, directing a host of dirty sharp points toward the invaders. The Blind Worm spoke to them in a kind of staccato rattle, like and unlike the language of the Wildland, which had, in various incomplete and bastard forms, replaced the human languages of old. Tamerlane recognized the language as based on the one he spoke, but could not make out what the Blind Worm said. The guards did not withdraw immediately, although they shambled slowly backward to allow them passage. The boneless ones lingered, menacingly, for quite some time, while Concuma fingered his sword and even the black king grew nervous.

As they passed through the gate the guards began to melt away but they were always near, always ready, and they took pains to make this abundantly clear.

The thorn maze ended and left them in a dimly lit tunnel which wound down into the mountain. Its floor was steep, but ridged in stepwise fashion, almost as though in concession to human feet.

The guards had gone completely now—melted away like silent, unpigmented ghosts. The tunnels were not long. They wound and curved, but even so it was mere minutes until the group emerged. They came into a cave which must have filled the interior of the wooden mountain. They stood on a ledge, level with the crown of the Wildland, which went all around the cave, sweeping out of sight on either side. The ledge was wide, and from its lip shone a mild white light emanating from the depths of the hollow mountain.

Except for the Blind Worm, they hung back. The cyclops turned, expectantly, and the black king strode forward. Slowly the others followed. Tamerlane looked over the edge into the great abyss below him.

It was like standing on the shore of a bottomless pit. Not far below was Sum, immense beyond the imagination of even John Tamerlane. Because Sum was a single cell. Sum, conquerer of Ocean, who glowed with a wan silver light like the lantern-flowers, seemed to be nothing but a mass of darkly sparkling fluid, like blood or wine, naked glutinous protoplasm turbid with subcellular membranes and organelles.

Sum was bounded by the great dome of a transparent membrane, within which could be seen a ramifying network of intracellular curtains, supporting millions of spheroid and ellipsoid bodies. Deep down, shining wtih a fiercer light, Tamerlane could see the nucleus, with an incalculable number of swirling chromosomes, sharply silhouetted by the inner light.

Through all its wooden walls went thin threads of the cellular material, out into the Wildland like the nerves of the hive, maintaining communication between mind and body of the Wildland.

Sum's pale light illuminated all of them—the Blind Worm, who was impassive, showing no emotion on his inhuman face; Vanice Concuma, who was confused by a feeling of awe and an unfathomable but furious hatred; Zea, clutched tightly to Concuma; Shadow, half lighted, half dark, almost lost in the conflicting shades he wore for concealment; Swallow, half crouched, eyes eager and mouth smiling wide. And alone stood John Tamerlane, the black king, ebony skin gleaming with sweat and the crown of thorns seeming to writhe in the odd light, like a prophet facing his god.

Zea slipped from Concuma's grip to kneel at the brink of the shelf, her face limned with a peculiar sharpness, as though she shone with a light of her own to oppose that of Sum. Yet every line of her face reflected the image of the being that was before her, twisting it somehow into her own face, which was the echo of another long-dead being: Ocean.

"You have the key?" said the voice of Sum: a deep, sourceless noise which filled the cavern.

"I have it," returned the black king, in a deliberately deep, rich voice which was almost the equal of Sum's.

"Show me."

"If I do, will you give me the Great Gulf on my terms? The Wildland will not touch it? I have my freedom within the Gulf?"

"I agree to those terms. I will give you all the help I can in adopting the Gulf, and all the isolation you wish when you have taken possession. I withdraw all claim to the city in the Gulf."

"Then the key is yours. Swallow is the key." There was a pause. Tamerlane, expecting his part to be over, merely stood and waited. The Blind Worm took the boy by the arm, and led him closer to the edge.

"I can join the Quadrilateral," said Swallow in a fearful whisper. He paused, gathering his composure, and continued in a more normal voice. "I have always been aware of the nature of the Wildland. I have felt its groping, the blind tropism which leads it toward these three other minds in different universes. I have felt the relationship between them, the nature of the disunity. I don't understand, but I do feel. I know that I can reach total empathy with these four minds, lock each one in turn into my own mind, and lock all four together. I can be the template which arranges the minds in the necessary configuration. Then, when I release the empathic link, the four minds will be one—the Quadrilateral.

"Can you not feel me? Can't you feel in my mind that I can do this?"

"I cannot reach your mind as you claim you can reach mine. But I believe you. I can lose nothing. I can take you into the four universes, one by one."

"All of us," said the black king.

"Is that necessary?" asked the Blind Worm.

"The key is mine. I shall stay with it until its job is done."

"It is easier to take all than to abstract one," said Sum. "There is difficulty for me in distinguishing between individuals. I am a hive, and I think in terms of hives. I am unable to comprehend individuality. I will transfer all the bodies on the ledge. It is quite safe."

From the tunnel mouth behind them came a sixth figure. The man stayed in the shadows, and none of the six turned. Even Shadow was unaware of him. The newcomer crept as close as he dared, and waited.

"Are you ready?" asked Sum.

It was the black king who answered "Yes."


## V

AND THEN there were stars, a dizzying sensation of great height without falling, but a spinning, wrenching around in a tight circle. There was darkness—an everlasting darkness with no beginning, no end and no genuine existence. There was a loud buzzing in each mind, as though every nerve in each of the seven bodies was vibrant with impulses. Certainly there was no ordered thought, merely a jumbled mass of emotions without references to explain their sequence. The greatest of them all was fear, and inside Concuma the hatred transcended even the fear, whipped to boiling point by the shifting of dimensions and mental isolation.

After a timeless interval, the sensation vanished. And then they were in a different world, all of them. The bioluminscent entity was left behind, but Swallow carried a part of it with him. Locked into his own identity was the identity called Sum.

The world into which they came was a world of colors. Their eyes could not adjust to the splinters and slivers of color which made up the space around them. There was nothing with which to orient themselves, nothing on which their eyes could focus, nothing to which they could definitely assign solidity. They saw each other as two-dimensional projections on the crazy mosaic background, frozen into the depthless world, unalive and out of contact.

It was like being hurled into the debris of a hall of shattered distorting mirrors. It seemed almost as though they were embedded in a great wall of crystalloid, to which their struggling eyes seemed to impart motion. The facets shifted their orientation, and the whole thing began to rotate, swinging in ever-accelerating pendulum fashion. They would pick out strange, only half-formed shapes which moved across and through the slashes of color with grotesque clockwork jerks. But they could not be real, because they would have been perfectly camouflaged against the patternless background. As in a kaleidoscope, there were hints of organization, but they were transient and more the illusion of the eye than a property of the canopy of colors.

Zea screamed a flat, harsh scream. It was something for their sensory apparatus to latch on to. But it was hardly enough. Only the Blind Worm realized that this was a world of only two dimensions, and that neither their bodies nor their minds were adapted to it.

Toward the black king there came a huge beast, which came ever closer although he could not make out at any one moment where it was or how it moved. There was nothing behind for him to track its path, nothing on which it moved. It existed, and it came toward him. He found that he could move and draw his sword. He saw the paper-like images of Concuma and Reander draw their weapons, but could not see what they did afterward, because his attention was on the beast.

He tried to run, but the directions he wanted to run in did not exist, and he performed sickening contortions in the single plane which trapped him.

The charging entity separated into four parts, but he could not judge the extent of their separation or the pace at which they approached. The universe seemed to curve. Somewhere away from him, Zea screamed again. Reander writhed, but went nowhere and accomplished nothing. Swallow had twisted himself into a fetal position.

Sweat on the black king's hand made his grip on the sword slippery and difficult to maintain. The beast of many colors seemed to be infinitely large now—it seemed to occupy all the space around him, engulfing him and moving through him. The others were gone, as far as he could see, even out of the corner of his eye. He was conscious of blood on his hand where he had somehow cut himself with his own sword. He felt no pain, and could not locate the cut. Blood flowed more freely and seemed to come from nowhere.

Then the crystal was frozen, its illusory motion stilled. And an instant later there was darkness.

"We are sorry. We did not know that you would be such totally different beings." The voice was thin, and came from no direction. The black king enjoyed the merciful darkness for a few moments before he thought of answering.

"Are we all safe?" he asked, meaning, Is Swallow safe?

"You are disturbed. We hope there is no damage. You were exposed for only a few seconds."

"This is the second fraction of the Quadrilateral," he heard a voice say, and realized that it was the voice of Sum, speaking to Swallow.

"They said *we*," the ghostly voice of the boy answered. "Yet there are not more than one."

"They are one. They are a hive mind, like myself in some ways and different in others. They are identical and numerous, with perfect communication and identical needs. They have no need of the caste system of the Wildland. Their condition is different. But they have the same tropism as the Wildland. They are a part of the Quadrilateral and they strive for its union."

Swallow said clearly, "They are in my mind. They are locked."

"What now?" demanded Tamerlane, beginning to dislike the cloak of darkness which protected him from the reality of the world around him.

"Continue," said Swallow. "I hope the next world is less unpleasant than this one."

"It is peaceful," promised the thin, fluting voice which was now the second voice of the Quadrilateral. "We are sorry for what happened here. It was unfortunate. We did not foresee that your senses would delude themselves in trying to rationalize—in your terms—the stimuli they received here. The only wound any of you have incurred was self-inflicted. There was no real danger. Our world holds no dangers."

"That depends who you are," said Shadow drily. "It is a reflex action to rationalize and interpret."

"We understand," said a voice that was compounded of the voice of Sum and the voice of the two-dimensional people. "We hope that nothing else will happen to disturb you. You will find the other worlds less fearful, we think. Remember, we shall not let any harm come to you. We need you."

Again there was a feeling of weightlessness, negativity, immensity, fear, and then light rushed in on them again. It was painful, yet a relief from the claustrophobic darkness which had shielded them in the previous world.


## VI


THERE WAS a desert. It was not like the salt-caked bowl that was the Great Gulf, or any of the other dead lands of Ocean, but a desert of red sand and red rock. It seemed to have no end, a sheet of sand blowing over rock fused from magma millions of years before. It extended, as far as they could see, in every direction. There were no hills of any size, but the evenness was split again and again by the sharp projections of rock, crazily shaped and scarred, which erosion had not leveled.

Above them, the sky was clear and pure, but not precisely the same shade as the sky on Earth—it had more red and yellow in it, and was a difficult color to name. The light was very bright to their dark-adjusted eyes, although it was gentle compared to the full glare of Earth's sun. There was no sound, not the slightest movement of the sand or the air. Yet there *was* air, for a blurring haze rose to obscure the further reaches of the desert.

"It is necessary to walk a little way," said the voice of the colored people.

Shadow at last realized the presence of the extra man. So did the others. "How did you come here?" snarled Tamerlane.

"It was not difficult," said Jose Dragon, smiling triumphantly.

"What do you want?" asked the Blind Worm.

"Only to travel with you," said Dragon, spreading his hands. He was moving away all the time.

"Kill him," advised Concuma.

"No," said the voice of Sum.

The black king had already half drawn his sword, but stopped. "What concern is this of yours?" he demanded.

"The man is not to be killed unless he tries to prevent the sealing of the Quadrilateral."

The black king hesitated. He did not understand. But eventually he sheathed his sword.

"Why did you not bring us nearer to the entity which we have to contact?" asked Swallow. The reply came from his own mouth, in a different voice.

"We could not. The universes have physical links, like bridges. We are not making new contacts, but transporting you by the routes which exist. A bridge ends where it ends, not necessarily in the place where we would like it to end. We can pass to a particular world, but not to a predetermined spot. We cannot select our place of arrival."

The voice was the voice of Sum. It was the first time the other members of the group had realized that the voices came from Swallow.

"Why don't they come to meet us, as the colored people did?" asked Tamerlane.

"They do not move," Sum answered. "They have no need. They are the ultimate in organization. They create what energy they need from nothing. They do not die, they do not reproduce. They share their minds in perfect harmony. All that they have left to do is fuse with the Quadrilateral."

"They are hardly alive," commented Concuma. His voice was rough, as if his mouth were very dry. Both Tamerlane and Shadow looked at him in surprise.

"You cannot understand them. They have an aim. That is sufficient to live upon."

"And when the aim is satisfied?" asked Reander.

"Then they will live for us. They will *be* us, and share our identity, as we shall share theirs. We will all have a common inheritance. We will be one instead of four.

"We are wasting our time. The Blind Worm and Swallow can guide, if you will begin walking."

"Where?" Reander asked Swallow.

The boy pointed. "They are there. Look to the northern horizon. Perhaps you can see them."

"There is nothing," said Tamerlane. "Nothing but the rock and the haze."

"I see them," said the Blind Worm. "I can lead us to them. But walk. We will come to them."

And so they began to walk. The sand was soft and their feet sank into it, and the rock was hard and ridged. For these reasons, their progress was slow. Concuma, after some minutes, picked up Zea and carried her cradled in his arms, carefully avoiding venomous glances from Tamerlane. Blood seeped from a small cut on his shoulder and stained the brittle chitin-scale garment which she wore. The black king looked at his own wound, and found that it had bled quite a lot, but was superficial and not painful.

Swallow was in obvious difficulties, and began to fall behind. Shadow was always with him, keeping between the boy and the yellow man who walked with them, but was not strong enough to carry the boy. Finally the Blind Worm picked him up, and Swallow rode on his broad, scaled shoulders. Reander and the black king moved into position just behind him, to protect his back. Dragon moved ostentatiously to one side as if to emphasize his peaceful intentions.

"Why should the Quadrilateral want Dragon alive?" asked Tamerlane of Shadow.

The slender man shrugged. "I don't know. What does the yellow man hope to accomplish? He can't do anything without being killed. He can't possibly hope to harm Swallow."

"He is mad," reminded the Blind Worm. "Watch him closely."

They stopped for a rest. As they sat in the sand, Dragon approached the black king.

"There is not much time left. Believe me, Tamerlane. The Wildland once betrayed me. It will betray you as well."

"It might. But why should it?"

"Sum had no reason to betray me, yet he did."

"If it were not for Sum, you would be dead. I don't think you have any quarrel with him."

"Sum has already robbed me of most of my life. I owe him nothing for his preservation of this small part of it. I am not grateful for the type of life Sum has given me. I once wanted much more, but Sum would not give it to me. I was cheated."

"You're mad," said Tamerlane.

The yellow man bit his lip. He was obviously angry. Reander had moved around behind him, and stood quietly caressing the hilt of his sword, in a characteristic manner.

"Don't draw your sword," suggested the black king. "Better still, give it to me."

Dragon hesitated, then slowly took the weapon from his waist and handed it to Tamerlane. The black king broke it effortlessly in two, and threw the pieces away. "Too old," he commented. "Tell me how the Wildland cheated you."

"I helped Sum. I gave him everything that I could. I built for him, I fought for him. Not against Ocean—long, long before that. I helped Sum to win the Earth. He gave me nothing in return. He would not grant me what I asked. For Sum, it was easy, but he would not give me what I wanted. He will not give you the Great Gulf either."

"You sound as though you want to stop me for your own revenge rather than for any reason which I would consider sound," said Tamerlane.

"You are betraying your race."

"I am assuring the future of the race. I am winning back our independence."

"I think that it is you who are insane, King," said the yellow man, "insane with ambition."

Tamerlane laughed. Dragon turned away.

Shadow instinctively measured the positions of himself, Concuma, Dragon and Swallow. Just as the yellow man began to run, he hurled himself forward.

Tamerlane stood up, kicked Reander's legs from beneath him in order to clear the way, and threw his sword. It was a mistake. The sword went in on the left side of Dragon's torso, above the lowest rib, and the point came through to protrude from the left breast, as the sword dug in to the hilt.

But it did not halt the madman's headlong rush. In his hand was a small dagger that must have been concealed in his clothing, and it flashed as he raised it for a downward stroke that would take Swallow's throat out.

Swallow rolled away, and the Blind Worm, with no apparent hurry, interposed himself between Dragon and the boy. He half-turned, apparently to take the thrust in his own neck. Instead, he swept it aside with an armored wrist and simply hit the yellow man in the face with his other hand.

Simultaneously, Concuma's blade took him in the side. Jose Dragon collapsed, sprawling on his back in the sand, as Concuma shook him free of the sword. The yellow man flooded blood from his wounds. His skull was crushed—smashed like a brittle piece of wood.

There was a long pause. "He was totally mad," said Shadow from a sitting position, with a glance of resentment at the black king.

"But why?" said the voice of Sum, from the body of Swallow. "I do not understand."

"He thought that he was cheated, once," said the Blind Worm.

"Why?" demanded Tamerlane, retrieving his sword.

"He knew Sum, a long time ago. So long, in fact, that Sum was merely beginning. The hive was a few plants only, and most of the Earth's vegetation was dispersed, uncoordinated. In those days, there were millions of men ruling the world from their cities. They had broken the back of every individual force which opposed them. They were sentient and intelligent, and had a great advantage over every other life form.

"The only life form which could possibly win the Earth was Sum. Jose Dragon conceived the idea of the hive organism uniting all the plant life of the planet and taking it by force. He foresaw a great battle—the Armageddon of his own race. And so he allied himself with the Wildland, because Dragon hated his own race. In a way, he was an outcast. He was deformed. Out of his deformity came his

41

obsession, to destroy mankind. He planned for the great battle which would annihilate the human race. To help the Wildland, he conceived an invincible army to fight and destroy. He built the prototype of his army. He built the Blind Worm.

"He went to Sum and offered his invention. The Wildland had no need of it. Sum refused his help.

"The Wildland never fought the human race: the takeover was peaceful. Sum refused to fight mankind for possession of the Earth, but Man did not contest the matter. And so Dragon thought himself cheated. He was, in fact, cheated of his goal, which was the genocide of his race. But it was not Sum who cheated him even of that, but mere circumstance. So the Wildland ruled the Earth, owing nothing to Dragon and without the slightest regard for him. He had only one hope left—one thing which would make possible his forcing the Wildland to follow his wishes. That was the key to the Quadrilateral, which he has been looking for for nearly a thousand years. The same freak of genetics which made him an outcast made him immortal. And then you came—you and Swallow. And that was the end of the search. Dragon had lost. That's why he didn't mind dying. There was no point in going on."

"I did not cheat him," said the sonorous voice of Sum. "I want you to understand that, Tamerlane."

"Why didn't you let me kill him earlier?"

"He once tried to help me. However misguided his help may have been, he was prepared to be an ally when I might have needed one. I owed him that much, surely."

"Why didn't you ever fight mankind?" asked the black king, trying to clear up the last point which still puzzled him.

"I *never* wanted to fight mankind—because of the Quadrilateral. That was far more important than owning the Earth. I would have been content with any role on Earth if only I could have the Quadrilateral united. But only a man could do that.

"As Swallow has said, the means to unite the Quadrilateral lay in a certain type of mind—one which could locate the minds of the Quadrilateral inside itself and fuse them into a single unit. We lacked that template, and could find no way of making it.

"What we needed was a pool of individual minds—discreet identities which varied sufficiently that recombination of genes would someday produce a mind with the properties we required. In all our four spheres of influence, there was only one such species, and that was mankind. It was the last thing I wanted—to have the human race destroyed. Rather I wanted to be in a position to protect Man and to guide him in the paths I wanted him to go. And so it is the Wildland which feeds and clothes mankind, and the Wildland which forces his evolution."

"We have been manipulated? It was you who was responsible for Swallow's existence in the first place?" demanded the black king.

"We did not expect success so soon. The requirements for the mind we needed must have been far less rigorous than we originally imagined. My plan was intended to encompass tens of thousands of years, not mere hundreds. Even with the mutagens which the Wildland continually fed you, the directed selective pressure should, in theory, have taken far longer to achieve the results which it has. It was, of course, a difficult program to put into operation. The design and training of my own component parts had to be carefully planned. I had to accelerate the mutation rate and selective pressure just enough to maintain maximum plasticity in the human species without placing them in any danger of extinction. In order to facilitate this program, I occupied the Earth. It was the only way to be sure. I did not occupy the Earth because I needed, or even because I *wanted* to expand physically. It was a mere convenience. Had Man decided to fight, of course, then I would have been forced to relinquish this part of the plan and do what I could with what I had.

"But war was avoided, and the plan went unhindered. In a way, we might be said to have had the cooperation of the human race. I do not know why they elected to let me have the Earth. It could not have been fear—they would have fought whatever the probability of their losing, if they had wanted to. Perhaps they were simply tired of civilization and had not the will to resist the return to the wild. More probably, they saw in the massively expanding Wildland the solution to their problems of food and raw material supply. They had run the world dry of all the food it could produce, and they were not good enough biological engineers to make enough of their own. Hence, *they dared not fight,* lest they destroy their hope of solution to the population problem. To them, I suppose, the Wildland might have seemed like a miracle."

"A miracle you might have been," said Reander, "but how many of us have you murdered over the centuries with your 'selective pressure'?"

"The Wildland's methods may seem cruel to you because they involve a great deal of hardship at the individual level. But within the concepts of my own morality, the plan was perfectly justifiable. You must remember that the individual level is impossible for any of us to conceptualize. I am a hive mind, and so are the other members of the Quadrilateral. A species whose units are separate entities is alien to our imaginations and alien to our morality. We live by our morality, as you do by yours. In our mentality the group is the operative thing. Individuals mean no more to us than the skin cells which you lose every day. I know that you think differently, but it cannot alter the way *I* think. I am what I am. My identity is inflexible. For me to destroy your race, as Dragon wanted me to do, would have been wrong irrespective of my own plans. But what I have been doing is *not* wrong by my standards. Dragon could not understand my point of view, and I cannot really hope that you will, because you are human just as he was. But I have tried to explain. I can do no more."

"What about Ocean?" asked Zea. Tamerlane looked at her a little sharply, but he was more surprised than angry.

"I encountered difficulties, of course. Ocean was one of them. I was not the only hive mind to have evolved—I might point out that both myself and Ocean probably owed our birth to the extreme selective pressure which the human race exerted upon every other living thing which shared the environment. Ocean precipitated a war. It was a sea-based hive including many marine forms of life, and we clashed over the extreme water requirements which we both had in order to maintain our expansion. Again, I would have avoided war if I could, but Ocean was the aggressor. What would have happened if Ocean had won, I do not know. Perhaps the Quadrilateral would have died; perhaps Ocean would have taken my place. Perhaps Ocean would have allowed me to continue living in a much reduced form, unable to carry on my key project.

"In any case, I defeated Ocean. My mechanisms for sucking the water from the seas proved more efficient than Ocean's means of securing the water. I took the water I needed by force. But I did not kill Ocean. That would have been contrary to my morality. I changed it into a form in which I could use it. The entity which had been Ocean became human—a group mind within the human species. I allowed the mental characteristics of Ocean to be imposed on synthetic, but in every way functional, human bodies. I had human assistance for this, of course. The group is small and offspring from crosses with normal humans are not necessarily members of the hive. But the numbers were maintained. It will not die out. I assume that the girl Zea is a member of that hive."

"I think," said Tamerlane, "that I understand some of what you have said. But it is too much to grasp fully."

"I am glad," said Sum. "I have done my best to keep the intelligence, and to a lesser extent the learning, of your race alive. That, in a way, is the purpose of the city men—to maintain knowledge which might be valuable to the race."

"I am grateful," said the black king.

"The knowledge has given you nothing," said the Blind Worm, with a peculiar edge to his voice.

"Enough," said the black king.

"I don't understand," said Concuma in a low voice to Reander. The slender man laughed.

The black king began to walk again, without any further word. "Wait," requested Swallow. The black king looked back. Concuma had gathered Zea in his arms again. Shadow and the Blind Worm were also on their feet. Without a word, the Blind Worm allowed Swallow to climb onto his back again, and they began to walk.

The Blind Worm took the lead again, and on either side of him walked Shadow and Tamerlane.

"He created you?" asked Reander softly, of the Blind Worm.

"Yes. For a forlorn purpose. It used to be said that no man could build a machine that was superior to him, but Jose Dragon did. It was his madness, I think, rather than his brain."

"So you were born into a world in which you served no purpose?"

"A world that was not mine. No one bore me any resentment save perhaps my . . . father, but I was not a part of anything: the Wildland had no use for me, and to men I was a hideous alien being. Sum, of course, knew me, and taught me a lot, helped me in what ways he could. The men who knew of me talked and invented stories. But that was all. I suppose I became a sort of legend.

"I was permitted no emotions by my creator, but I think that I learned to feel something over the years. I think somewhere in my life I learned to hate him." The Blind Worm inclined his head to indicate the direction from which they had come, where the inert body of Jose Dragon lay.

In the distance, Tamerlane could see a structure or group of structures like a row of broken teeth. It occurred to him, really for the first time, how old Dragon had been, relative to his own short life span. He even began to see why the yellow man had accepted inevitable death in order to try to stop the completion of the Quadrilateral.

The black king realized that in the days when Dragon had been born there had been no such diversity of shape and form in the human race as there now was. It was by those standards that the yellow man was a freak, and it was because of those standards that Dragon had come to hate his own race.

He dwelt on the irony of what the Wildland had done in spite of Dragon. Instead of gratifying the yellow man's hatred, it had removed the reason for it. In the world of today, the variations from the normal in Dragon's body were no more strange or repulsive than a great many of the physical types which had arisen from Sum's meddling. Sum, far from cheating the man, had done, incidentally, everything possible to help him. It was the intractability of the madman which had made Dragon unable to accept the new order. Another man might have pitied Dragon, but Tamerlane was not the type to indulge in emotions of that kind.

## VII

FINALLY they came to the place where they were to meet the intelligence of this world. Seven pockmarked towers of inert stone stood in a rough circle whose center was rock, smooth as if it were polished, and clean of sand. But there was nothing else—simply the seven monoliths.

"Fuse the second link," said the voice of Sum to Swallow.

"What are they?" asked Reander.

"We are stone," said a new voice from the mouth of Swallow—a slow, dry voice. "But we are nevertheless sentient and intelligent. To your eyes we seem simple, but on the level at which our consciousness exists, we are complex and very large. The quality and matrix of our life is not on the molecular level of protein in water, but on the atomic level of electrons in a subatomic stratum. All that is necessary for thought is the flux. The replicative properties of living tissue is superfluous. A thing does not have to be alive to be sentient."

There was silence. Concuma had set the girl down on the piled sand outside the circle, and stared at the monoliths without understanding. Shadow, willing to accept almost anything at this time, believed.

"It's all right," said Swallow. "We are ready now."

"The next link," said Sum, glorying in the words, "will seal the ring. My work will be finished. Your purpose will have been fulfilled. All is justified. We shall go on to the last of the four universes."

There was the same jerk into the in-between for an infinite moment that they had encountered twice before. It was familiar now, but the tight fear was still present because it came not from within, but from without.

And then Tamerlane discovered with a shock that he was wet and cold, that he was not supported by solid land, but gasping for breath as his head went under water. Horror and realization struck him at the same instant. This was *the sea!* Tamerlane had never known an ocean, had never stood on a shore and looked out to sea. He had never been immersed in fluid since the womb. He could not swim. The only water he knew was to be extracted from the leaves of the Wildland or tapped from the sap-carrying tubestems. He had seen the emptiness of the Great Gulf and imagined it full of water, but it was a difficult concept and the reality was quite a different matter.

He panicked as soon as he realized that he was in danger of drowning, but somehow retained sufficient presence of mind to avoid sucking his lungs full of water at the same moment. He thrashed and fought, and was immersed again and again as his flailing plunged him into crazy acrobatics in the salt water. From very far away, he seemed to hear a triple scream as the voice of Sum, the voice of the two-dimensional people and the voice of the monoliths together displayed their discovery that they were on the wrong world. Then he was unconscious.

He awakened choking and coughing and vomiting. There was a foul taste in his mouth and breathing ripped his chest with bursts of agony. But he was alive and intact. As soon as he was in any condition to think about his surroundings, and about the fate of his companions, he sat up. That started a fresh spasm of coughing, but he recovered quickly.

He was on a beach, and the ocean was mere yards away. The beach was located on an island—a long slender spur of gray rock and silver sand and mud. There seemed to be no native life—perhaps the spur was too small, or subject to periodic battering by the sea. The Blind Worm was bending over the prostrate form of Swallow some feet away, and the black king sighed with relief.

"You pulled me out?" he asked the Blind Worm. The cyclops nodded.

"Him too?"

The Blind Worm nodded again. Some distance away, Zea sat in the sand, naked, staring out over the calm waters with an identity in her eyes which he had not seen there before, but was far more alive and aware. Zea was no longer an echo of something forgotten, but a reflection of something alive. Shadow stood behind her, talking to her, but Tamerlane could not hear what he said. To judge by her face, Zea could not hear what he said either.

The black king rose and went over to them. Shadow looked up as he approached, without the slightest expression in his face.

"Concuma?" asked the black king. Shadow spread his hands.

"*Dead?*" It seemed inconceivable.

"It used to be said that Concuma could never be killed by anything which he hated," said the girl, very quietly and almost dreamily. "That was true. He loved me. I killed him."

"You? How? And why?"

"By bringing him here. I didn't want to kill him. I didn't want to bring you. Just Concuma and myself. But it didn't work. I couldn't do it."

"What did you do?"

"I tried to cut away while we were in transit. I have very little power left, but I could manage that. But I hadn't the ability to distinguish between some of us and all of us. Sum was right—it's so much easier to think in terms of groups. And Concuma died. It had to be him—not Swallow, or you, or the Worm. Concuma. The one I didn't want to hurt. It's always been that way. I shouldn't have tried."

"Who are you?" asked Shadow quietly.

"Don't you know?" she said bitterly. "You are a wise man, Shadow. Don't you even know now?"

"Ocean. The defeated Ocean. Part of the group mind."

"There is no group mind any more. We didn't breed. We just died—there is nothing in the Wildland's morality about suicide. I am all that is left. Sum was never wasteful—he made Ocean into a part of its pool of psychic clay. But that was Sum's justice, not mine. Ocean elected to die. But when I had the chance, I decided that the decision had to be set aside in favor of me. I wanted to do something for myself. I ceased to care about Sum and Ocean and morality. I am Ocean. Ocean is dead. I wanted a new life. I had to take the chance. I had to try. I should have known that I wouldn't succeed."

"Didn't Sum realize that you might do this? He knew who you are."

"He must have thought that I was just one of the group. Perhaps he didn't think that I had the power. Perhaps he simply couldn't see a reason why I'd want to. Sum is narrow-minded. I didn't do this to stop you, John, believe me. I didn't even want to involve you. It was for me, only me. You didn't matter any more, nor Sum and his twisted morality. I suppose Vanice Concuma was just a pawn too, in a way. It was no use, though—I've always lost when I've tried to win."

Tamerlane turned away, keeping his anger controlled. Shadow had another question to ask. "What now?"

The Blind Worm stood up, straddling the inert form of Swallow.

"He will die," said the cyclops simply. "Within minutes. There's nothing I can do." The words sounded in the black king's mind. Then they seemed to amplify and echo hollowly. And then another echo, and many others.

"What happens to Sum?" asked Reander, while the black king stood still. "And the other two minds? Are they still linked? Or will they die with him?"

"They'll come to no harm. They'll be released from the template as he dies, and will return to their bodies, still linked. Three parts of the Quadrilateral are joined, but no more."

"It must be hard to come so close and fail by accident."

"It is not easy," said the thin voice of the colored people, with difficulty. Swallow's lips barely moved. It was clear that Swallow himself would never speak again.

Tamerlane's fist went to the hilt of his sword and folded around it. It gripped tight until the sweat came and, in his fury, clutched it still tighter. Then he drew it, turned and lunged toward the sitting girl. She made no movement, but looked at him, merely looked, with big round eyes like oceans.

But Shadow was between the black king and Zea, his own sword drawn to take the blow. Tamerlane's sword stroke ricocheted from the smaller man's blade, but even before the stroke was complete, it whipped back to catch the other blade again.

"Stop it!" yelled Shadow, retreating rapidly, half stumbling in the soft mud. But the enraged king swept on. The girl did not move, and Reander nearly fell over her in his attempt to keep between Tamerlane and her. She seemed to realize finally that she was endangering Shadow's life by remaining, and so she leaped to her feet and ran.

Tamerlane lost his balance as he turned to follow her, and Reander could have killed him in that instant. But instead the slender man danced back into the way, so that the black king was unable to follow Zea. But the black king's insanity had him in a terrible grip now, and Tamerlane came straight in, determined to go through Reander if he was not to be allowed free passage.

Shadow realized, with a feeling of coldness, that he was now fighting for his life, and not protecting Zea from the black king's anger. He had diverted the big man's fury to himself. There was no chance, and he knew that. Tamerlane was a great fighter, whether in possession of his senses or completely berserk. Concuma might have stopped him, or even the Blind Worm. But the gliding form of Reander could only run, and there was nowhere to run to.

When Shadow was ripped by a score or more slashes, the silvery sand caking his thin body, slowly forming a paste with the seeping blood, Tamerlane stopped, and sank to his knees on the sand beside the still-living body of his friend. He breathed deeply for several minutes.

During that time, Shadow said: "I suppose I loved her too a little. Is she to blame for my death too?"

The black king did not answer. He looked up again. The Blind Worm still stood beside Swallow's supine form, staring out to sea, where the white form that was Zea tried to be lost in the waves. Tamerlane watched the lithe body for a long time. Then he returned his attention to the Blind Worm. "I'm sorry," he said. It did not occur to him that the Blind Worm was an odd person to apologize to. The Blind Worm flicked his eye at the black king and said nothing.

"So," continued Tamerlane. "I cannot complete my side of the bargain. What happens now?"

"We can only return to Earth," said the Blind Worm.

"No!" said the voice of Sum. And, incredibly, it did not come from Swallow, but from the unwilling vocal apparatus of the Blind Worm. "You can complete the Quadrilateral, Worm! I do not understand, but the template is here." There was a dead silence. The Blind Worm folded his arms.

"What is this?" demanded Tamerlane incredulously.

"Sum has decided that I have a key as well as Swallow."

"You *do* have a key. All the years I worked, you had the key. Why? Why did you withhold it?"

"What has happened?" demanded Tamerlane, still mystified.

"The partially linked Quadrilateral was released from Swallow's mind as he died. It looked for another template, and found one. I allowed the fragment to locate in my own mind."

"*You* can complete the Quadrilateral?" protested the black king, still finding difficulty in believing.

"Why not?" asked the cyclops. "I am more than man. I know more about the human mind than any man alive. I know my own mind. I have an empathy with the Wildland, just as Swallow had. I also had an empathy with Swallow, but he did not recognize it for what it was. I copied the key, King. I took it out of his mind and put it in mine. It wasn't hard to do."

"When? And why did you let Sum make the bargain with me if you could provide the key?"

"Not long ago. While I guided you through the Wildland. The bargain was already made then. Besides, I knew that a time would come. There was something I had to do first. Something I have wanted to do all my life: I wanted to destroy my creator, Jose Dragon. And I have done it, using Swallow as bait."

"You could have killed him at any time."

"No, that is not so. You know that I am more a machine than a man. I am a synthetic being, built to specifications. I had a prime directive built into my mind: to work in the interests of the Wildland. And I have a secondary directive: not to harm Dragon. He should have reversed the directives. But he built me to be a tool of the Wildland. He was my creator, but the Wildland was to be my master. Therefore there was a way I could kill my creator—by placing myself in a situation where I stood between him and his revenge upon the Wildland for the imagined treachery. You cannot know, King, how long I have waited for the chance to crush his skull. I only wish that he had built sufficient emotion into me for me to have found great pleasure in the act."

"Follow your prime directive now," said Sum, "and complete the Quadrilateral."

"I will do that," said the Blind Worm, "but I would like to ask something of you in return. You do not have to grant it, because I cannot help but seal the Quadrilateral. It is a matter of identity, not choice. But I think I am entitled to ask."

"Agreed. I can give you the emotions you lack. I can give you ambition and purpose. I can erase the directive from your mind. *But I cannot change your identity.* Remember that if you ever come to accuse me of having cheated you. You are mistaken when you confuse your directive and your identity. But when you find your identity, remember what I have said.

"I can give you more. I can give you a universe of your own—I can make you a god. I can give you everything that the Quadrilateral has. The freedom of all the worlds of all the stars. An infinity of experience and the emotions to enjoy it. That is what you want."

"That is what I want," agreed the Blind Worm. "This is what I need. The man who created me built me imperfect and conscious of my imperfections. He is dead. Now I want what he did not give me. I want to be complete just as the Quadrilateral wants to be complete."

"I could have asked for all that," mused Tamerlane. "But I asked for so little. Even so, it was what I wanted."

"One more thing," said the cyclops.

"Yes," said the second voice from the same mouth, granting it before it was asked. The incomplete Quadrilateral was too impatient to bargain.

"Leave Tamerlane here."

"Why?" cried the black king.

"It is your world. It is where your mistakes have led you. I'd like you to stay here and live in it." The Blind Worm's eyes went to Silver Reander's prostrate body. "Shadow was a good man," he added.

"But it was no fault of mine that Swallow died! Zea brought us here, not I! What have I done?"

The Blind Worm made no reply. In the single great eye there was no pity, no friendship. There was nothing, because there could only be nothing. Tamerlane realized that he was alone, that he had achieved isolation, of the kind he deserved rather than the kind he wanted.

The Blind Worm vanished silently, carrying in his mind the three linked hive minds, taking them to their destiny.

There was only a slender island in the great, empty ocean. Tamerlane laughed slowly and bitterly. Then he looked up to watch the slim white body a long way away as it slid even further from the sliver of rock and sand. And there was no longer hate or rage in his eyes, but only despair.

## VIII

PERHAPS there might have been hope and triumph in the single eye of the Blind Worm, had he been able to experience and express it. But there was emptiness, as always, as he stood at the edge of a great waste on a desolate, lonely world.

"Where is the fourth limb of the Quadrilateral?" he asked Sum. There was a soft laughter. It was his own laugh, but it was Sum that used it.

"I am here," whispered a new voice inside his mind. "I am beneath you and above you and all about you."

54

"The entire world?" asked the Blind Worm without awe. There was more susurrant laughter. "Not a world," was the answer, "not a solar system, nor even a galaxy. A universe."

"A universe is infinite," said the Blind Worm.

"Yet there are many of them," said the fourth link. "I am infinite, but basically no different from the other hives of the Quadrilateral."

"An infinite organism?" asked the cyclops. "And even then, incomplete?"

"Dimensions are immaterial. Fullness is of the mind. But I am tired of being so much. When the Quadrilateral is free, I shall go with it, out of this universe. I shall diffuse myself among the other three minds. My physical manifestation will no longer be necessary. It is a burden I have carried too long.

"It is your universe now. All the worlds of all the stars were, I believe, what you were promised. You have them. You can take my place as a god. You can create and destroy. As my mind flows into the Quadrilateral, yours will flow out to encompass everything I leave. You will be one gigantic hive mind, like me, but you will have the advantage of a body to live in. I never had that. My sentience was corporate in every atom of this universe. I could never limit myself.

"Good luck."

The Blind Worm nodded, ostensibly in understanding.

And then the Quadrilateral was complete. There was no word, no sign, nothing. The sealed ring was gone from his mind. And then his heritage came flooding in. One moment he was alone on the edge of a great waste on a lonely world, the next he was all-powerful, all-knowing. His mind opened to time and space, and he felt love, fear, joy and despair in rapid succession, bathing in their separate beauties.

The Blind Worm had found his freedom.

PART 2   BLIND GOD

## IX

THERE WAS a limitless silence on the dead world. The Blind Worm stood very still, his head bowed. He looked deep into his own mind, testing the power he had received, searching from without the universe which he had inherited. It was like a drug, like a dream of amaranth to feel the drifting fragments of his mind coalesce into images and ideas.

He could not take it all at once. It thundered inside his skull and he had the terrible urge to retreat from it, to fly back into his old mind, powerless and emotionless. The dread and the horror passed, but he still floated as though in a dream, his mind disordered and disoriented. It would take time, time to get used to it, time to rationalize, learn and control. He needed a great deal of time. . . .

He was on a new world, elsewhere in the universe. He walked along slowly, in the middle of a great plain. The landscape was shifting, very slowly, eddying, rising and falling. The small, bright sun rose and set in mere seconds and the scene flickered in the rapidly changing light. The ground below was unstable, changing so quickly that it often looked hazy. The sky was changing too, like curtains of vapor continually dragged back and forth in patternless array. The Blind Worm walked on, ignoring the insubstantiality of the ground, his great cyclopean eye roaming in bewilderment. He let his mind sink into rest as he stopped wrestling with his problems, and allowed himself to become acclimated to his new powers.

Some distance away he could see the outline of a city

which stood on an elevated plateau that curved gently to the floor of the plain. He began walking toward it, watching without paying a great deal of attention. It was quite small, smaller even than the cities he had known on Earth, but as he watched he saw that it grew slowly. New outlines appeared at the edges, usually squarer and taller than the ones in the center.

His brain attuned itself so that the focused gaze of his single eye compensated for the stroboscopic effect of night and day, and gave a three-dimensional quality to the fluid city. But it was too far away to see much in depth. He watched the buildings at the expanding rim of the city spring from the ground and soar into the air. Their growth was sporadic, but he could not make out the individual time lapses. They were too short to do anything more than give a collective effect of unevenness.

The expansion grew more rapid until the whole border of the city was in constant and violent movement. The central area was changing too, but more slowly. Its asymmetry was never quite completely transformed into the regimentation of the suburbs, but its rougher lines were smoothed, and it grew taller.

It was larger now than Ylle, and still in violent flux. Buildings sprang erect in groups some distance from the body of the city, and the city marched on to engulf them. The Blind Worm was witnessing the birth of a city the like of which he had not seen since the early days of his life, when the human race still ruled and the Wildland was barely suspected. This was a city from his far distant past, reinstated into his new future.

Creation continued.

The buildings no longer huddled for protection, but lay ranged far and wide, arrogantly, like the jagged outline of a row of broken teeth. It changed as it decayed and sprouted anew along the whole of its still-increasing length. The pace of enlargement still increased. The entire skyline seemed to be wavering and oscillating in outline.

Suddenly, he saw roads radiating in many directions, descending from the plateau to shoot across the plain and unite the city with some super-civilization that was taming its environment with tyrannical force. There were no people or vehicles visible—their presence was too ephemeral for him to detect. Only by the hectic pseudo-life of the silhouetted city was life on a smaller scale manifest. The resemblance of the city to a hive struck him forcibly, and he rather enjoyed the comparison of the city to a weird Wildland of stone and metal.

Almost without thinking, the Blind Worm stopped and shot out a hand, straight in front in a dramatic salute, and the city fell. The towers were toppled and the sprawling outline collapsed into ruin. In one moment it was complete, a system of dynamic growth, and in the next there was a transient thin swirl of black smoke and more than half of it cascaded as though vaporized into a thin smear of rubble. There was only the merest glimpse of a halo of flame, and then it was gone, swept into the skies by the surge of time, and only ruin was left.

The Blind Worm stared with what was almost naïve wonderment at his outstretched fingers. He felt no jubilation at the discovery that destruction was as easy as creation, but a little awe at the sweeping majesty of the stroke. He felt no sorrow for the city. It was only a shadow on the horizon, a puppet on jerky strings.

The pantomime went on—feeble, spasmic growth, slowing and ceasing. The wavering stopped, gently and without fuss. There was no rebirth.

There was none of the thrashing of a wounded animal, only a tranquil passiveness. The city began to disintegrate, very gradually. The flick-flick-flick of night and day had not altered, yet the scene was more sedate, as though a great tiredness had descended upon the plateau.

The city was dying. It slowly surrendered its memories of the chaotic life it had once led. The blunt, angular figures abandoned their reach for the stars and slid to the ground. The roads were washed gently into oblivion by the tidal flow of the sands, whose waves swept lethargically across the plain. The towers which had carried power lines parallel to the roads fell, made mounds in the sand for a while, and were eventually swept into smoothness by the marching plain.

The plateau sank deeper and deeper toward the plain as the horizon assumed a regularity it had never had before, and finally it curled away to lose its sharpness in the ever-present duststorms. The sands shifted and stirred. The skyline was dead, the city was buried without a monument to signal its passing. It was lost and forgotten. Peace had come: peace and emptiness, hand in hand, held the plain.

The Blind Worm carefully curved his fingers and relaxed his arm. It was over. He breathed deeply for several moments, listening to the rasp of the cold air as he expelled it from the opercula on his chest across his scaly skin. He looked up at the sky and slowed it down, banishing the sun and holding a still, cloudless night. He looked at the stars, which were multitudinous in the blackness, and knew that the cycle was in progress a million times on the worlds of the stars. Creation and decay, growth and death, in different forms, all over the sky.

"Freedom can be very impressive," said a soft, dry voice as the scene faded.

"It's what I wanted for a long time, King," said the Blind Worm.

The king laughed quietly. "I wanted something like that, too. I remember that."

"That was another man in another universe."

"That one was abandoned on a lost planet in a lost cosmos. Why did you recreate him? What am I doing here?"

"I made you. I have to make things I know. This is my universe. It reflects my identity and my memories. You are still fresh in my memories, King."

"You'll bring us all back? You'll recreate Zea and Shadow and Concuma so that we can live our lives again? Why, Worm, why?"

"I want you. I want to see all of you in my world. I need an anchor—something to remind me that I am the Blind Worm. Something to save myself from being lost in my own mind."

"It won't be the same."

"It isn't the same. It's mine."

The king clenched his jaw. "I remember the other king," he said. "The one you left to die."

"I created you," said the Blind Worm, as though the two acts counterbalanced.

"Am I supposed to be grateful? Remember Dragon, Worm. Remember your own creator. I'll remember that. We all will, when you've built us all."

"Forget it, King. I'm not your enemy. I'm a wanderer in a wanderer's universe. Use it for what it is, King, whether you're grateful or not. It's a great stage with an infinity of sets, a series of shifting realities. It's *my* universe. You have power, King, power to see those worlds in the sky. You're trapped in what *I* wanted. Try and get what you want from it, if you can. Discover new ambitions, or hold the old ones. I hope you find something worth finding.

"I'll see you again."

"Goodbye, God," mocked the tall black figure with the crown of thorns.

## X

THE BLIND WORM stared moodily into the semi-darkness. From mist-shrouded mountains which surrounded a large river basin like plumed helmets, he watched a battle.

The smoke-veiled ground sloped away from him for a long way. At the foot of the mountain, a number of tiny figures slipped and struggled in deep mud trying to shift a huge cannon or similar piece of artillery up the slope. Its giant wheels were spinning uselessly as its motor whined, failing to gain any purchase in the fluid earth. The men wielded levers and towropes, and the field piece moved laboriously in the desired direction. Similar weapons already ensconced higher up the incline lit the dimness with streaks of flame accompanied by loud reports. Where the shells hit was impossible to see.

There were hundreds of the machines, of like design and of several different shapes, but the Blind Worm could see that it was the men who were really important. They worked unceasingly in hundreds and thousands to move the weapons—or even to keep them in place—in the appalling conditions. Where the machines could not be taken under their

own steam, men pushed, carried and coaxed them. They
fed them with ammunition and fired them at some hidden
enemy below them in the valley and on the slopes on the
other side of the river. The oily pall of smoke hid the
second army from the view of the cyclops.

Half a mile away, a large tank with thick treads and a
huge bulbous cupola lurched to a stop on top of a narrow
ridge. The long barrel of the gun bounced madly, but its
sound could not be isolated from the general clatter coming
from that direction. Whatever effect the gun might have had
was completely undetectable. Men suddenly erupted from
hatches on top of the turret and in the side. They sprinted
madly downhill and threw themselves flat as the tank exploded in wreaths of rose-tinted flame. Bits of flying
metal spiraled in the smoky air for a long time, and the
twisted hulk left behind was hardly recognizable. A curtain of explosions followed a ragged line leading sideways
from the wrecked tank and across the ridge, but nothing
further of any size was hit. Several of the men who had
escaped from the tank must have died, though. Yellow and
scarlet splashed the ground at several points where the
grass had caught fire, and running men were momentarily
illuminated by the flames.

All the time, the men strived to keep their machines moving, not merely to gain good firing positions, but to avoid
allowing the enemy to pinpoint the positions of their artillery.

He moved down the slope a short distance, into the
fringes of the army's lines. A man raced past him shouting
unintelligibly—he seemed no more than a shadow in the
dusk and smoke. A vehicle of some sort—small and unarmored—bounced toward the man. He ran downhill a
short way and dropped into a ditch. Seconds later a large
body hurtled into the ditch some way to his right. The
Blind Worm heard heavy breathing, and a burst of racking
coughs. Then the man was gone again, and the Blind Worm
scrambled after him.

A silver missile—some kind of rocket—flew into the air
on a tail of fire from a peak a long way to the east. Puffs of
smoke burst around it as there were frenzied attempts to

shoot it down in the few seconds during which it was in flight. It landed, fragmenting as it did so, letting loose a vast explosion which lit the slope for half a mile and sent four cannons hurtling aside, splintering. Before the after-image had faded, the enemy had taken advantage of the momentary illumination and two of the exposed field guns boiled into flame under a hail of superbly aimed shells.

The black pinnacle from which the missile had come became a target for as much as the army could throw at it. Half a hundred flames erupted from it before honor was satisfied, or vengeance satiated, and by then the peak must have been severely altered in shape.

A rain of the silver missiles swept from the far mountains to bathe the nearer slopes in a pattern of devastation. There was a tangible tremor as the mountains reverberated to the multiple impact. On the steeper hillside there were rock-slides which carried men and metal down with them in roaring cascades of rubble. There were sheets of flame and a vast burst of sound that went on and on. The heat was intolerable, but dying rapidly.

The men were running. Scattered groups tried to strike back with all they had, but it was pitifully little in the face of what the opposing forces had just done. The guns they had struggled long and hard to keep in operation were abandoned as they ran uphill and down in a belated attempt to escape the ceaseless blast from across the river. Burning men swarmed down to the plain, scattering. Black ash filled the air, choking the Blind Worm and sending him to his knees, writhing, his chest opercular heaving to suck in air. The bombardment ended with a final squadron of cylindrical rockets riding white cones of flame in shallow arcs to terminate in what was left of the nearer army's ranks in the roots of the mountains.

And then the charge and the pursuit: out of the smoke raced amphibious vehicles, bouncing into the water and leaping out on the near shore on thick-tired wheels once again. And with them came a running tide which ran across the shallow river without bothering to swim, clumsily splashing, waist-deep in the water. Shambling over the scarred, cratered surface came horde upon horde of the conquerors—with hard, jointed bodies like human locusts, naked, with a cyclopean eye in the center of each bobbing head, and cusp-shaped breast opercula. The Blind Worm stood, paralyzed with shock even though he had *known*, watching thousands of his duplicates tear into the human forces, killing. . . .

He felt an urge, somewhere in his abdomen, to shout at the top of his voice that it was all wrong and that the Blind Worm was a man and that the war should not be. He wanted to raise his arms and bring peace, or banish the whole scene into everlasting darkness and silence. But something made him hold himself there, impassively watching the wave of replicas come on and on, in deadly array, with magnificent discipline and superlative efficiency.

*Is that what I want?* he demanded bitterly of himself. *Could that ever have been what I wanted? I wanted to be a man. I don't hate men. What is there in me that can see worlds like that?* But he knew no answers to those questions.

They were important questions, and he wanted to think about them. He went away to somewhere quiet, to the attic of an old house whose roof was full of holes where tiles had slipped or gone altogether, letting in a great deal of light. The air was still and gentle. It smelled pleasant, and he knew that it must be summer. The attic was shadowy, but not gloomy. The rafters were coated with thick white dust and had been eroded by dripping water, but they looked secure. The air was heavy with dust, and the filtration apparatus which protected his breathing membranes was darkening with the grains.

He watched a woodlouse ambling along the roughened wood from one crack to another.

*It's so long since I have seen a woodlouse,* mused the Blind Worm. *Where did this place come from? It's like a memory, but I'm sure I've never been in any place like this. It doesn't feel like an artifact of my imagination. What is this I'm feeling? Nostalgia? It seems impossible—nostalgia is embedded in the past, like an echo. How can I be feeling the echoes of lost emotion? I never had sufficient emotion.*

He looked around him more closely, inspecting his surroundings with a critical eye.

There were a number of flaky white patches of mildew, streaks of orange rot and numerous different species of mold. There were dark-bordered pits in the wood, showing that it was the home for a large number of burrowing arthropods.

*The detail is fantastic,* thought the Blind Worm.

In every corner and crevice there were cobwebs trailing in tattered rags and threads. On the other side of the battered sheet of tiles he could see fresh spiders' webs glowing with reflected sunlight with, here and there, the indigestible husks of their victims swaying in the slight movement of the air like corpses on the gallows. He watched a spider paralyze a newly trapped fly and begin pumping digestive juices into the stilled body to liquefy the tissues before sucking them up. While it fed, its web oscillated, gleaming like sticky silk.

The tiles had once been a granular brick red, but time had cloaked them in gray and had engraved pits and fissures in their surfaces to wrinkle them with age. In the gutter outside, grass and weeds had usurped the channel where rainwater had once run. Many of the roots penetrated the rotten metal to hang like thin string, shriveled by the heat, while they futilely searched the empty air for water. The roots hung in pitiful clusters, often knotted about one another as though in consolation.

Much of the grass was yellowed and the few weeds wilted sadly. Their invasion of the heights had not been very successful.

*How can I explain the affinity I feel with this place?* The Blind Worm ran his finger over a stained beam. *I never noticed these ridiculous creatures with armored backs and many legs when they were alive to be noticed. I saw them—I knew of their existence. But to see them now so closely, to know them so intimately. This is not my world, yet it came from my mind. It is like the Wildland, but so very different in its flow of life. These creatures cower instead of ruling; they are small instead of huge.*

*This scene belongs to Earth's remote past. I never saw it there. I am a creature of the Wildland. Why do I not understand what is happening in my own mind?*

He looked around in questioning bewilderment, turning

his head so that his monstrous eye scanned the whole room, taking in the architectural symmetries and what had been done to conquer them by the invading wild. He saw the conflict between the stark, angled wood and the glassy seas and colored stars of lichens and fungi.

He looked down at the steadily accumulating carpet of bird droppings, dead grass and simple dirt, and watched a centipede work its way through the microcosmic jungle in search of prey. He listened to the pleasant, soothing hum of flies, smelled the musty senility with the chemoreceptors on his gill membranes. He looked closely, his great lens swelling and sinking like a quiet sea as it focused and refocused. And he looked within as well, at himself.

He remembered what Sum had said to him on the Ocean world. *I cannot change your identity!*

And he remembered Jose Dragon, the man who had made him. *I had no mother,* he thought. *I had no other teacher. Dragon made me. These are his memories and his emotions. I took my independence when I killed him, but he is still in my mind. I am tainted with his ideas, his memories, his hands making my body. Perhaps, somewhere, I'm still harboring his motivations. Perhaps the battle was real; perhaps I still carry his hatred of mankind built into my flesh. Is his insanity flowing in my veins, as well as in his? Is it his blood that I carry there? Blood he made, pouring his sweat into it, and his tears, as like as not. Dragon built me, and Dragon alone shaped me—am I only an extension of him? Have I then only inherited his emotions and his worlds?*

*It can't be,* said the Blind Worm in a silent voice. *It can't be because I haven't lost the hate I had for him, the repulsion I had for his ways and thoughts. And then again, what if Dragon hated himself as much as he hated all men? I could believe that. No, power has not changed my identity.*

*But who am I?*

A small brown wolf spider scuttled across his hand where it rested on a rafter. He flexed his fingers absently, and the spider passed on, walking into what was apparently its regular hunting ground, for several of its less aggressive kin lay dead and desolate, their legs intertwined into black caskets and their bodies empty of flesh and fluid. The wolf spider picked its way tastefully through the debris of mummified chitin ghosts, searching for its next meal, having no time to spare for contemplation of its former triumphs.

*The corpse of Jose Dragon lives yet,* thought the Blind Worm. *Even now, I am not finished with him. Somewhere, on another world in another universe, he is dead. But the black king is there, too—and he wanders my universe. Dragon is here too, or his ghost. They're all here—all the ghosts in my mind. Sum could not change my identity, but I can. Zea will know how. Zea had known power, when she was Ocean. She can lift the answer out of my mind. Dragon is still alive!*

*I'll have to kill him all over again!*

## XI

THE BLIND WORM walked steadily, the brilliance of the sun irritating his lidless eye just a little. To his right was a sheet of dark blue water that sent waves rustling along a great curve of dazzling white sand. The beach stretched away for a long distance until it was hidden by cliff faces extending far out into the sea.

The sea reminded him strongly of the world where he had abandoned the black king, but the beach was very different, taken from a great deal farther away in his memories. It was a great deal more pleasant than the lonely island he had encountered more recently.

To his left there were tall dunes, some shifting like desert sands, others anchored by knots of marram grass and held as a windbreak protecting the dunes behind. Beyond the sandhills there was a forest of conifers, but that was a long way. There looked to be very little animal life on the wind-swept dunes.

This was a young world with a young sun. The star was a clear, blinding lemon yellow and seemed to be surrounded by a great golden aura which extended its diameter by a factor of three or more. The sky was deep opalescent blue.

There was abundant life in the sea, though. Not far from where he walked was the debris left by the last high tide. It contained a fair range of dead marine algae, and the occasional corpse of some primitive animal. There were a large number of shells which had not so long ago been tenanted by animals. The shattered remnants of the shells probably represented a substantial component of the pale sand.

The Blind Worm knelt and stirred the fine substance. It was silky as it ran through his fingers; when he squeezed it, though, it grated harshly on his armored skin. Meticulously, he dusted impacted particles from the palm of his hand. The sand was warm and comfortable to walk on. He continued on his way.

She was waiting, as he had known she would be, sitting in the sand, staring out to sea in her characteristic manner. He knelt down beside her and suppressed an impulse to reach out and touch her. She turned quickly so that her blue hair rippled as it ran across her face. She smoothed it gently with a delicate hand.

"Why?" she asked, very explicitly.

"I had to. Do you like it?"

"I don't feel it properly. It's like being in a dream."

"I feel exactly the same. There is that same sense of impotence, of illogic. The same feeling of detachment and periodic hyperacuity. Yes, that's it—it's like a dream."

"It's not the same for me. It feels as though I'm in someone else's dream."

The bitterness of the comment did not escape the Blind Worm. "I have done what I could," he said softly. "I have not been cruel."

"All creation is cruel," she stated.

"And wrong?"

"I think so."

"Ocean would not have said that. That is a young girl speaking. A bitter and lonely girl. Forget the other Zea and try to start again."

She stared into his eye. "You can't change my identity," she said.

"I know," he sighed. "We are who we are. I imagined that power could solve all problems. I was right, I think. But I was wrong in thinking that the solution came intrinsically with the power. It does not—one has to find it. Everything that was wrong before I won what I wanted is still wrong, and I do not know how to right it. Every mistake I ever made remains a mistake.

"I think, now, that in any conflict—with others, with one's own past—it doesn't matter at all *what* you are. It only matters *who* you are. Life is a battle of identity."

"What do you want with me?" she asked.

"I'm not sure. To talk, I think. Perhaps I need your help. I know that I wanted to ask for it."

"I can't help you. You're the creator, the powerful one."

"How do I change my identity? How can I take something from my own mind and destroy it?"

"What?"

"Dragon."

"He's dead. He was killed a long way from here, some time ago."

"He might be dead, but he isn't destroyed. He's still in here." The Blind Worm tapped his forehead. "He made me, and he's still alive in every fiber of my flesh and every thought in my head."

"Then kill him again," she advised.

"How do I destroy the idea?"

"Recreate him and kill him in a way which will eradicate him. Take him from your mind and put him back in his own body. Make the thing which you create everything which you want to destroy. And then kill him again."

"Like sticking pins in a wax doll!" the cyclops sneered.

"Precisely. Except that it's yourself that you're trying to change. Everything in this universe is an embodiment of you. Every atom in this universe was part of a vast hive. It still has that unity. Your identity *is* the universe. You are everywhere and everything in it is you. When you create and destroy, you are pulling the puppet-strings of your own mind. That's what the power has given you. Use it. Isolate what you don't want and destroy it. This is real, material symbolism. Sympathetic magic can work in this framework. Ritualize the killing. Make as much use of symbolism as you can, and you can tear your own subconscious out by the roots."

"I'm not sure," said the Blind Worm doubtfully.

"It's true. What do you think really happened when the Wildland destroyed Ocean? Do you imagine that it was a simple matter of securing the waters of the seas? How did you think that Sum embodied his enemy in a group of humans? There never was an Ocean, really. I never existed save as the synthetic scapegoat of the Wildland. There never were two gigantic hive minds struggling for world domination. There was one hive mind struggling for mastery of itself. I represented all the unwanted ideas that the Wildland had collected while Sum was being born and reaching maturity. And so I was isolated and destroyed. The physical part of it was never more than the appropriation of the Earth's resources for its own use. Everything else was ritual. Do you understand?"

"I didn't know," said the Blind Worm quietly. "It is harder than I thought. There is much more to it than I imagined. It is not easy to become a god."

"You can learn. It is no more difficult than being a man."

The cyclops laughed softly. "I was never a man either. I'm a machine. That is what I was built to be. That is what I shall always be."

"You have the power to be anything you want," she said.

"All I need is the knowledge. I have to learn. It will take time."

"You have a great deal of time."

There was a pause, then the Blind Worm spoke again. "Yours must have been a strange existence. A scapegoat without any real life of your own. Were you human, Zea, or were you just a machine as well?"

"Neither. I am like this." She had been digging in the sand, and had unearthed the corpse of a many-legged crab-like creature with a scratched brown carapace. "It's a relic—a dead thing. It retains its shape, but it's hollow inside. Its guts are gone; it's a futile, meaningless thing. What's left is what the carrion-eaters couldn't eat—neither use to itself nor to anything else. Can you blame me for not wanting to live—for shrinking from a hive to a lone individual, so that when I die there will be nothing left? Can you blame me for trying to find *something* by loving Vanice Concuma? And does it surprise you that it resulted in his death?

"Every day I curse the Wildland. More than anything, I hate Sum's concept of morality which made him destroy without killing. That was Sum's justice, to strip me of everything I had and everything I was and then to leave me, still living, like a ghost. No matter what I do, I can never be anything else now. Not human, not even a machine."

Zea rose to her feet and hurled the corpse of the sea creature to one side. It shattered, the legs flying from the body.

The Blind Worm stared at the wreckage which marked the tide-line as the girl walked away from him. Soon, there was no sign of life again. Only of death. The sea lapped gently up the beach toward the line of detritus. A few strands of dead seaweed were visible beneath the surface, where waves and eddies tossed them about.

The Blind Worm began walking back the way he had come.

## XII

IT HAD BEEN raining recently and the ground was muddy. The mounds of dirt and rubble on either side of the road had been leached over the years so that they had spread, drowning the pavements and the tarmac and making a new floor for the dead city. There were plants almost everywhere, but they looked unhealthy and stunted. There was too much metal in the ground—tin sheets and tendrils were more common than living leaves and roots.

Among the gullies and blackened bricks walked the Blind Worm. He paused for a moment beside the remains of a car. The bodywork had been stripped bare of paint and was a mass of splintering rust. Its wheel-less axles were buried deep in the mud and the car listed to one side. Rammed into its interior were the remains of a much smaller vehicle, its roof crumpled and torn, its wings folded up and its wheels and engine missing. Strewn around the metalwork were shapeless tangles of undecipherable origin.

Towering over the wrecked buildings was a crane, corroded arms pointed tirelessly at the regathering rainclouds.

Glass seemed to have preserved its identity better than metal, but it existed only as shattered pieces, gouged and scored. At least it had not degenerated into shapelessness.

Pieces of wall still stood—mostly at the corners of houses. Where their shelter had protected the soil from being transformed into the life-devouring dust, the squalid plant invasion had done its best job. Dark red and dark green abounded, with some yellow. There was no lushness, though, only the depressing coarseness of willowherb and chickweed.

The most remarkable feature of the landscape was a church, older than most of the blighted city, yet hardly touched by time. Its roof was in disrepair, and the wood of its doors was partially rotted, but that was all. Where the tiles were gone, it showed its beams, and the small bell could be seen still hanging in the crumbling steeple. The bell might even be able to ring, although its tone would be ruined by rust. But it existed defiantly, refusing to be lost in the floods of time which had engulfed its surroundings.

The Blind Worm hurled a brick into the rafters, aimed at the bell. It missed and fell inside the church with a rattle. A man appeared in the doorway, moving the great door gently, as if afraid that it would fragment while he held it.

"You had to be here," said the Blind Worm, almost whimsically. "You always needed a church to add sanctity to your sermonizing. So I've given you one. A dead church in a dead city for a dead man. I've begun to adjust—I've begun to make things the way they ought to be."

"You're going to kill me again, aren't you?" asked Dragon with easy scorn. "You're going to kill me over and over until you've driven yourself mad. I can't be destroyed. I'm too close to you, too much a part of you. I made you, Worm, and I know. I created you, remember?"

"And I've created you. That makes us even."

"Following in my footsteps? That's good. You'll follow me all the way to your own little hell, when you go insane."

"I won't go insane. I'll get rid of the devil which is

possessing me. I'll cast him out, exorcise him. I can do it, Dragon. You can't run away, because you have nowhere to escape to. I have the power; I can kill you. It's like cutting out a cancer—a surgical operation performed with precision. My plan is forming—soon I'll know exactly how it will be done. I'll be free of you then."

"You're wrong, Worm." The Dragon was mocking, as always. "The cancer is all of you. You must know how much the created is a part of the creator. I created you and you created me. We're one and the same, Worm. It's a paradox. You can't separate us."

"That's arrogance talking," said the Blind Worm with assurance. "You never exercised so much control over me that I was nothing without you. I'm better than you in every way. It couldn't have been your meager brain that created me. It was something else, something I don't recognize in you any more. You lost it when you went mad. Whatever drove you when you created me is no longer there. It's not in the Dragon I want to expel, it's not in the Dragon I've created.

"The thing I've created is the thing I killed. There's nothing carrying you except hatred. You've changed your identity since you created me."

"You're a fool, Worm," said the yellow man. "The identity of mine that's in you is the identity that was in me when I created you. You can't get rid of it by destroying anything else."

"What I want to get rid of is the taint—the seeds of madness, all that is wrong in me that I inherited from you. Whatever you had that enabled you to create me then, I'll keep. I don't want to destroy that. All I want to exorcise is the evil. I can keep the rest. That's why I can do it. That's why there is enough in me which is not in *you*."

"You can't do it. You can't make distinctions like that."

"I will."

The Dragon shrugged. "You have the power. I have no choice in the matter. But I tell you, you'll lose."

"You have all the choice in the world," said the Blind Worm, smiling derisively. "A god has no power over the choices of his creations. That is why free choice is no paradox. My power is only to mold myself. You are on your own—your only limitation is the self which I gave you, which is no different from the self which you shaped for yourself on Earth. What you choose is determined by what you are. I can't make you choose any differently. This will be no mock battle, I assure you. If you can, you might even win and destroy me. I'm not invulnerable."

"I'll do my best, Worm," promised Dragon. But it will make no difference. Even if you do kill me, you can't get rid of me. Go away, Worm. Come back and kill me if you must, but leave me in peace until you do."

Dragon turned and walked back into his ruined church. The Blind Worm walked on down the lonely, devastated road.

*I wish I could be sure,* thought the cyclops. *He scares me; even now he scares me. But I know, at least, how to kill him. The question remaining is—who? Who wields the sword? Who would choose to take my side against Dragon? The black king will not do it. Shadow will do nothing without the king's approval. Vanice Concuma is the only one, but how can I make him do it? If only I could do it myself!*

*But the ritual is the important thing. The symbolic killing is more than the physical death. Striking him down with a lightning bolt would be worthless. It has to be an execution, and I need an executioner.*

*There is a way, if I can find it. But they are all working against me. Why can I create nothing but hatred?*

## XIII

VANICE CONCUMA, who had been lost in a great ocean on another world and had been created again, walked down a hillside into a great, high-ridged crater. The saucer of the crater was dull and somber under the illumination of a cloudy, dark sky. The sun was invisible, but it was probably early afternoon.

It would have been a drab scene to any eyes, but Vanice Concuma hated it. He hated every part of this weird universe whose worlds shifted and changed. Most of all, he hated the person who had put him into the world, the Blind Worm.

As he walked through the ugly landscape, he felt a cold fear and some anger. Both were born in loneliness, part of which was in his own mind and part of which was built into the world in which he was. He compared the crater to the blasted loculus of the Blind Worm's own skull. This world was no less and no more real than the Earth he had lived all his life on, but he could not help remembering its origin. The Vanice Concuma who walked beneath the cold crater walls and looked at the distant, cloud-tipped peaks was not the same Vanice Concuma who had lived on Earth, but the hatred and the memories were the same.

Deep within the crater, near the center, was a crevice filled with a light clay, like dirty snow in color. It was not wide, but it stood out quite clearly from the blacks and browns which surrounded it. The darker colors formed a mosaic pattern, blending little as they spread in macabre array from the livid scar all the way out to the rim of the bowl.

The ridge, which ran all the way around the crater, was uneven, with numerous chopped-off pinnacles. A few trees could be seen in silhouette on the skyline. There was no life in the crater itself. Whatever the black, brown and gray soil was, it was totally hostile to vegetation.

The stuff was solid beneath his feet, and there seemed to be little or no difference in texture between the scabs of various colors. The patches were not smooth, but whorled and lined. Here and there were imprints which appeared to have some specific design, but the forms which he saw there he assumed to be figments of his own imagination. In his mind, he made a circle around the white slit which gave it the appearance of a lidded eye; then he made the crater the head of a sleeping beast, diseased by the cloying phlegm of clay and rock, its slack, furrowed skin sagging from its cheeks, and the sick white of its eye turned sightlessly to the gray firmament.

The king waited with Shadow on the brink of the white crevice. He raised his right hand in greeting. "We are together once again," he said.

"No," said Vanice Concuma. "It is not once again. It is the first time. A new world and a new time."

"Inside, you are the same."

"Because you are the same? We are never the same from one moment to the next. I had changed before we talked to Sum. I was changed when I was plunged into the sea. I don't think we are together again. That is ended."

"Because of Zea? I am carrying no grudge because of that. I am willing to forget, if you are."

"No, I am not. It's nothing you've done, nothing you are. It's in me, just me. I'm going to find Zea."

"What is it that you want?" asked Shadow.

"Nothing you can help me to get."

"I'll help you in any way I can. You know that."

Concuma shook his head. "The old days are over. This is a new world. I don't want the old one back. In the old world, I would be dead. This is a new start."

"That's no reason to throw us aside," said the king.

"Perhaps not. Perhaps in time—"

"There is no time," said the king. "We need you now. It is a matter of taking sides again."

"And who are you fighting this time?"

"The Blind Worm."

Concuma laughed. "You are a strange man, John. Always the same fire and the same ambitions. What can you hope to gain by fighting the Blind Worm?"

"His power. The power to give me what I want. It's rightfully mine. I should have completed the Quadrilateral, not the Blind Worm."

"You can't fight him. He's too powerful. This is his universe. He created us and can destroy us just as easily. It's his now."

The king shook his head. "We can take it away from him. We have free choice. We can control our own destinies."

"Don't be a fool. You have only what he gave you. He cannot possibly be fought."

"He is not safe yet. He is not safe while Dragon lives inside his mind. By isolating Dragon as an entity, he has given himself the chance to get rid of him for good. But he

has also given Dragon the chance to destroy *him*. I am ally-
ing myself with Dragon. I want you to do the same."

"You have talked to Dragon?"

"Yes."

"He has infected you with his own madness. You cannot
possibly do what he says. I will not work for Dragon."

"Then you are on the side of the Blind Worm?"

"You dramatize too much," answered Concuma steadily.
"I am on no one's side but my own."

"And what about Zea?" asked Shadow.

Concuma ignored the question. "Have you joined this
ridiculous plot?"

Shadow spread his hands. "I seem to have. But I think
that if a fight comes I shall treasure my own side more than
the black king's. I made the mistake once of not thinking
like that."

The king looked angrily at the slender man, but said
nothing. Shadow waited for Concuma to reply to his own
question.

"Zea?" said Concuma. "She won't help you. She won't
want anything to do with any of this stupidity. She's finished
with power. All she wants is peace."

"The greatest fighter on Earth," sneered the king. "And
you want to stop fighting. *Peace!* I hope you and the girl
enjoy your peace."

"I hope we will. I hope you enjoy your war. If I were
you, I'd forget the black king of Earth. Leave your fanaticism
on the ocean planet and find some new way to live."

The king coughed. "I can't do that, Vanice. Perhaps you're
right and things have changed, but in this world as in any
other I have to be what I am. If I am an atavism, it is the
fault of my creator rather than myself. I can only do what
I must. If you are not with me, then you can only be
against me."

"I'm not against you, unless you place yourself against
me."

"I will if I must. If you stand in my way, through your
own fault or not, I'll kill you."

"Perhaps," said Concuma, not believing it.

"I will," repeated the king. "I must have the power which is owed to me."

"You can't take it from him when you're only a character in his dream."

"This is no dream. This is a universe as real as the one in which he abandoned me. Do you feel unreal, or flesh and blood? Nothing is different except the ways of the worlds and the balance of power. I am working for the same ends as always. If I fail, well and good. But I must try."

"You have been infected by Dragon. You're chasing his lost cause. Has he made you hate your humanity yet?"

"Who are you to talk about hatred?" cried the king. "You hate your race as much as he did. I can see the hatred in you now, Concuma, in your face and behind your eyes. Your hatred is your strength, remember? Don't preach to me about *my* hate."

Concuma shrugged. He said nothing.

"It's no use," said Shadow. "Goodbye, Vanice."

"There is still hope," said the king.

Vanice Concuma had turned away, and was walking back up the slope toward the lip of the crater.

"Is there?" asked Shadow cynically.

"The Blind Worm can never force Concuma to kill Dragon. Concuma hates him and Concuma's hatred is insurmountable."

"And unpredictable. I don't know what he'll do. There's more in him now than hate. Perhaps there will be a new strength. When he takes arms—if he does—I warn you that it will not be me who tries to bar his way. You can do it alone."

"I can win. I am the greatest fighter in this or any other universe. There is no one more powerful."

"There is Concuma," said Shadow confidently. "And behind Concuma, there is Zea."

## XIV

THE ROAD WAS roughly hewn stone, worn to smoothness by the treading feet of many generations. It was flanked by dense forest, oak forest of great age.

Beyond the forest, or perhaps within it, away to the east, were four very high narrow towers. Fires burned at the top of each one, making them beacons in the dusk. The sun hovered low in the part of the sky most remote from the towers, and barely outshone them as it set in a bank of dull blue cloud. There were clouds behind the towers too, but thinner, paler clouds that floated slowly along in a wind that barely stirred the leaves on the trees.

The Blind Worm sat by the bole of an ancient oak, watching the towers and thinking. Numerous black birds sat in the branches above him, mournfully contemplating the dusty road some feet away. Further away, a bird was singing melodiously, but that too sounded a little mournful.

There were other lights, barely visible, some way down the road. They represented houses in a loose community which was not even large enough to think of as a village.

Hoof beats sounded on the cobblestone, approaching slowly. There was a rustle in the trees as the black birds grew slightly agitated, but they calmed down and returned to their semi-torpor.

The rider dismounted and came toward the Blind Worm. He wore a flowing purple cloak, high fur boots and leather jacket. His head was bare and his long blond hair hung loose about his shoulders. It was Vanice Concuma. He left his horse without tying it. It stood quietly.

"Hello, Vanice," said the Blind Worm.

"Are you collecting allies, too?" asked Concuma. "I wouldn't have thought it necessary."

"It's necessary. Far more than you might think. All the power in the universe isn't without its limits and its faults. I need help, just as anyone else might."

"Just to fight the black king and Dragon? Surely they can't harm you."

"Harm me?" the Blind Worm repeated absently. "No, they can't harm me. But I have to destroy them. It's a personal matter, you see."

"No, I don't. You can destroy them as easily as you created them."

"It isn't easy," said the Blind Worm. "It's not the killing that's important, it's the way it's done. I have to cleanse my universe, wipe out the disease. It's not enough just to banish them from it physically. I have to erase what they stand for."

"And what do they stand for?"

"Dragon for evil, the black king for tyranny."

"And what do you want from me?"

"Your help. I can't buy you, Concuma. I can't force you. What I need from you is inside you, and only you can bring it out. You live within me and because of me—I don't expect you to be grateful for that—but your life is your own, your will is yours. I won't bribe you or threaten you. I simply ask you to find out where you stand, and hope that it will be with me. It's your own affair—you can choose to side with the black king if you want."

"I don't want to take *any* side," complained Concuma.

"You have to. You are in the center of the battle. Its outcome may depend on you."

"I can't see why."

"I need a warrior. I need a hero, a champion, a disciple. I need someone to perform an operation on my universe and remove a cancer from it. It has to be someone other than myself. I can create and uncreate, but to strike something from myself is something someone else must do."

"But I'm a part of you. I have no existence except in you."

"You have free will. You are who you are. Even when I create you, I must give you an identity of your own. That identity is what I need to exterminate Dragon from my mind."

Concuma's eyes wandered to the road. They looked up at the tall, beautiful towers with their beacon fires at their peaks. He looked at the black birds and breathed deeply of the cool air.

"I'm finished with fighting," he said.

"You can't be," replied the Blind Worm. "It's in your blood. You don't premeditate fighting, you either *need* it or you don't. I think you need it. Irrespective of motive, with no reasoning, no loyalty, without even knowing why, you'll fight. You'll be driven by the ache in your belly, the screw in your mind. It's your decision, and you have free will —but there's only one way you can decide, and that will be determined by who you are. Go, if you like, think about it. But I think you'll do it."

Vanice Concuma remounted the silent horse.

"You might be right," he said. "If you are, I'll come back and admit it. I hope that you're wrong. The waiting's yours, though, Worm. The uncertainty and the fear are yours."

"I'll see you again," promised the Blind Worm in farewell.

The Blind Worm watched Concuma ride away in the direction of the towers. Behind them, the sky was dark and starlight was gathering to halo the yellow fires, which now seemed so tiny against the backcloth of night.

The bird which had been singing was silent now, but there was still an occasional rustle from the black birds in the branches, which could still be seen as dim shadows.

The Blind Worm rose wearily to his feet and began to walk. There were other places to be, other people to talk to. But he was confident now that he knew Concuma, and knew that Dragon would be destroyed.

He had formed his plan. He knew how to wake the blond man's anger. He saw clearly the spur which would have to be applied to drive Concuma into blind, unreasoning madness and hate. The hate had to be so intense and immediate that Concuma would not for one moment contemplate joining the Dragon and the black king in their quixotic quest, but would need a flow of real blood in the shortest possible time to appease it.

While he considered the details of the scheme, he walked from one world to another, from passive night to vibrant day.

The sudden light disturbed him momentarily, and he could see nothing but heat haze and hot mist for some seconds.

Then his vision cleared and he saw the sweating jungle of green leaves, large and spatulate, growing from twisted trunks and multitudinous branches. There was a superabundance of light and humidity. The sun itself was only a blur in the steamy mist, but its light was profuse. The riotous lushness of the vegetation might have been confusing under other circumstances, but the Blind Worm at this moment knew exactly where he was going and exactly what he had come to find. He stepped forward confidently.

The ground beneath his feet was mobile brown swamp mud, liberally splashed with pools and puddles of stagnating water. There was a great deal of deep green grass in the more secure mud, and where the water was more than an inch deep it was a soup of algae and diatoms spread thickly in the muddy matrix. There were animals in the water too, but for the most part the animals kept to the surface, skimming or splashing in the shallows. Larger flying insects like dragonflies darted low over the surface again and again, voraciously taking their fill from the clouds of smaller insects which swarmed close to the ground, humming loudly and persistently. Occasionally there would be a surface disturbance to indicate the presence of larger creatures in the deeper pools.

The roots of the trees were usually embedded on tussocks of grass which elevated parts of the ground, but often the roots sprawled messily for quite some distance. The ground closer to water level was colonized mostly by smaller woody plants and tall plants reminiscent of vast rhubarb sticks.

The trees themselves were crawling with insects; larger animals, like reptilian squirrels, constantly ran over the branches, feeding from the multitudes.

As he walked, he had to brush from his path hundreds of jewel-winged insects—mostly flies and midges. There seemed to be an incredible biomass of small insects feeding on the plant material and being fed on in turn by a series of predators. It was like a fantastic multiplication and acceleration of life in the Wildland, with the insects reincarnate.

His eye was persistently troubled by landing mosquitoes,

and the tear glands wept continuously as his nictitating membrane flicked across the lens again and again. He felt the hordes of landbound arthropods which his feet encountered slowly ascending his legs, and he stopped occasionally to brush them off. But it was impossible to keep them away. By sheer weight of numbers they invaded the crevices between his scales. Sometimes they stung, and many of them tried to suck blood from his tissues, but his skin was too tough and thick for them to bother him. The only irritant which mattered was the continual sensation of their crawling over him. In time he got used to it and began to ignore it, troubling only to keep them clear of the slits beneath his opercula.

He crossed a stretch of muddy sand which was strewed with rotting shellfish and covered by worm castings. His feet sank deep into the cool moist sand and relieved him of a great number of the pests he had collected. The humidity was making him sweat profusely, and many of the insects on his skin could not have dislodged themselves had they wanted to.

The smell of the place was strong and unpleasant. There was a tangible air of decomposition and decay. There was a profusion of sound. In the background there was the eternal hum of the dipteran clouds, but superimposed with musical irregularity were the plops of larger animals in the water, the sawings of grasshoppers, the sighing of the wind and the suckings and hissing caused by the constant mobility of the swamp and the release of marsh gas.

He paused to rest, stretching his back muscles to try to alleviate the constant itch, but failed. He almost regretted the world, but not quite. This explosion of life and death was exactly appropriate to its role in his living play.

The sun shone through the mists for a few brief moments and he bathed in its burning heat, letting it dry the sweat from his skin and drive the flying insects away to the shade of the trees. The sun was oddly small, considering the incredible amount of radiance which it threw out. It was whiter and brighter by far than Earth's old sun.

A shadow passed across the sun, its shape indeterminate

in the glare. Diffraction blurred its outline as it flitted a-
round in a fast spiral above the swamp.

He glimpsed bat-like wings as it wheeled around, and
a long whip of a tail. Then suddenly it plunged, skimmed in
between several of the trees and was lost from sight. The
cyclops caught a glimpse of leathery gray skin. He followed the object at a run, guessing the object of its swoop.

He found it gibbering and darting toward its intended
prey and kicked it away. It chattered angrily as it stumbled,
then leaped clumsily into the air and half-bounced, half-flew
away into the jungle.

The carrion which it had been after was the body of Zea.
He had known that it would be here, in this particular spot,
for this was what he had intended should happen. Her
skin was blued in several places by the poison which had
been pumped into it by the bites of various creatures. They
crawled over her now in thousands, eating the flesh away
and drinking her blood, and eating each other at the same
time.

He knelt beside the mud-stained body. He took a handful
of water from a nearby pool and splashed it on her face to
get rid of most of the insects. He brushed her eyes and
lips clean with gentle strokes of his horny hand.

Lying beside the body was the damp, dirty, never-
alive form of a miscarried child. It was smothered in blood
which still oozed slowly from her vagina. The blood became
a thick broth of insects before it clotted. There lay at the
feet of the Blind Worm the first sacrifices to a new god.
They would ensure the destruction of Dragon and the victory
of the Blind Worm.


## XV


VANICE CONCUMA stood on the reef looking down into the
clear water. The sun made silver patterns on the surface,
which sparkled as it moved and rippled. There was some
depth of water, but it was so clear that he could see every
detail of the golden sandy floor of the lagoon. Hundreds of
strange fish glinted as they flew through the sunlit water.

Others hid their bright colors against the gem-like pebbles scattered on the bed of the pool.

Near the edges, some distance away where the water was quiet, there were long tresses of seaweed. On the reef itself, where the waves bobbed and bounced more violently, there were only sedentary mollusks.

Beneath the surface of the water, he could see the polyps in the coral sweeping the water with gill-nets, trapping food too small to be visible. A hairy crab, with clumsy, spider-like legs and big red chelae, scuttled across the sand. It moved very quickly considering its wobbling, mock-dancing gait.

Clouds of tiny opalescent firefish continually slid aside to allow larger fish passage. The shadows of the tiny fish were hardly distinguishable on the sea bed, and looked like a fine mist, dispersing at the approach of phantoms.

Concuma's eyes idly followed the furious darts of the shoals of diamond bright fish. He thought them purposeful, yet futile. But the darkness and pain in his eyes made it clear that he was not thinking about the fish at all, except in the merest surface thoughts running across his mind. Almost blindly he watched the soaring of the larger fish and the snake-like motion of a shark. The patterns on his retina registered in his brain, and he pretended to look at them, but he did not remember them.

"There is so much life," he said aloud when the shadow fell on the water, signaling that someone stood behind him. "You have brought so much life into your worlds, but I can only find death. Is the profusion too great? Can't you sustain it?"

"There's always death," said the Blind Worm. He held the body of Zea cradled in his arms. The insects were gone, and the poison of their bites was dissipating, but the body retained its discoloration and its ugliness.

"You killed her," said Concuma without malice.

"She died because of the miscarriage. It was your child."

"I killed her, then. It is all the same in the end. It was the way things went. This is your world, my existence. She is gone from both of them. I'm burned out—everything is lost."

"Not everything."

"No," spat Concuma, "I still have my hatred. I'm alone with it again. Everything else is dead. I'm Vanice Concuma again, the man who hates, the man who kills. That's what you wanted, isn't it? That's the man you wanted, not the man I was yesterday, not the man you created. I had to be shaped, didn't I? Rehabilitated! You had to make a hero."

"I didn't change you. That was in yourself."

"You could have stopped her dying! Even if you didn't murder her yourself, you could have saved her. Why should I do anything for you after you did that? Why should I?"

"You don't have to do anything for me. It's your choice. I can't force you."

Vanice Concuma took the corpse of Zea from the arms of the Blind Worm. The blood was gone—the cyclops had cleaned the body. "Give me the sword and give me the strength," he said bitterly. "I'll use them. But I won't promise to win. I won't promise to stay alive long enough to do that. I won't promise to try to stay alive at all."

"The sword will come," promised the Blind Worm. "And the strength. You won't see me again, like this. When my identity changes, other things will as well. This body is part of the heritage of Dragon. I don't want it. You'll see me again and you may know me. Remember the eye. Remember this whole universe is composed of shadows in an eye. I'm going now."

Vanice Concuma made no sign, nor did he say anything. He simply stood with the burden in his arms, watching the receding figure. Another figure could be seen, coming toward him. The two must have crossed, but neither was aware of the other or, if they were, they showed no sign.

The approaching man was the black king. He walked forward silently until he was only a few feet from the blond man, then looked at the body of the girl for long moments.

"I'm sorry," he said, but there was no genuine compassion in his voice.

"It's over," murmured Concuma.

"Who killed her?" demanded the king.

"Myself as much as anyone. My son, too."

"I don't understand."

"You can't understand. You never will. It happened, that is all. Justice or injustice, guilt and innocence, it doesn't matter very much. The end is always the same."

"What will you do now?" asked the king.

"Kill Dragon. Kill anyone in my way. Kill and kill and kill. Feed the hunger that's left."

"But why?" protested the king. "What has Dragon done to you? If you want some sort of revenge, take it out on the Blind Worm, who's to blame if anyone is. You hate him, remember."

"How can I help but remember?" returned Concuma. "How can I mask the hatred now? It's all there is. It's consuming me."

"Then appease it! Help us against the Blind Worm."

"You can't ever understand, King. You're a barbarian with ambition instead of credulity. You have no gods; you have nothing to put in their place but icons of yourself. You can't hope to understand because you would have to believe, and you don't believe in anything except your own failure. What I have to do, King—it isn't to gratify my desires, to achieve any ends, to serve any design. It's because of a need, a thing inside of me which tells me what to do."

"You're illogical. You don't know what you're saying."

"Fight on, King. You don't know anything but your own visions and schemes. They won't ever work because they're impossible. But keep fighting, because it's all you can do. Keep losing, too, because that's all you're worth."

"Concuma," said the king in carefully controlled tones, "has there ever been a man who could kill you?"

"If there was, King, then it would have been you. But you wouldn't be fighting *me* if you fought now. You'd be fighting the thing inside me, the thing with the power. Yesterday you could have killed me. Tomorrow only I can kill myself, only I can choose to die. You will lose, King, if you try to stop me. No more aims, no more dreams. I'll kill you, King."

"I'll remember."

Vanice Concuma shook his head and held up the body of the girl. "She too is against you now. Zea, the Blind

Worm and me. You have the chance to forget what you want and find something else."

"I have no choice. None at all. The will may be free, but I am bound. The course is already decided."

The black king turned away.

"He will fight," whispered Concuma, as though to the inert body which lay in his arms. "He does not believe. He knows that I can kill him, and that he cannot kill me. What's the use?"

## XVI

HE ENTERED the cavern, avoiding the slimy water which dripped steadily from the roof and made a discontinuous whir as it splashed on to the floor. Dirty white stalactites hung everywhere, and water ran down their uneven sides to hang for a moment before being forced to drop by the steady trickle.

He went deeper into the cave, which wound tightly, so that he was soon quite isolated from the outside world. The dim light shone from the roof and the walls, throwing no shadows. The source was visible as a number of star-like silver points scattered in the granite walls.

The running water formed a stream which gradually widened and deepened as the tunnel burrowed further down into the ground, twisting like a spiral staircase. Soon he was walking on a narrow ledge beside the underground stream. The slope became steeper and the water rushed faster and faster toward the center of the world.

Finally he reached a right-angled bend in the ledge. The water rushed in the same direction, falling into empty space. The pit appeared bottomless from where he stood, looking down the sheer face of rock which swept away beneath him.

The ledge went on for some yards and then ended in a solid face of rock, into which was etched an alcove. In the alcove was a pedestal on which rested a sword and a skull. The skull had only one eye socket.

He reached forward to take the sword and felt a rustling

in the skull. Tentatively, he tipped the skull over. It rolled to one side and a white shape emerged from the hole where the spine had articulated. It was hairless and eyeless, and seemed to bear most resemblance to a short-tailed lizard. It croaked faintly as it ran around on the pedestal, seeking some means of escape.

He picked up the sword and was about to decapitate the beast when the skull spoke.

"Leave the animal alone," it said. "The sword is for a different purpose."

"Who are you?" demanded Concuma.

"No one. I ceased to be a long time ago."

"Where do I find Dragon?"

"In the Wildland. In the Wildland the Blind Worm has created. Go there and wait."

"The strength. I was promised the strength."

"When you need the strength, it will be there. You need no external help. It is inside you, inherent within you."

The lizard at last gathered enough courage, or sufficient desperation, to leap down from the pedestal. It disappeared behind the structure of stone. Vanice Concuma tested the weight of the blade and found it comfortable to his hand. The hilt was ornate, and the blade short and broad. He sheathed it in his belt, where he already wore a dagger.

Then he retraced his way along the ledge, up toward the daylight once more. For the first time, he felt the coldness of the air and of the silvery light from the walls.

Eventually he emerged once again into the outer world. It was not the same world from which he had entered the cavern. He shivered briefly, because it was as cold and damp out here as it had been in the cave. He walked forward.

A light mist swirled gently about him, recoiling as he walked through it. The light filtering through the fog was bluish and carried no warmth with it. He saw dim, half obscure shapes of violet and magenta, dull brown and many shades of green. The foliage was dense but ghost-like in the clinging fog.

There were tall plants with spiky leaves projecting in clusters, with ridged stems and wrinkled apical buds creased like pulpy paper. The roots were partially above ground, forming a cage-like structure half buried in black sticky soil. Around the stems crept lavender colored parasite stems with wide leaves that were blotched with blue and white, swollen and bulbous. The flowers were miniature splashes of greasy red and pink.

He saw other plants like traps or netted baskets, with curled supporting ribs and thin cross-filaments. Luminous flowers like lures glowed softly inside the bowls of the nets. The thick stalks were gray and off-white in color, streaked and branded with pale yellow and ocher. Near them lay fungi like inflated bladders filled with water. They were of many colors, tiger striped with black or dark blue.

Concuma peered into the mist, trying to make out more. The colors seemed abnormal and unnatural. The forest stretched as far as he could see on all sides, fading into the mist. It was unbroken by rock or pool or path. The height of the vegetation was remarkably even, considering its diversity, and was never higher than seven feet. There was no wind and no movement at all except for the steady fall of condensation from the dough-textured leaves. The water seeped into the soil, turning patches of it into thick mud.

He walked, picking his way carefully, avoiding the damper patches and the leprous fungi which were scattered throughout the forest. The time passed slowly; he seemed to walk for hours. The sky grew no darker, but the sunlight—if there was sun behind the cloud—was no more than a weak glimmer that might have been moonlight or starlight. The plants were more strongly illuminated by the eerie gleam of the lantern-like influorescences in the trap plants. By this weird illumination he watched the water droplets wavering as they trickled down the leaves like the water running from the stalactites in the cave.

The fog began to fall as frost, which sparkled and glinted on the ground. The stars at last shone through; the sun was visible only as a silver sash on the horizon, which heralded the dawn. On the opposite horizon, sinking out of sight with only a thin sliver still visible, was a second sun. Even with the new clarity, he could see no limit in any direction to the dense vegetation. It was not like the Wildland he had known, but it was a wildland. It was not sentient, though. It was mindless. He felt that as he looked at it.

There was no skeleton, as in the Wildland he knew, no womb-like quality. It was alien, as if every individual plant bore the identical imprint of an anti-human architect. Somehow Concuma found it difficult to associate the landscape with the Blind Worm, despite the unhumanity of the cyclops.

The silver light limned some of the plants nearer to him, and their listless carriage seemed all the more oppressive. Then, not far away, he saw a break in the canopy, a small circular clearing. At its center was a small fire made of the flesh of some of the plants. They burned reluctantly, with a strangely white flame. Curls of smoke drifted slowly upward into the cold air. At the edge of the clearing, between the blond man and the fire, stood the black king.

"I am impatient," said Vanice Concuma evenly.

The black king drew the long sword from his scabbard and held it loosely, pointed downward. He was unarmored, but wore some garment wrapped around his left wrist. "It's always been too late, my friend. I have to fight. There is nothing else I can do."

"I know."

"It's not my world, Concuma. But there's nothing very much changed. There's no way to retreat, no way to change aims. This is a wanderer's universe. Only a wanderer can be happy here. I want to rest. I want to own something. There's nothing at all for me here. I don't fit.

"Once, the strings were in my hand. I know that was another me in another universe, but nevertheless it was my hand. And in that universe, even though I lost it, I still had a chance. Here there is no chance. I don't want to play when the whole world's loaded against me. But I have to, because that's the way I am."

"I'm coming through now," said Vanice Concuma. "It's your choice now. No matter what the odds are, it's always your choice. You have that much freedom."

The black king shook his head. "That freedom is an illusion. If there were any real freedom, you wouldn't be

here either. You'd be with Zea, never dreaming of fighting
for the Worm. When did you have a choice without your
hand being forced one way or the other? Come and kill me,
friend."

Vanice Concuma moved forward, easily and relentlessly.
In his left hand he held the sword which he had taken
from the cave, in the right was his own dagger. He
warded off the black king's first stroke almost casually, flick-
ing forward a feint of his own that was countered with
equal facility. Then, with a flurry of feet, the duel began in
earnest.

The very real difference in skill became quickly apparent
as Vanice Concuma was forced again and again to avoid
by speed thrusts which his guard failed to cover. Twice his
clothing was brushed lightly, but his own weapons never
passed the defense of the black king. The single blade was
easily a match for the pair, and more besides. Eventually,
it licked the blond man's face and cut a long diagonal slash
from temple to chin, the point dancing close in front of the
eye without making contact.

The black king suddenly laughed aloud. His tongue
flashed over his dry, black lips. *He's not afraid!* he realized
exultantly. *His strength is gone; he's nothing. What has
happened to him? The Blind Worm must have made a mistake. This is not Vanice Concuma!*

Vanice Concuma found with acute horror that he did not
hate the black king. He was empty. The strength which
the Blind Worm had promised him was not there. It was as
though the pain which had accompanied the death of Zea
was dead, and the death of his hatred would lose him
the fight. He was helpless before the black king, and the
black king sensed his helplessness. The king did not know
if his advantage would last, and so he fought with demoniac
fury. He was no longer fighting a losing battle.

And then the Blind Worm acted.

Sweat was running into the black king's eyes. There was
a terrible heat in Concuma's belly. Each man could feel his
heart pounding at a thunderous pace. The blond warrior
grew stronger with every blow. As the hatred flooded his
lungs and his wrists every stroke gained him ground over

his opponent. The black king was finished. He felt Concuma's raw power growing and growing and never stopping, as though nothing could ever stop it. He lost the ability to judge the blond man's movements individually. The dreary landscape whirled around his darkening mind. His eyes seemed swollen and would not see the dancing wild man.

Then his sword hit home. Half-blind, having given up hope, he felt his sword sink deep and a warm, sticky substance gushed over his hand. He swayed and lurched, but with a burst of triumph which multiplied his strength, twisted the blade within the wound and pushed it even deeper.

As the black king sank to his knees, he yelled as loudly as he could, "I have killed Concuma!" Then he felt the blade enter his stomach and run right through till it penetrated between his ribs and pinned him to the damp earth. He lay there, his right hand still clutching the sword buried hilt-deep in the mangled stem of a trap-flower, the wan lure hanging just above his ecstatic face, sap dripping from the plant flesh into his open eyes.

Vanice Concuma stepped away, not bothering to withdraw the sword. All of a sudden he felt tired and afraid. As the black king's last defiant shout had stirred the bobbing crown of the flower, he had seemed to feel a blade within his own body. But he was completely unharmed save for the cut on his face.

The black king's black blood ran into the soil where he lay impaled. There was the first breath of wind in the mock wildland; there was a strange humming music from the plants, and the clouds obscuring the dawn began to clear.

Into the clearing came the figure of Jose Dragon, lighted with an aura of its own and carrying a great hammer. The creator of the Blind Worm seemed ethereal and powerful, like a devil. Vanice Concuma saw that he *was* to fight a devil. This was the being that created the creator. This was a being who had no status adequate to describe him— the devil, the dragon, the enemy. And it would destroy the Blind Worm and his worlds if he could not stand in its way and prevent it. In Concuma's eyes and heart, this was no longer a fight between man and man, but between man and idea. He needed more than physical strength now, more than conviction and faith. Now was the time for fear and pain, and above all hate, pure emotion that would eclipse everything but itself. The power which had destroyed the black king was merely the pilot—it guided, it initiated. But Vanice Concuma's weapon now was beyond mere power.

Hate washed over him like the tides of Ocean. It numbed his mind and eradicated all thought from his brain. There was one thing now and one only—the object of his hatred.

It moved before his eyes. It shouted mightily and meaninglessly. It swung the giant hammer and wave after wave of fear rocked Concuma as the great gray head swept at his face.

Then he was beneath it, snatching at the wooden handle and smashing it with his fist. A mailed glove hit him in the mouth, breaking teeth and pulping his tongue, but the pain only added to the vast well of pain already in him. A boot drove hard into his groin, but he was hardly aware of it and did not stagger.

Irresistibly, one hand gripped a burning, stinging neck and gripped tight, locking in an unbreakable clasp. His foot was bedded in the knee joint, forcing the shin to the ground. His knee dug into the back just above the last lumbar vertebra. Slowly, irrevocably, he pulled backward.

The body of Dragon bent like a great bow, snapped once, twice, then again and again until Vanice Concuma threw it away like a useless doll and sagged to his knees. A river of blood issuing from his mouth cascaded over his fingers as he tried to wipe gummed lips. Then he stood up again, with pain shooting up his own spine from the exertion he had put into breaking Dragon's body.

He looked down at the smashed body of the yellow man. It did not bleed, simply lay limp and ragged. The sword from the cave, which Concuma had no memory of even retrieving from Tamerlane's body, was driven deep into the skull from the top.

He began to walk away—the reaction from his great burst of hate sending tongues of fire through his mind, so that he could not think.

His eyes blurred and the blood still flowed from his

mouth. He felt the delicate touch of hands on his forehead and knew it was Zea, though how and why he did not bother trying to guess. He grasped her hands between his and tried to speak, but found he could not, because his tongue was lacerated and blood filled his mouth and welled down his throat. He might have felt a kiss on his lips, or it might have been the moment when he drowned in his own blood.

Anyhow, a second or two afterward he realized that the Blind Worm had come and taken Zea away. That was to have been expected. Zea had always belonged more to the Blind Worm than to him. Even her son—Vanice Concuma's son—belonged to the Blind Worm. No choice was offered, but it would have been free if it had. Then he began sleeping and forgetting. Only once more did he open his eyes, and that was to see the bright cyclopean eye of the Blind Worm rising on the Eastern horizon to bring a real dawn to dispel the faint distasteful memories of the false one.

But he did not imagine, in his dream, whose eye it was, and he imagined that the tears he saw in it were irrationalities in the vacuum of his own eyes.

## PART 3   THE ARMY OF THE DEAD

## XVII

TAMERLANE watched the waves beating against the rock, and waited. There was nothing to wait for. Zea would not come back, nor would the Blind Worm. Swallow was dead, Concuma lost in the vast ocean. Shadow, very weak from loss of blood, and well on the way to death, looked at the king with mute eyes. He did not hate and he did not question.

"Don't look at me like that," said Tamerlane.

"You're a strong man, John," purred Reander. "It takes courage to sit and watch me die. I couldn't do it to you." His toneless voice held no trace of any resentment or mockery.

"All you have to do is die," snarled the black king. "I have to live with my failure."

"You're obsessed with your failure. You were doomed to fail. If you had another chance you'd fail again, and you'd wallow in your self-pity just as you are now."

Tamerlane shook his head. "There will be no more failure, except for death."

"She won't leave you to rot."

"Is that what you believe?"

"She won't leave me here to die."

Tamerlane laughed. "You! What are you? What am I? What was Concuma, even, to *her*? She is as fathomless as the seas around us. Don't expect anything of her."

"Maybe you aren't right," suggested Shadow.

The black king did not trouble to reply. The sky was blackening and it had begun to rain. He was not cold, but shivered and huddled to shelter himself nevertheless. The sea was not rough, but quiet and calm. The waves did not roar, but simply muttered as they hit the spur.

There was no lightning and no thunder, just rain and darkness.

"Look out to sea," said Shadow in a loud whisper.

"There is nothing."

"She's coming."

"She's gone forever."

"I can see."

"What can you see?"

"Horses. White horses—*pulling the sea!*"

The black king stood and moved forward, but there was nothing but the hiss of rain in the sea. The moist sand moved beneath his feet and he felt hard ridges of rock cutting into his soles. He moved further back and along the islet, crouching high on the flat slabs of stone which formed its spine. Above the everlasting rolling of the sea, he heard Shadow wailing something ever so faintly. It was as though Shadow were a long, long way away. It was as though he were falling deep into the bowels of the unknown world, and further than that. On and on, deeper and deeper —still the echo of Shadow's voice whined in the distance, in the recesses of his memory.

There was no dampness beneath his feet. The stone he crouched on was as cold and dry as a tombstone. The air around him was static and opaque. Sweat ran from his forehead into the corners of his eyes. He could feel a pulsebeat in his temple, and another in his neck, and another in the base of his hindbrain where the spinal cord entered the brain matter. The third was not the pumping of blood but the resonance of nerve tissue still trying to hear what Shadow was saying or had said, trying with memory to gather the shards of his senses and relocate them.

There was no time between the pulsebeats. There was only one beat and it lasted forever. He might have lived a thousand years and not seen them pass. While a single thought remained elusive in his struggling mind, he might have journeyed a million miles. . . .

The stars, blurred and multiplied by refraction and reflection, shone through beaded walls of ice. He was in a castle of ice and glass which—unsupported—floated free amidst the stars.

"I enjoy watching the stars," said a voice. "I like their company, their closeness. I like to live in a cage of stars, imprisoned from *inside*. Do you know what I mean?"

"Who are you?" said Tamerlane. He looked around and blinked away the tears from his eyes. The figure sat in a womb-like web of some soft, firm substance like plant flesh, visible only from the waist up, and sunk deeply into the cocoon-like structure. The figure wore a gown of dark brown cloth with a high hood, which bunched and creased around the neck. The sleeves were long and poised, as though the figure were resting invisible hands on the ridge of polished wood before it. Like the hands, within the hood there was no face.

"It's difficult to say. I don't think you would understand who I am. What you want is a name, and I can tell you that—Warwand, I call myself. But that means very little. It is a new name that I have taken since I last saw you, King."

"What you have said means nothing to me."

The figure named Warwand never moved. The voice from within the cowl never wavered. "You can't understand. You don't know what's happened. You're only a man."

"What do you want?"

Soft, murmurous laughter—melodic, like a vocal expression of Zea's visible echo of Ocean. "What do *you* want, King? What do you want from me?"

"What can you do for me?" The black king was relaxing slowly.

"I can send you back to Earth. Isn't that what you want? To run home? Having lost a little dignity, a little purpose, a little ambition and a little of your senses?"

"Who are you?"

Laughter again. The black king recoiled from it, twisted in confusion, and stopped dead. There was more laughter. Tamerlane reached out and touched the other body which lay on the stone floor. The man was unconscious but alive. His face was peaceful with no trace of pallor, and he was not wet. He was Vanice Concuma.

The black king turned again. "Shadow . . . ?" he asked.

"No use. He died. *You* killed him. In a fit of blind rage, you slaughtered him."

Tamerlane was silent. He made no apology, no excuse, even to himself.

"Do you even care?" sneered the voice from the hood.

Tamerlane remained silent, waiting for Warwand to begin explaining.

"I'll take you back to Earth," said Warwand. "I'll give you what you want. You can have Earth if you can defend it."

"Against the Quadrilateral?"

"The Quadrilateral has no tighter hold on Earth than you have on your soul. Earth is passing into the hands of the dead. Its dead past has come to reclaim it. There is something in the city of the Great Gulf—the city which you once thought that you could own—something that wants the Earth. It has an army—of men long forgotten and men never known. An army of the dead, marching on the Wildland to destroy Sum.

"The power of the Quadrilateral is useless. It is not the appropriate kind of power. It is power of the mind over the structure and laws of the universe. But it is not fighting the laws of the universe. The thing in the city has no mind. It is dead."

"I don't understand you."

"On Earth, the Wildland will burn and fall. The waters will return to the ocean beds. Sum will be destroyed—the Quadrilateral broken and banished. Every last human being in the world will be destroyed. The dead have come to retake their world for their new master. All the dead men are marching to war against the living.

"I don't know what this thing in the city is. I can't quite understand it myself, but I understand why the Quadrilateral can't fight it. The Quadrilateral is afflicted with one great handicap: it is a hive mind. It is too mechanical and too defined. A hive mind *is* all its components, and all its components work by reflex. They cannot receive direct instructions from Sum because they are all parts of Sum. They are coded for one pattern of existence, one pattern of behavior, each serving its own function in the great organism. The loss of one unit means no more to the Wildland than a cut in your skin. But the Quadrilateral cannot say to any part of Sum 'Cut your finger.' Each element has its own program, its own directives, and cannot violate them, even if it is imperative to the existence of the Wildland.

"The Quadrilateral has the one insurmountable problem of its own identity. It is powerful. It *had* to be powerful for its four units to have survived in their own universes with their inherent disadvantages with respect to individual-oriented species. The Quadrilateral needed the linkup as an additional defense, an additional compensation for its Achilles' heel. But no matter how much power it wields, it will still have that point of vulnerability.

"The war the Wildland is fighting now—the war on Earth—is a war of identity and not of power. The nature of its opponent is such that the Quadrilateral cannot reach it. It is immune, or can make itself immune, to every blast of mental power the Quadrilateral can send. It is not receptive to force that would evaporate any other mind because it is —or can be—mindless. It is dead already and cannot be killed.

"The Wildland cannot stand against such an army. Its limitations prevent it from mustering a rival army. The Quadrilateral members cannot provide an army: the Wildland is a plant hive, with few motile elements; the two-dimensional people can have no real existence in our three-dimensional universe; the monoliths are obviously excluded; and the fourth member no longer has an existence independent of the other three.

"The only army available is a human army. Only men can defend the Wildland. Only a man can go into the city in the Gulf, find the enemy and destroy it. Only men can be heroes; the Quadrilateral can never be more than an animated machine, despite its power."

"You want me to be your hero?" asked the black king.

"Concuma is the hero." Again the melodic laughter swelled to a cruel crescendo.

"Then what do you want me for?"

"I want you to lead the army. The Quadrilateral needs

someone to unify and direct its army. Only the wild men will fight, and they will not fight under one another. The only leader who is known to them all, who is respected by them, and whose commands they will accept, is you."

"Why should I help the Quadrilateral?"

"Because you are defending your home, your world, your own kind."

"And what about you? What do you stand to gain?"

"That doesn't concern you."

"Who are you?" demanded the black king for the third time.

"No one you know," evaded Warwand.

Concuma opened his eyes. His hands moved toward his face. "I thought I had died," he said dully while he ran his fingers over his face as though doubting the reality of his existence.

## XVIII

"WHO AM I?" asked Concuma of the faceless voice. They were alone. Tamerlane was elsewhere in the castle of ice, watching the stars go around him.

"Vanice Concuma, the greatest man on Earth."

The blond man shook his head. "I died," he said quietly.

"Then how are you here?"

"What happened between the worlds? I died, I know it."

"What is death?" said the faceless voice. "Death is a personal thing. The black king went through what you did, yet you claim that you died and he knows that he lives. Death is nothing immutable. Life is like the ashes of time running in an hourglass. It finishes, but the glass can be turned and the cycle started again. Death can be reversed, death can be endured, death can be ignored. It is not necessary for death to destroy. Identity is what matters, not life."

"I had a dream. Perhaps it was in the dream that I died."

"Forget your dreams. You can never see them clearly. They can only distort you."

"What do you want from me?"

"Only that you do what you can to defend what you believe in. You are a wild man. The wild men are at war. You must fight for them in the best way you can. That is all."

"And the king?"

The voice hummed its macabre laughter. "For a simpler task and more complicated reasons. He is very strong but, like the Quadrilateral, he has his limitations. He is a pawn in all our plans."

"He is a dangerous man to play with."

"Dangerous? Not to me. Never to me."

"Am I a pawn too?"

"Not in my hands. Ultimately, who can say? What are we but shadows cast from somewhere else? We may all be pawns and never be allowed to know. You might think, if you like, that your identity is only a pattern, and by the mere fact of your existence you are a pawn."

Concuma wiped his lips with the back of his hand.

"No?" asked Warwand rhetorically. "Perhaps. Living out here with the stars has ingrained a philosophy of abject humility into me. I watch them, whirling with an odd kind of majesty, like the arms of a gigantic clock or the blind eyes of a great beast. You can learn, just looking at the stars. They are a more perfect mirror than the best silvered glass. There is no reflection, no distortion. They do not turn images or twist them. The only image you can see is the real one."

"It would drive me mad!"

Laughter again, chiming from the abyss inside the hood. "My friend, the melodrama in that statement sounds like Tamerlane. Or perhaps it is my influence. I'm sorry if my mock philosophy disturbs you."

"You don't mean what you say?"

"I only say what I mean."

Concuma turned away, reaching out a hand to run his fingers over the wall of ice between himself and infinity. It was pleasantly cold and he felt it turning liquid beneath the warmth of his touch.

"What is happening on Earth?" he asked.

"Nothing wonderful. The army of the dead is merely gathering. A few isolated beasts from the Gulf have come up the cleft and into the Wildland, where they are caught and torn apart. They are useless. Their dead brains cannot be reprogrammed properly. The thing will have to use men. But the Quadrilateral is afraid. The Wildland cannot kill them. They are already dead. When the army of the dead marches, the Wildland will be helpless. But there is time yet.

"The human army is gathering as well. Thousands of wild men are flocking to the edge of the Wildland overlooking the cleft. The word spreads slowly, but the men who have sufficient empathy with the Wildland to know the message are respected and believed. They will have a leader soon. They will be organized. They might well be committing generic suicide, but they have no choice—there is no joining the enemy."

"Can they win?" asked Concuma.

"They *can* win. It depends on their leader, their strength and the strength of the opposing army. If the human army fails, then the army of the dead will overwhelm the Wildland by sheer weight of numbers. Each of the elements of the Wildland will act in the way it has always done, without self-interest, and without interest in the invaders. Their passage will not be seriously impeded until they are too close to Sum to be stopped.

"A man is different from a part of a hive. He will destroy and destroy and destroy, and jealously preserve himself against all harm. Every plant in the Wildland is a potential martyr to its cause. A man has to be defeated before he becomes a martyr. Only an army of individuals can fight an army which outnumbers them to the extent that the army of the dead outnumbers the human army, and have a chance."

"And what will I have to do?"

"Your type of man is something else again. The thing in the city has a certain type of strength because it is a certain type of identity. If that strength is matched it can be killed. That is the only way to destroy it. Earth needs the right man to go into the city in the Great Gulf and fight whatever is there, to destroy the dead thing which has reanimated the dead in order to pit Earth's past against its present."

"I am that man? Why? What do I have that makes me that man?"

"Selflessness. In a perverted sort of way. You are the man who hates everything. You hate dead things and living things and inanimate things. You are the loneliest man in existence. You have the strongest identity. In a battle of identity, you cannot be defeated. And yet you are selfless because you need no strong motives to make you act. You need no greed and no love—nothing for yourself. All you need is to be hurt.

"It seems something of a paradox that you will act on behalf of the people you hate. Perhaps it is because you hate yourself more than you hate them. If you were to ask 'Why should I?' as the black king did, then I could not answer you. I could not force you, because if I had to do that you would have lost before you began, simply by being what you would be.

"You can fight and win, and only you. The human army and Tamerlane are the defenders of Earth. You are its attacker."

"Is it inevitable that I win?"

"It is never inevitable. There is no law which says that the strongest man must win. Primarily, it is a question of identity, but ultimately it is chance which decides."

Beyond the womb of ice, chance moved the stars patiently in their rhythmic paths.


## XIX

THE CITY OF Ylle had not changed. But it seemed colder and less familiar. It was silent, and through its ruins the wild men passed on their way to the edge of the Wildland, and the lip of the Great Gulf.

Into the dead city rode three men—the tall figures of John Tamerlane and Vanice Concuma, and the hunched, heavily cowled Warwand. Concuma wore armor of polished wood and his blond hair spilled over its tight neckline. He rode a powerful unicorn, almost pure white, with a short, broken horn.

The black king too was armored, his head also unprotected save for his crown of thorns. He rode a jet black mare with a long, upward slanted horn sharpened to a needle point. He had regained his regality and arrogant manner. The experience he had gathered while away from the Wildland had not been lost, but its marks were hidden. Once home again, he had slipped back into character with an ease which surprised him.

Warwand was not armored, nor was he armed. He wore the same robe and hood of gray that he had worn in the citadel of ice. His hands were gauntleted, his feet encased in boots. No living flesh, if he had flesh, could be seen. Warwand remained a voice.

"We should stop here," said Tamerlane.

"For a while," agreed Warwand.

They dismounted and left the unicorns to wander. The unicorns were the only animal life form of the planet of the monoliths, and had been the only contribution any other member of the Quadrilateral had been able to offer toward the Wildland's war.

Warwand curled himself up and almost lost himself in the shadow of a slab of stone, in the manner of Reander. The black king sat easily on the steps of what had once been a great building. Concuma wandered restlessly, as usual. He, too, had reverted to his old character.

"We shall reach the edge of the sea in two days," said Warwand.

"Soon enough," muttered Concuma, pausing in his stride.

"I expected more from the City of Sorrows," muttered Tamerlane, half to himself.

Warwand sighed. "City men are city men. Anachronisms. Relics of the past. Almost akin to the army from the Gulf. They cannot fight, any more than they can desert their way of life and become wild men."

"I, too, am a city man."

"You never were. You are too strong. You were born out of place."

"But not *one* of them joined us. It doesn't seem that they are the same people I fought for."

"You never fought for anyone except yourself," said Concuma.

"I fought for you once, and Zea and Shadow."

"You killed Shadow."

"I fought for all of us. I tried to win something for all of us."

"You wanted the city for yourself."

Tamerlane, angry but not disposed to argue, said nothing.

"In time," said Warwand, "you can fight for your people. You can lead the wild men against the thing in the Gulf and its army of corpses."

"I will lead if they will follow me."

Concuma rested uncomfortably, leaning against a wall. "They will follow you. Even though they are wild men, who boast no allegiance to anyone, they will follow you. We will follow you because we have no one else and we are afraid. We all know of the black king, and when we are scared we forget how much stories grow in the telling."

"There was a time when you used *we* to include myself and not the wild men," said the black king without rancor.

"I am a wild man."

"Even so, something has changed."

"I have changed. You have, too. And the world as well."

Warwand watched in silence. Slowly moving down the steps toward the black king came a long black leech. Tamerlane moved away, drawing his sword. Its black head followed him around, waving slowly and blindly in the air, searching for him. With a quick slash, Tamerlane swept away the first seven or eight inches of its body. The rest writhed convulsively and dull red blood splashed around, spraying the steps.

"Vermin," snarled Tamerlane, squashing the severed head beneath his foot.

Warwand laughed silkily.

Figures appeared in the oily mist, walking lightly, hands poised near sword or dagger.

"It's Concuma and the king," said one, and came forward quickly, relaxing.

"Graycloak," acknowledged Concuma briefly. There were

four altogether. Graycloak was a small figure, with long muddy hair and gray eyes, who looked almost frail. He reminded Tamerlane of Silver Reander.

The others were introduced as Axel Harm, Jolas Darkness and Loder Wrath. All were typical wild men—tall and broad-shouldered, light-haired, with pale eyes. Harm was particularly heavy in build, with immense hands. He carried a large iron-bladed ax with a long curved handle. Jolas Darkness was taller, with skin almost as dark as the black king's. His eyes were as yellow as his hair, and seemed to glisten even in the dimness of Ylle's fog. His most prominent weapon was a large bow. Wrath was less distinctive in build, save for being longer in the legs. His face was scarred and pockmarked.

"Some of your followers," said Concuma to the black king. Tamerlane looked at them without enthusiasm.

"How many of these have you got?" he asked Warwand.

"Not enough."

"Have you got mounts?" he asked Graycloak.

"Yes."

"Bring them into the city. You might as well ride with us when we leave."

Without perceptible hesitation, Graycloak nodded. There was no testing of strength, no suspicion of insubordination. Apparently, it was as Warwand and Concuma had said. The wild men were willing to follow him. Even so, he was not impressed.

"How can we make them into an army?" asked Tamerlane of the hooded figure of Warwand. "They can't cooperate. It's just not in them."

"It's in *you* to give them heart. Discipline doesn't matter."

"It matters a lot. They'll be no better than the city men.

"They don't really understand what they're fighting for, and they certainly won't fight as a group. They might just as well have no leader. They might follow me in a bunch, but they won't be fighting like an army—each one will be on his own."

"It's all we have."

"Then how can we win? How dare we even try?"

Warwand remounted his unicorn with an unnatural fluidity of motion. "The real battle will be fought within the city against the real enemy. The wild men are paper dolls in a defensive gesture. Only if we lose the real battle will the slaughter on the seabed be disastrous. Otherwise, it is just a delaying tactic to keep the army of the dead from reaching Sum and overrunning the Wildland. We have to hold them while Concuma kills their operator."

"The Quadrilateral—"

"—is powerless."

"Why?"

"Because of what it is."

"And why should we be able to do what it cannot?"

"Because of what we are."

An erne flew high above the empty sea, slowly spiraling, neither losing height nor going in any particular direction. It was watching patiently for something interesting to appear, interesting (as far as an erne is concerned) being synonymous with edible. It did not hope. If it had, it might have yearned most of all for a man. Failing that, a luth would do, or a diome. Even a moloch would be welcome. But for the moment, there was nothing.

It almost decided to fly somewhere else—back over the Wildland where there was sure to be something interesting skulking in the rafters of the canopy of endless green. Then it saw the army of the dead emerge from the city far below it in the cleft.

They looked like men. They had once been men. Now they were puppets. They danced and hopped along in jerky scuttling fashion, which was the best that decayed synapses could manage.

The erne did not wonder from whence they came. It did not care who had opened the door to the past through which they poured. It did not know that only the dead can come out of the past, because the living are the seeds of the future. Out they came in a long ragged stream, armed with stone and rusted metal, unarmored.

Intent on the flood of prospective food, the erne did not even notice the thin line which emerged from the edge of the Wildland to watch its doom approaching.

With a flip of its wings, it dropped a hundred feet, and waited for an individual to separate from the horde. A lame, sightless corpse staggered clear of the phalanx as one of its rotten femurs snapped within its leg from the sheer effort of carrying its body, wasted though it was.

Down went the erne.

With unnatural awareness, the useless cadaver lashed at the descending bird with a length of metal pipe. The erne squawked and sideslipped, landing a few feet away and stumbling. Then, with a deadly accuracy, it thrust itself forward within the dead man's guard, snapping its curved beak at his eyes. A ribbon of flesh tore loose, but no blood emerged.

Then the claws went to work, ripping intestines. Its powerful wings smashed the bones in the flailing arms. The erne shook the shattered hulk like a ripped rat. Then it began to eat the flesh.

After two mouthfuls, it vomited. Bewildered, the erne perched on the corpse and contemplated its surprisingly uninteresting qualities. It might also have observed that the broken limbs still wriggled and jerked in an unfamiliar way. If it did, it did not care very much.

The experience was enough to deter the erne from eating human flesh for the rest of its life.

## XX

"How MANY can there be?" asked Tamerlane in an awed voice.

The army of the dead fanned out and came on. They blackened the seabed for half a mile in width and almost as much in length. And the flow was not abating. More and more emerged from the cleft.

"We can't possibly hold them," said Graycloak.

"How many men have we?" snarled the black king.

"It's impossible to count them. They're spread out over nearly a mile of the edge. Several thousand, I think."

"What about unicorns?"

"Not nearly so many. Nearly a thousand, perhaps. Possibly only eight hundred."

"Are all the men watching?"

"I assume so."

"Ride up and down the line. Try to even them out into a line long enough to cover the entire width of that army."

Graycloak rode away, shouting to some other riders nearby.

"It's spreading them very thin," said Concuma.

"What else can we do?" The black king shrugged. He turned to Warwand. "What else do you want me to do?" he appealed.

"Just stop them," said Warwand.

"And how do you expect me to do that?" snapped Tamerlane.

"You are the leader. You're doing the fighting."

Tamerlane returned to his contemplation of the approaching horde. "What can we do?" he asked again, hopelessly.

"It will be dark soon," said Concuma.

"They'll be here before that."

"The battle won't be over by then. They might still gain a big advantage from it."

"We'll light beacons every few yards. We can fight them with fire. They have to come up the slope. It will be like storming a citadel. We hold the position of power. The beacons are being built. Wood is being felled. If the Wildland can't help us, at least it will provide us with raw materials. Powerful plants still burn. They are only plants, after all. They might as well be useful if they won't be helpful."

Warwand had moved a short distance away. Concuma looked at the hooded man speculatively. "I wonder about him," he said. "Whose side is he on? If he is fighting for himself, I should like to know who he is."

The army of the dead, like a column of soldier ants, came on. Many of them fell, useless husks of crumbled flesh and cracked bones. The ceaseless feet behind them trampled them into the dust they should have been for thousands of years. The fallen did not matter. There were enough who stood.

"Time is against us," said Concuma.

"Time is always against you," said Warwand, who had moved closer again. "But sometimes you can cheat it."

The black king mounted the unicorn whose reins he held, and turned to face the silent group behind him. Graycloak and Jolas Darkness were away organizing the men on both flanks, but Axel Harm and Loder Wrath were both there.

"Carry these orders," he said. "Every mounted man is to be ready in one hour. At the sound of this horn"—he held up a curved horn of hard wood—"they are to charge. We won't wait for them to start the fight. When I blow it again, it will be the signal to retreat. Then they get back here as fast as possible and get ready to fight again. In the meantime, the rest are to continue building the beacons as large as possible."

"You're mad," said Harm. "Why split us?"

"What do you hope to gain?" asked Concuma.

"The battle," said Tamerlane somberly.

Concuma laughed. Tamerlane clenched his fist. "I'll smash their column," he boasted. "Break it into fragments. They won't have enough coherency left to storm the heights."

"*They'll* smash *us*. Every last one of us. We won't dent their column," protested Harm.

"You'll die then," said the black king unpleasantly.

The army of the dead never faltered. The column was still half a mile wide, but it was at least six times that in length. It was impossible to estimate with any accuracy how many there were, but it must have been several hundred thousand, mock-marching in a great wedge, tapering a little toward the front.

With two hours yet to go before dusk, out of the Wildland came a thin line of unicorns, no more than three or four deep. They moved carefully down the steepest part of the slope, picking their way and slipping often. At the bottom, they began to pick up speed. The ground leveled out to the rough seabed, caked with a carpet of salt and sand. As the horses found much better footing than on the treacherous slope, they broke into a canter, horns bobbing, as their heads dipped and reared.

From high above and very far away, the army of the dead had seemed huge. From nearer its own height and at moderate distance, it seemed infinite.

To the black king, in a way, it was the fulfillment of a dream. With the human race beside him and behind him, he was riding into battle. Objectively, he was a part of a much larger pattern. Subjectively, he was the leader of humanity, fighting for his world. He gave up his doubts and despair to the battle he was about to fight. He thought neither of beforehand nor afterward; he immersed himself totally in the present, in a glorious—if hopeless—dream.

To Vanice Concuma, the battle was a sick taste in his mouth. Before him were three miles or more of death. For him the battle was not an end but an interim. His goal was the city, where he would have to fight the real war. The sheer immensity of the thing in his path numbed him, but it did not prevent him from thinking. While they rode, he directed his mount far away toward the right flank of the enemy formation, intending to cut it at an acute angle and plow his way clear by nightfall.

Warwand, from behind him, saw his design and followed him. Deep inside Concuma there was growing an uncontrolled, violent hatred. He felt it billowing within him, swelling to the tune of hoofbeats. He felt warm and wild and bigger than he was. He thrilled to its heat—he had been lonely and uncomfortable while it lay dormant. He forgot Zea and remembered only the hurt that her absence left behind. He was whole again. Vanice Concuma was a hero reborn.

Warwand felt no exhilaration, no satisfaction. It was not in him to do so. He saw the massive army only as an obstacle, a part of his plan which he had considered, evaluated and integrated into his project. Warwand had faith in himself, and in Vanice Concuma.

To Axel Harm, Graycloak, Jolas Darkness, Loder Wrath and many hundreds of others, the army was fate. It was a threat to their way of life and to their own individual lives. It was a climax to the continuous futile fight that was their nomadic existence in the Wildland. Essentially, the wild men were just as anachronistic as the city men. They were better adapted and stronger, but they lacked the will and personality of the black king. As a race, they were as flaccid and lethargic as the city men. They had the strength and the lust to fight, and they had the will to win. But the will to live was to a large extent missing. They were riding to their deaths, and they did not care. It might almost have been their purpose all along.

Tamerlane edged his mount into a slight lead. He began to dictate the pace, increasing it slowly and drawing his ragged line of followers into a gallop. While the closing factions were still a quarter of a mile apart, he snatched out his sword, stood in the saddle and reached full pace.

The big white unicorn that was Concuma's was far away now. At the black king's shoulder rode Axel Harm, his ax held high. The wild man let loose his pent-up rage and defiance in a loud, wordless howl. Many of the others joined in with similar war cries. The silent army of the dead came on, not responding in the least to their presence.

The dust cloud accompanying the advancing horde was whipped by a sudden flurry of wind into the faces of the riders. Tamerlane was blinded for a brief moment by stinging particles in his eyes, and when he had blinked them away, he was just in time to feel the shock as his unicorn tore into the front line of the enemy.

The faces which had been before him were suddenly all around him. Their disinterest changed abruptly into a frightening and savage mechanical compulsion to kill them. The black unicorn trampled three or four as he plowed into them. The beast whinnied and bucked, but the black king held it steady by pure brute strength. The first sweep of his sword decapitated two corpses, but that did not help. The headless bodies, hardly even oozing blood, continued to move in. A rock hit him in the chest, but without much force.

Rearing the unicorn up, he slashed in wide arcs at arms and torsos. What he hit broke easily, but what was broken was not necessarily destroyed. With snapped spines, they twisted like venomous snakes; armless and headless they still walked, still clustered around him and pressed closer.

He realized that his principal danger was not from the

crude weapons they wielded. Instead, he saw that they could imprison him with their bodies, reduce him to immobility, and then simply crush and beat him to death.

He smacked the black unicorn to keep it moving and took a drunken path through the mass of animated corpses, leaving a wake of fallen but still struggling bodies.

He looked out over the sea of heads and once more the enormity of what he had tried to do swept over him. He could see no end to the rank upon rank of once-human marionettes. He remembered that every one of his men had many hundred to destroy if they were to win the battle. On both sides, he was conscious of unicorns being forced down— by rocks, by swords or by weight, and their riders disappearing into the emotionless tide of flesh.

"Keep moving!" he roared, and was surprised that his voice was starkly clear. It occurred to him what a *quiet* battle they were fighting.

All the while, his sword never ceased to lick out, cutting the wrists which held clubs or blades or stones poised for throwing. He did not trouble, for the most part, to destroy the dead men physically, nor had he the time. It was more than enough simply to protect himself from their weapons and let luck protect him from their numbers.

As he plunged deeper and deeper into the column, yet barely scratching its surface, he saw with a shock how much of a single lunge his charge had been. The first few lines of the remorseless army had been obliterated, but the unicorns had by now penetrated to different depths, and the never-very-straight line was now hopelessly disordered. There was no chance of getting them all out again to regroup and charge again. The rabble had suffered for their lack of discipline and each man was now committed until he fell or fled.

Axel Harm was doing his job better than most. His horse was gone and he was on foot. Using his ax as a circle of prohibitive destruction, he moved swiftly sideways and forward. He aimed always to cut the dead men in half in the waist region, that being the most damaging single blow that he could deliver.

He realized the necessity for keeping always on the move,

even before the black king shouted, and kept as far away as possible from the still mobile and purposeful dismembered parts which he strewed in such profusion. But he was also horribly aware of the fact that he was using an enormous quantity of energy in keeping the ax whizzing around him, and that he was not nearly strong enough to keep moving forever. Sooner or later he was bound to slow down and make himself an easy target for the perpetually grasping hands that were all around him.

He contemplated running, but moving backward was for the moment impracticable, and so he moved on, trying not to get too far into the ranks of the army, wishing that he had not come quite so far already and feeling like a rat in a trap.

As Axel Harm achieved a bare patch of ground which enabled him to rest for a brief moment, he saw the unicorn which Jolas Darkness rode moving down some distance to the right. He began moving in that direction immediately, but there were far too many of the enemy in the way. He never caught a second glimpse of the dark man.

Darkness had landed badly after the leap from his mount, which had been felled by a knife thrust in the neck. He stumbled again as he tried to move away, and found the arm of a headless and legless body gripping his ankle firmly. Panic-stricken, he tried to kick it off, but the fingers clung tight, and by the time he had cut himself free, he had lost too much time and space. A solid wall of dead flesh surrounded him and closed in. He had neither room enough nor speed enough to cover all the blades and clubs which faced him. He tried to cut his way through the wall at its weakest point, but had no chance whatsoever.

A blade scored his deltoid muscle and scraped his rib cage. A blow at the base of the neck staggered him and an upward slash cut its way into his mouth from below, penetrating his lower palate and impaling his tongue. He wrenched his head back as the blade jerked convulsively backward, and his lower jaw was ripped clean away.

He could no longer scream, but the fountain of blood from his throat made an odd muffled whistling that was representative of one. He was already dead then, or at least very soon after, but they kept slashing, cutting and thrusting until his heart, lungs and gut were a mess of pulp. Then they separated and resumed their forward march.

Graycloak, crouched high in his saddle, was at a disadvantage compared to his fellows because of the slightness of his build. He found it impossible to hurl his sword around in massive arcs, and it was soon apparent to him that his rapid flicks and twists, although individually effective, had not the cumulative power necessary to keep the throng away.

Desperately, he kept his unicorn wheeling and swerving. The beast afforded a great deal of assistance by lashing out hard and often with its back legs. Each time it did so, Graycloak had to hang on tightly, but the slashing hooves earned a little more space every time. Eventually, it was inevitable that the contortions the mount was undergoing, both at Graycloak's insistence and of its own accord, were going to have disastrous effects. Realizing this, he began to guide the animal back the way it had come. The way back was long, but he had the advantage of moving with the surge, so that the corpses before him did not meet him like a coherent advancing wall, but turned slowly, in a disorganized array that he found easy to cut apart.

With a large amount of luck, perhaps bordering on the miraculous, he made his way out of the horde, and ran well out of range before turning. The scene was one of absolute chaos, from the human point of view. The plunging unicorns seemed so few in a sea of lurching puppet men. Thousands of the dead men must have been totally disabled, yet the ranks had closed so as not to give the cavalry any chance whatsoever of using the maneuverability which was their greatest asset.

Graycloak contemplated running back to the Wildland, and actually turned his horse to look at the plumes of smoke now rising from points several yards apart all along the edge of the vast fringe of wood and leaf.

From this place, the wall looked impregnable. The idea of the army of the dead penetrating that barrier of fire and men after scaling the steep hill was difficult to stomach. Yet he did not doubt that they could do it if their numbers were not sufficiently thinned by the battle on the seabed.

Although he saw that clearly, it was not really for that reason that he turned again and galloped back. He did not know why he did it and he demanded no reasons from himself.

This time, he did not plunge into the morass at full speed, but hung back, darting at the oncoming wave again and again, fighting and leaping back, away from danger.

Loder Wrath had followed Concuma out toward the wing of the attack. They hit the wall side by side. Instantly, Concuma began cutting a diagonal path through the phalanx, aiming to get clear at the side, which was no longer very far away. He did not hear the words which Warwand, who had not entered the ranks of the enemy at all, screamed to him. The hooded figure hung back and maintained a course along the advancing front, aiming for the same point as Concuma, apparently, but by a much more indirect route.

Wrath somehow got in front of Concuma, having aligned himself the same way, and went forward full tilt, hardly pausing to smash at the groping dead to either side. Concuma followed, and although his sword was stained with blood almost as black as Tamerlane's, he did relatively little damage.

It never occurred to him that entering the enemy host at all was a grave mistake, or even that it would prejudice his chances in the battle he was to fight in the city if he tired himself here, or—even worse—was wounded. In his own mind, he was taking the most direct line practicable to his proposed destination, and he would ride straight along it, stopping for nothing and eradicating everything in his way. Anything which threatened to hamper his progress in any way was to be completely destroyed. Concuma had ceased to operate as a man; he had been transformed into a hate-powered machine. He was berserk.

En route, he lost Wrath, which made things a little more difficult. The lead man's unicorn went down and its rider was catapulted clear. With remarkable presence of mind and fantastic agility, he made dead straight for a large rock standing shoulder-high in the salty sand. With a colossal vault, he was on top of it and whirling to hack and stamp at the fingers of the dead men who tried to climb the boulder.

It took him several minutes to realize that he was practically invulnerable. The jerky, spasmodic movements of the reanimated corpses were sufficiently efficient for their inexorable tramp across the salty sands, but were woefully inadequate for hauling themselves over the lip of the boulder while the dancing figure above them tried to throw them down. Wrath could strike their hands from their wrists, or simply prise their fingers loose, as he chose. Even better, though their hands were gone and their chances of success were remote, they kept trying, blocking the lump of rock from their fellows, who might have been more successful.

On the other hand, Wrath had nowhere to go. He was trapped tight.

For a very long time, during which Wrath came to feel quite secure on his island in the midst of an infinity of dead heads, the corpses did not vary their tactics. Eventually, however, they began throwing things. For Wrath, it was the end.

Their aim was bad, but they had all the time and all the ammunition that they needed. Rocks and bits of metal stung him at first, and then began to hurt. There were more and more. They used the same rocks again and again because he could not trap them on the small surface of the boulder.

For a while, he continued attacking his tormentors, then began to concentrate solely on defending himself. His arms became a mess of cuts and bruises, blood ran from his temple over his eyelids and down his cheeks. The more hurt he became, the more rocks seemed to hit him. Finally, inevitably, he toppled from the rock into the cluster of assailants. They crowded around and continued showering him with missiles until his body was a thin red smear on the salt. In the end, just before they gave up and went on, they were stoning him with his own skull.

Meanwhile, nothing could stop Concuma. With phenominal speed, he drove through the marauding army toward his chosen point of exit. They might as well have tried to stop fire or wind. The white unicorn was a magnificent animal, strong and fast. It showed no sign of slowing down—it was as insane in its surge as its rider.

The black king stopped once for an instant as he was blocked by the oppressive welter of bodies and looked for Concuma. But the white unicorn and its rider were far too distant by then to be seen. Sweat rolled from Tamerlane's crown of thorns and his arms ached from fatigue. His massive chest heaved and his heart hammered like a devil drum. He was not surprised that Concuma could not be seen. He knew that the blond man ought to be well on his way to the city by now. He knew that Concuma, and only Concuma, could and would reach the city in the Gulf.

The black king decided then that he had had enough. He turned to head back the way he had come. It seemed to take an interminable time to get back. Lather flew off the glossy skin of his mount as it doggedly went the way it was urged, horn bobbing and fiery eyes weeping tears of effort.

As soon as he was clear, he unclasped the signal horn tied to his belt. He stood in the saddle, facing the Wildland and waved his arms in two wide arcs. The light was very dim, but his tall black frame and black mount were easily recognizable. During the battle, the army had moved very close to the edge of the slope leading up to the human defenses, and the beacon fires blazed close.

He blew the retreat and from somewhere high in the branches of the Wildland came a long penetrating fluting which echoed and prolonged his own call. He turned back to see how many answered the summons. No one was fleeing backward. He counted the mounted men in the sea of dead men. There seemed so few, and their fight to be free to run appeared so futile.

He almost went straight back into the fray to give his help, but paused, sword lowered and head down, as he realized how weak he was and how little help he had to offer. Out of the pack, riding hard for home, came Graycloak, still waving his sword in mock gestures of attack, laughing from bloodless lips and furious eyes. When he saw the black king standing silent on the quivering unicorn, he

118

paused and turned to stare. In a gargantuan line, appearing concave but in fact almost dead straight, the army of cadavers stretched away to either side. Its depth was still immeasurable from where they stood.

"So many," said the black king gently and almost inaudibly.

"Too many," agreed Graycloak, in a voice cracked with fear, his throat dry and seized with the paralysis of utter exertion.

"Where are they?" said Tamerlane.

Graycloak pointed with an incongruously delicate hand. All along the line, figures detached themselves from the leviathan body and ran for the Wildland with the desperation of the defeated. The black king counted nineteen.

Graycloak reached out and grasped his sword arm. "Come on," he said roughly. "They'll be around us again in a few minutes.

Sullenly, the black king turned his horse and spurred it into a slow, labored trot. He looked back once, his eyes searching the endless battlefield for a glimpse of Concuma, Warwand or more survivors. Nothing could be seen save a lone straggler breaking free and riding at an incongruously slow gallop away from the army of the dead. He could visualize Concuma a long way off, still relentlessly plunging through the enemy, consumed by hatred and rage, mindless save for his identity and raw, hot emotion. Tamerlane lifted his sword again, close to his face, and gripped it hard. It was scarred and bent, splashed with black and red, morsels of decayed flesh clinging repulsively to it where the edge was nicked.

"Quickly," pleaded Graycloak, and the black king became aware that he had stopped again. Raising his eyes to the flames in front of and above him, he let the firelight play on his wide-open eyes. It was painful to blink, painful to move, painful just to sit in the saddle and ride. He was almost broken. His will alone held his body from folding up and his mind from slipping into peaceful oblivion.

He woke himself up by telling himself that there was still an entire night's fighting to be done.

## XXI

ALL OF A SUDDEN, Concuma was free. It was not quite dark—the last vestiges of twilight lingered, and there was a bright three-quarter moon. He did not stop, but pressed on. He was to the right of the cleft, but he could vaguely see it in the distance like a long scar. Between it and himself were the last few lines of the army of the dead, but he rode around them. Slowly, the madness ebbed away, leaving him cold, drained of energy but still alert. His teeth began to chatter. The reaction was a pain deep in his abdomen, sucking at his kidneys and making his spine grate. His nerves hurt horribly but dully.

Behind him, there was the sound of hooves on the rock. He turned and saw Warwand coming toward him at the steady but slow trot which was the best his mount could manage by this time.

"I had to be sure," said the faceless man.

"That I was still alive? That I would go to the city?" Concuma's voice was thin and echoed oddly in the night air.

"I'm sorry. I had to know. I was worried when you rode into the army. It was a foolhardy thing to do."

"Go home, Warwand," said Concuma.

"Where is my home?"

Concuma nodded toward the Wildland. "There it was, once. When I first knew you. It will do for the time being. It might well be your home again, one day."

"I don't think so," said Warwand slowly. There was a pause. "Kill him, Concuma," the faceless man said in a low, intense voice. "Destroy him the same way that another man like you destroyed Dragon."

"The Blind Worm killed Dragon."

"He did not destroy him."

Concuma shrugged. "I'll do what I can," he said. "I'll see you again."

"I hope so."

Warwand and his tired unicorn began the long walk back to the Wildland. Several miles away, the fortress of fire glowed magnificently, with the monstrous bulk of the Wildland occulting the stars in a ribbon of darkness looming behind the flames. From here it looked defiant but forlorn. He remembered that it was the last hope of the wild men and city men alike, who were about to be massacred by their own dead ancestors. Then he thought further, and contemplated the size of the planet. Try as he would, he could not see the great impending battle as anything but a minor skirmish.

Concuma rode slowly on toward the rift in the seabed. It was too steep for the unicorn to descend safely while he was mounted, and so he led the animal down the wall of the narrow valley on foot.

When they reached the bottom, he took a long torch from his saddle and kindled it. The torchlight cast flickering shadows which were forever blending and changing as he moved. He saw nothing moving anywhere. If the army of the dead had left guards to protect the city, then they were not in evidence. He relaxed slightly as he began to believe that he might reach the city unchallenged.

He rounded the buttress which had hidden the city from Reander's eyes when the latter had first found it. He saw the city in the distance. The moon was hidden and his torchlight wan, but the city was visible by its own lights. They were perfectly still and silvery white—not dots or lines, but long, easy curves, serrated but unbroken.

The city shone like a spider's web—concentric but irregular rings radiating from a center of pitch blackness, with radii of light issuing from the innermost ring. It gave the city a pattern which Reander had been unable to see, a regularity and focus which seemed to direct the eye to the geometric center of the web. Concuma was convinced that whatever was in the city would be found at its focus, in the disc of darkness at the eye of the web.

Without hurrying, he moved on.

"Spread the fires," ordered the black king. "Build a solid wall of fire a mile long."

The shouting began, relaying the order along the thin line of the human army. The beacon fires were already high and close together, being constantly fed by the toiling wild men.

"There's no time," said Axel Harm. The wild man lay on the ground, propped into a semi-sitting position. His left leg was broken. He had survived, somehow, the entire duration of the fight on the seabed without harm, but his leg had been broken as another wild man had picked him up during the retreat and cut his way clear.

"We can't fight," said Tamerlane. "All we can hope to do is use their own relentlessness against them. We'll build a wall of fire and they'll try to walk straight through it. They're animated, but mindless—they won't stop. Our only possible defense now is to set the Wildland alight."

"How do we stop the fire afterward?"

"The Wildland will do that. It has inherent defenses against fire. Our problem is not to stop it, but to keep it alight. The Wildland's reflexes will be straining to put the fire out and we'll have to fight it tooth and claw to keep the fire going."

Harm laughed bitterly. "Why do we bother? Why not just run and keep running? They'd never catch us."

Tamerlane sighed. "Eventually they would. They'll destroy Sum and the whole Wildland. They'll exterminate us."

"We don't know that. Let's leave them Sum—we don't owe the Wildland anything."

"We owe it everything. Home, food, clothing—everything. Besides, we have no choice. How do you make terms with the dead? How do we even surrender? There's nothing we can do but try to destroy every last one of them."

The black king walked away, leaving the crippled wild man to his ghostly laughter. He did not bother to order anyone to carry Harm out of the way; he assumed that the wild man would arrange his own transport, and he did not care anyway.

"Flame," he whispered to himself. "The entire Wildland aflame. They can't possibly get through." He looked up at the silent heights stretching far into the distance above him and completely hiding the sky. The ruddy fireglow and the white gleam of the lantern flowers made oddly beautiful patterns in the darkness. In fact, he knew, he had only changed the situation and not won the battle. The battle now was against the Wildland. Deep inside the Wildland were the waters it had long ago sucked from Ocean. Hundreds of the living pipes which ran everywhere throughout the Wildland carried water almost exclusively. Desiccation and burning cracked the pipes and brought the water in a never-ending stream to gush out into the Wildland until the fire was drowned and dead. Only when there was no more heat was the message conducted back to the metabolic pump to stop.

The battle now was not to be fought with swords and courage. The humans had to locate the sutures in the water-conducting vessels and block them. They had to keep the water in and the flames alive. It was an almost impossible task because of the vast area which had to be covered—along the edge of the shelf and right up to the top of the Wildland.

He knew that he would have to keep the fire alight along the ground only, but there was no way to stop the flames spreading upward and bringing water cascading down from above.

The all-powerful Quadrilateral was no help at all, he reflected. It could not hold up the normal bodily processes of one of its members for one night. Its hold upon the planet depended on its keeping the fire burning in one tiny fragment of itself, yet it would devote every effort to putting out the fire because it could do nothing else. The plants were part of the hive, programmed for a particular function just as the dead men were programmed. There was no direct motor control, no mechanism for voluntary suspension.

Sentience, when all was said and done, was not a great deal of good to a plant.

They worked ceaselessly—tired, stripped of their clothing—searching out the water leaks, blocking them. All the time they worked close to the towering, slowly moving mass of flame. The wind, sucked through the trees by the great heat of the fire, whipped the sweat from their backs.

They did not understand. Hardly one in three realized that they kept the fire alight to burn the army of the dead while it marched. Those who did not know worked as hard as those who did. The black king's "officers" screamed at them persistently, telling them what to do and getting it done with the mindless determination which characterized the wild men.

The black king himself was chief of the furies—running ceaselessly, pausing only to lend his great strength to a struggling man striving to hold back the flood which threatened to eclipse their giant funeral pyre for the army of the dead.

As he was running quickly, like a great black beetle with crown of thorns and large sword, he saw a screaming man retreating from the flames. He caught the man by the shoulder, spun him around and hit him hard with the flat of his sword across the face.

"Your nerve breaks and I'll break you," he said through gritted teeth, hurling the unfortunate back the way he had come.

The man was sobbing and wailing. He rose to his knees and pointed at the wall of fire. "They're coming through!" he cried. "They're coming, they're coming, they're—"

The black king kicked him into quietness.

He turned and widened his eyes to the furnace-like brightness. For long moments, all he saw was blinding yellow and the falling masses from above where the canopy of the Wildland collapsed to the floor as the fire ate away its foundation.

Then he saw them, moving slowly and relentlessly, jerking and shambling in their eerie fashion. Black, burning corpses. Unstoppable.

He nearly screamed himself. "They'll do no harm," he yelled. "They're burned, falling to bits. They can't hurt you."

But he could not be heard over the roar of the fire. And he knew that he was lying; that the water was pouring from a thousand cuts despite their efforts; that within the fire where his men could not go, there was a fountain of water which would extinguish the fire well before dawn.

The battle was on again—not the men against the water against the fire against the enemy, but the terrible free-for-all where everyone had to be aware of every danger.

Howling his battle cry, he went forward to fight a burning swordsman by the light of the curtain of fire.

He swept the sword away without any appreciable force

and split the burning man from head to groin like a brittle stick.

"How many?" he screamed. "How many can we fight? How many can come through *that?*"

They came, no longer in ranks, no longer in a single irresistible mass, but in ones and twos, in blazing platoons, to spread more fear and despair than death. Even though they came and even though the waters sprayed, the men were winning their battle.

But when they saw their enemy doing the impossible, walking through the impenetrable barrier, they lost heart. They stayed; they fought. But their tiredness fought them and their wills could not withstand the struggle.

As the night died, the battle died. The men and their enemy dwindled in numbers to a mere handful on either side. If there was any victory to be won, it would be a victory of total negation.

The black king was there right up to the end. When dawn broke, he was still defending the dying fires, aware that there were hundreds of ways through the useless barrier, but staying nevertheless.

The one thing which disturbed him still was the memory of a burning corpse which had come through the flames a long time ago—a corpse with glittering eyes, who looked vaguely familiar. It had been impossible to identify the dead man, because he had had no lower jaw.

## XXII

WARWAND RODE as fast as his tired mount could take him. He was a long way from the battle and even Ylle was behind him. Ahead of him was the mountain of wood which was the skull of Sum. Somewhere in the city in the Gulf, Concuma would be fighting the battle which really mattered to him. Warwand's own campaign depended only on the outcome of that fight. He raced for the position which he had chosen to occupy while he played his own hand in the game of glory.

# THE BLIND WORM

The moment Vanice Concuma rode into the city of the Gulf, he knew that he was in a different world. There had been no interdimensional transfer as there had been on the journey around the Quadrilateral, and yet he was elsewhere. Perhaps there had always been this fragment of elsewhere buried in its crack in the seabed, relic of some forgotten age and lost universe.

Torch held high in his right hand, left hand resting on the hilt of his sword, Vanice Concuma rode into the web of time, the pale light of another world.

He crossed a street which he named in his mind the Street of Memories because the light made images of the past float around him. They were painful memories because they were lost, and he was lonely even in their midst. They were long gone, for the most part, and should have been dead. It seemed to him that the thing in the city was able to achieve resurrection even in living men.

Another place he named the Echoing Gardens, and fancied that there rested ambitions under tombstones because he imagined that ambition was the only thing which would be allowed to die in the city of the Gulf. Destinations were also there, as stark crosses above the all but empty graves.

He shook his head to clear it of the crazy ideas, but could not. It was as if the air itself were hallucinogenic.

He passed a golden gate beyond which were row upon row of silent statues. The thing in the city could force the dead to walk, he thought, but would not breathe life into its own people. Concuma somehow identified the statues, immortal and intransigent, with the people of the city.

He passed the Hall of the Shapes, where grotesque figures of cold stone lurked in special shadows of their own. Wild beasts and demons, he suspected they were the ghouls which wandered *beneath* the city. Mercifully the thing had not sent these particular minions on its marauding quest. These, too, belonged here. Even in his waking dream, Concuma knew that that made no sense, but he could not disentangle himself. He was trapped in his own imagination with nothing to scare him out of it.

He passed the junction with the Street of Nightmares, where a cold wind blew, and in the unbelievably far distance—on worlds other than this—he could hear the murmur of macabre voices. Most of those voices, he knew, were not human voices. It was from here that the army of the dead had come, for the Street of Nightmares was a road straight down to Hell.

In the penultimate circle were three cages of darkness, whose prisoners might have been immovable since time began. They were made of flesh—petrified, but inhuman. One he named the Wanderer, because of the soulful searching light that lingered in his ruby eyes. One he named the Man with the Mask, because of the identity-less quality of the paper-textured face. The last he named the Laughing Jester —an anti-heroic figure decoratively dressed and gay of manner.

Before the ultimate circle of light, he peered across brightness into blackness. The pale thread of light extended no more than sixty feet across and then stopped dead. Beyond was nothing—a stark, unimaginable nothing. It might have reminded the black king of his journey from the Ocean world to Warwand's tower of ice, but it was not the same.

Despite the fact that there was nothing beyond the last pale circlet of light, he felt convinced that it was into the focus of the city where he must go to find the enemy. He suspected for a wild moment that the feeling might be a trap and that he might better ride down the Street of Nightmares, but deep in his hatred he knew that while the Street of Nightmares was only a figment of his imagination, this was intensely real.

Out of the nowhere came Silver Reander.

Perhaps, after all, the thing in the Gulf had saved its best defense of all as a personal guard.

Shadow was dead, there was no doubting that. His lips were still parted into his last plaintive cry about white horses hauling the sea. His body retained the lax frailty of fresh death. Across his forehead was a long slash which still oozed moist blood.

The corpse spoke. It said: "Go back, Vanice."

Concuma dismounted, sword in left hand, torch in right. He stepped forward.

"Are you Shadow talking, or the city?"

"I am the city and I am Shadow, now. The mind that was Shadow was lost in the winds of time, but I have replaced that and everything else is here."

Concuma shook his head slowly. "Shadow is Shadow. No thing can have more than one identity. If I am talking to the city, then I am not talking to Shadow."

"I have many identities," said the city.

"Shadow is not one of them."

"This body is a pawn. A device. No more and no less than all the dead men which I sent against the Wildland. But its nature is not important. Its identity is no longer defined."

"It has no identity. Shadow is dead."

The slight figure barring Concuma's access to the focus of the city came forward slowly. In its right hand it held Reander's slim sword, poised in the familiar style of the wild man.

"I am Shadow," said the city.

Like a streak of lightning, the dead man lashed. There was no trace of the awkwardness of the animated cadavers which Concuma had fought during the day. This was Shadow again, alive and in full possession of his skill and speed. He had not been dead long enough to have decayed.

Concuma moved cat-like away from the thrust and swept his sword around in a tight, swift arc intended to catch his opponent's sword and flick it away. He failed. The small figure moved again and Concuma was forced to parry the stroke. He attempted a riposte which achieved nothing.

The blades licked out in a lengthy testing of strength. They flickered, touched, were gone again and then returned.

"I am Shadow," said the city.

All the time, while he moved like a snake, warily and wound up for each spring as it came, Concuma asked himself: *Can I kill him?* He knew that it did not matter how much of the animated corpse was Reander and how much of it was not. Whatever counted, whatever it was that would win or lose the duel, was within himself. The real struggle was deep in his own mind and heart. It was, as Warwand had called it, a battle of identity. Concuma had fenced with Reander a thousand times. Reander was his friend. Reander had given his life to protect Zea. Concuma had loved Zea. Could Concuma do what the black king had done with the same cold-blooded determination?

"I am Shadow," said the city.

*Can I kill him?* asked Concuma.

All the while, the blades kissed and parted, touched and slid. There was a feeling of unreality, as though he was fighting a mock duel and Reander was not trying to kill him. Sometimes he thought that the corpse was only fighting for sport, despite its master.

He fought his memory and his emotion. Bitterly, he almost tried not to hate Reander. He found that he had to. He was not berserk, but cool as ice. He wondered at his own hate. He felt sick with himself.

As suddenly as that, it was over. His own blade cut the biceps of Shadow's right arm. The slender sword dropped to the lighted stone. In the strange pool of light, Concuma watched the dead face. The vacant eyes throbbed. The pupils dilated and contracted without reason or rhythm. The blueness of the irises flicked on and off in weird, random succession.

Concuma was aware that the face was very close. He was almost paralyzed when the teeth closed on his throat. Absently, as though narcotized, he slid the sword in his hand into Shadow's body. It passed into the groin, up through the intestines. It stuck, but a slick wrench freed it from the pelvic girdle, and the point went through the diaphragm into the heart.

Blood began to flow from his larynx. Cartilage twisted and broke. After Concuma released his sword and tore the smiling corpse-face from his throat, he could never speak again.

With deliberation but no malice, Concuma cut the dead man into pieces. He squashed the eyes in their sockets with strokes of his fingers, broke the neck with a jerk of his thumbs and snapped both the collar bone and the humerus on the left side.

Incongruously, the corpse still stood, with the sword hilt still protruding obscenely from its groin, with blood running down it and dripping into a puddle on the glistening ground.

Gently, he pushed. It collapsed like a man of brittle straw. Carefully, he took out his sword.

Then he walked out of the ring of light, into the center of the city in the Gulf.

## XXIII

THE DARKNESS was only the wall. The city had been elsewhere; the core of darkness was elsewhere again. It was almost a return to Earth, but an Earth a very great distance from the one he had left. He now stood in the remote past or the remote future, if anywhere on the world of his birth. He thought perhaps that he had returned in time to the day of the city. Back long past the age of man, via Cenozoic, Mesozoic and Paleozoic to the pre-Cambrian era, he might have gone—into the erased eons wiped out by the cataclysm which accompanied the wedding of planet and moon, obliterated by the giant tides whipped by the close passage of the satellite before it settled into orbit.

Then he looked into the sky. It was a pristine sky alight with a million stars he had never seen from Earth. And he saw, like a vast blister on the cushion of the diaphanous galaxy, the yellow planet.

He breathed the sharp, clean air and knew that if the eye of the night above him was the Earth, then this was a very different moon from the one of his own age.

It did not matter. The where and when were not important to him. This was not the world for which he was to fight, but the arena in which the fight was to be staged.

He lowered his eyes and looked around him. A city had been here, a long time ago. Older by far than Ylle, now mummified like the city in the Gulf, it had been gone for some time. It was no longer easily identifiable. It was not even the skeleton of a city. It was the ashes and dust. Only the patterns, the lines of the dirt and bright grass, revealed that he was standing on a gigantic grave.

The invasion of the wild was at a minimum. Grasses, lush but short and silky, were everywhere, but no trees and no flowers. He could see the carpet of grass for miles around him, for although it was night the clear air and the abundant starlight and the silver splash that might have been Earth permitted him to see the horizon plainly.

A trickle of blood ran from his torn throat, inside his shirt and onto his chest. When it had leaked from his veins it had been warm. It felt very cold on his torso.

His opponent was approaching. The thing in the city was no giant. It did not seem so fearsome. It was tall for a man, long of leg and arm, with multiple joints. It was scaled all over and its head was small with big eyes which bore no lids. Its mouth was slit-like and very wide, its nostrils tiny. Its neck was long and bore a membranous flap of scaled skin which stretched from temple to scapula, concave and extended. It looked more human than the Blind Worm.

It spoke in a slow sibilant voice. "You cannot kill me, Vanice Concuma."

Concuma could not reply.

"You were the greatest man on Earth. If only you had stayed there. I would have wanted you on my world. Did you think that because I sent your dead into battle I wanted you destroyed? Once men who saw my armies would have known me for their god. What manner of men live on Earth now, who fight their gods? Who sent a hero beyond the end of the world to kill me? The age of the innocents must have passed yet again, and the age of miracles returned. Aye—and the days of glory.

"Come, then, Concuma and kill me. Kill all of us, for I am not alone. I am a hive, like Sum or Ocean, but all the individuals who are my units are in this one body. They do not live—you cannot kill them in your sense of the word. And you have the power to destroy. Even the almighty Quadrilateral does not know the power which will destroy the dead."

The enemy carried a long, curved rapier like a serpent's fang. He moved forward now, reaching with the weapon to engage Concuma's heavier, broader blade.

With incredible smoothness and speed, the scaled one slipped the larger blade aside and flashed inside the blond man's guard. By inches, Concuma sidestepped the blade and was forced to give ground rapidly. The scaled creature was faster than anything he had ever seen before. His own lunges and parries were sluggish by comparison. Time and time again he went backward to avoid the thin blade of his opponent. The wisp of steel whipped perilously close every time the other struck.

And as time went on the fang-bearer seemed to get faster. Like a whip, hate forced Concuma to keep pace. The fury in his heart and brain drove him to every effort his body was capable of. It never let him misjudge any maneuver by the slightest fraction. It never let him pause.

The enemy moved faster and faster; the rapier became an invisble thread woven so rapidly that Concuma had almost to guess where it was. His own sword was a vast weight in his hand, but his hatred would not permit him to relax the muscles which held it and moved it. If there was to be a chance—if he did not burn himself up before he killed his opponent—the chance lay in the sword. He needed time to spare, time to attack. The slender blade of the scaled one could never turn Concuma's aside.

He ducked and ran, waiting for a spare inch. Whether the other made a tactical error, or whether tiredness was having an effect, he did not know, but he gained the fraction of a second he needed. Swaying back, he flashed his sword arm out at full stretch, leaving his right shoulder vulnerable.

With ecstatic ease, the enemy avoided the thrust and struck. Bending backward, almost double, Concuma intercepted the blade with his right hand. It passed through the flesh between thumb and forefinger, an inch from the edge. Reflexively, Concuma's hand closed and wrenched. The thin blade bent like a spring and for a moment it was held between them. Then, with a snap, it was out of the scaled hand.

Concuma brought his sword arm around in an extravagant arc and trapped the other in a single-armed bear hug. In vain, the stubby, scaled fingers raked at the blond man's back. It was like crushing a soft fruit.

Save that something was wrong. The broken body flew

away, spinning Concuma aside. The scales burst and white fluffy flesh splashed out, growing, expanding, changing.

The creature of the Gulf stood again. "You cannot kill," it said in a grating whisper. Its head was black, scattered with coarse hair and bristles. Its mouth parts looked like a complicated trap. Its eyes were as large as its head, bulbous and compound, one on either side. Its arms were horny and its hands bore talons. Its chest was brazen. Its legs were striped black on red, and the big rounded feet bore long claws.

"No matter how many you kill," it said, "you cannot destroy me. I will kill you in the end."

The chimaera leaped. Concuma met the charge with a full-blooded blow to the breast. It struck full on. The sword broke.

Concuma dived to the left, releasing the hilt and jagged stump that remained. The chimaera passed over him, but did not fall. It whipped around and spread its talons, poised to leap again.

Concuma was already up, legs spread in a fighter's crouch, arms held in front ready to grab and break.

The chimaera lunged again. Concuma went for each hand with one of his own. His right hand was hurt badly and his thumb would not be able to grip properly. The pain was no serious inconvenience. Concuma noticed no pain and no weakness. Until he fell dead, he would continue to fight.

The hands locked, the talons closed but could do no damage to the backs of Concuma's hands because the tightness of his grip prevented the muscles from contracting with any force.

With one foot, Concuma stopped the chimaera from bringing the claws on its feet into effect. Gradually, he began to flex his muscles experimentally to discover how and where he could do the most damage. All the time, the black grotesque head was mere inches from his own. He could see his reflection in hundreds of the elements of the compound eye. He watched dark, sticky saliva run over the chitinous mandibles of the mouth and saw the bulbous tongue expanding and relaxing as blood was pumped in and out of the flaccid organ.

Slowly, he bent back the thiny horny arms. His breast came into contact with the bronze exoskeleton of his opponent. He could feel its hardness and he also felt upon it the beating of a heart. He did not realize that it was the rhythm of his own heart reflected from the unyielding surface back into his own intercostal muscles.

The arms began to bend inward as the elbow joints began to give way before Concuma's relentless effort. Inward and backward came the feebly groping talons. At the same time, Concuma forced the other back, trying to make the chimaera fall so that he would be on top.

It was not easy. But Concuma's strength was superhuman. His muscles exerted their maximum power and sustained the effort. He could have forced a man of supple steel to the ground. But the chimaera was improbably strong. Its spine would not yield to being bent like a bow. The knee grinding into its groin would not force it to give an inch.

But its arms could not hold themselves still. Ever inward came the talons, toward the creature's own gigantic eyes. The chimaera tried desperately to curl its claws but could not. With infinite deliberation and tremendous exertion, Concuma scratched its eyes with its own fingers. The ocelli burst and splintered. Fluid cascaded on to the broad shoulders, splashing the bronze breastplate. Deeper and deeper bit the claws, tearing and carving in helpless savagery.

Eventually, when Concuma's wrists were deep in repulsive moistness, the nails began ripping at the brain. The chimaera did not go limp, but its limb muscles began making convulsive flicks.

The blond man let the body fall. The chimaera finished tearing its head to bits by itself with the last reflexive kicks of its own motor nerves.

Then, once again, the body exploded and got up again.

With the sour taste of blood and vomit in his mouth, Concuma watched a new opponent grow from the wreckage of the old.

*I can't keep killing them forever,* he thought. *I must destroy it completely, somehow. How can I do it? How can I destroy instead of killing? What's the difference? What is destruction?*

His hatred could give him no answer. It could give him the endurance, but not the method. He would have to search elsewhere for that. If only he could think. But his hatred would not allow him the opportunity to think. It was preparing him for battle—holding his body in ruthless tension, directing every vestige and energy into the berserk rage which was all that could keep him alive.

The new enemy was soft and obese. It was like a bloated dwarf, all misproportioned and ugly. Its limbs were multifold, with no skeletal support. The entire body seemed to be innocent of bone, cartilage or chitin. The skin glistened and bore millions of tiny hairs.

It looked particularly horrible, but not in the least dangerous.

His hate permitted his brain to whisper: *Poison.*

It came forward slowly, with a disgusting slither, wobbling on a great many tentacles, while many more reached blindly forward. It had a head, all mouth and nose, with pinpoint eyes and no hair. Bulbous lips moved all the time. It may have been trying to speak, to tell him yet again of the fruitlessness of struggle, of the inevitability of defeat.

Warily, Concuma circled, keeping well out of range in case the monster should be capable of a sudden burst of striking speed.

He looked around and gathered the stub of his own sword. It was not that he wanted, though. He noticed that the creature kept itself diligently between Concuma and the needle-like sword which one of its previous incarnations had lost.

No matter how fast he moved, Concuma could not get into a position to snatch the longer weapon. He dared not close in. Instead, he stopped to rest. If the creature wanted to kill him, it would have come to him.

Slowly and hesitantly, it did. Almost reluctantly, it left the sword a long way behind and attacked.

Concuma waited for the right moment and then charged. Taken aback, the pulpy dwarf stopped and displayed its tentacles protectively. Concuma jumped. As he did, he hurled the dagger-like remnant of his weapon at the belly of the creature. Momentarily, the tentacles recoiled to deal with the metal sticking into itself. In that moment, Concuma's booted foot slammed the monster in the tiny head. Then he leaped wildly, a long way clear, and landed on the run.

His stratagem was more effective than it had any right to be. There was only the briefest brushing contact with one or two of the tentacles: on his right arm, on the back of his wrist and forearm. These began to sting and become inflamed. He reached the needle-like sword and slashed the wound boldly and bloodily. He hoped it would prevent most of the poison from reaching the rest of his body—there could not be very much of it, and most of it would remain superficially in the subcutaneous tissue.

He turned around to dispose of the creature, but it was no longer there. Apparently, it had decided not to wait to be killed. His enemy was probably susceptible to fatigue.

The thing in the Gulf seemed to have settled once more for armor, after its brief attempt at subtlety.

The new manifestation of his enemy was very long, many-legged and many-jointed. It was worm-like in form, but its anterior end reared to a height of six feet, swaying slightly back to balance itself. Its foremost legs were long and flattened like sword blades. Its jaws were massive and saw-edged.

Unsteadily, Concuma waited to see the tactics that his opponent would adopt for its new body.

The head reared higher and higher. It towered above him. The segments of the body—particularly the hind body —seemed very simple. The actual worm was thin, but there was added bulk and stability by virtue of complicated spike structures of chitin. It appeared that his opponent was of fixed size and could become larger only by proliferation of nonliving material. It appeared that the limitations of the creature were not so different from his own limitations, except that the monster only had to kill Concuma once.

The slim sword did not seem to be much of a weapon in this particular encounter, but Concuma did not want to discard it while he was effectively reduced to one arm.

With an odd rattling, and a gait almost as jerky as one of the members of its army of the dead, the worm lumbered forward.

The head was so far above him that Concuma had no chance of reaching any spot which might be vulnerable. There was no advantage to be gained in dodging and running—that would only waste energy. He could not win this fight by waiting for the flaw in his opponent's strategy to expose it. If there was a gap in this beast's armor, it had to be physically accessible or he was finished.

And so he waited for the head to strike, planning to deliver himself into the worm's jaws and fight from there. The forelimbs stretched down, clacking like a pair of scissors. He did not try to evade them and they caught him tight. He had assumed that they would attack like blades, but they did not. They grabbed him and lifted him high. They curled around his waist with a flexibility he had not imagined that they could have possessed and held him like an iron girdle.

Then they fed him toward the jaws. He looked closely at the big head, searching for an eye, something into which he could slide the curved fang he still held. But there was nothing. The beast's pale eyes were behind a transparent mass of substance far harder than the metal of the sword. The entire face was armored in this way.

Sickly, he probed unsuccessfully with the point. The jaws were very, very close. His hatred would not let him give up. He switched the sword to his limp right hand and raised the left, palm rigid and aligned with the major suture of the worm's face—the seam where the chitin had to crack every time the monster shed its exoskeleton to allow for growth.

He had no time to compose himself, but the intensity of his hatred automatically adjusted his glandular balance and psychological and emotional pitch to the correct magnitude. Like an axblade, the edge of his hand struck. The skull of the monster burst asunder like an eggshell. White frothy flesh flooded out, and he felt the vise that held him relaxing as the creature metamorphosed.

He fell heavily to earth, but instinct relaxed him to take the fall, then tensed him into a leap which could take him clear of his new enemy. He lost the thin sword again.

There was a blaze of light and color. The dimness of the night was shattered by the sheer glory of the new shape which faced him. It radiated from itself an astonishing quantity of light.

Concuma shrank before it, shielding his eyes with his wounded arm. There was a blast of intense heat, as though the thing were burning. It was literally violent in color; shifting reds, yellows and purples hit him physically. It dazzled and confused him. He had no weapon to resist with, but it did not matter in this battle. The creature had switched from physical fight to an attack on his mind with an onslaught of terrific power. The enemy was weakened by its continual defeats. It was afraid. He could feel the fear in the mental lash.

The monster seemed to have the shape of a giant bird, long of beak and cruel of eye, with a salt gland which wept tears of fury. It wore the fire like a living cloak, its outthrust breast showering sparks and balls of flame. Its all mighty wings beat and beat, spraying fire and light. They seemed to grow as they threw off more and more brilliance and to beat in graceful curves which enfolded the frightened Concuma, hugging him and gathering him into the center of the visual crescendo.

The light which showered from it lit up the sky in a vast auroral display that hid the stars, and then the flames trailing from the primaries lit new stars within the new sky, in a blaze of splendor.

In another time, in another place, but in a moment inextricably linked with this one, John Tamerlane was battling the burning warriors in his self-inflicted cage of flame.

The fire could not burn, the light could not blind, yet Concuma wilted before the curious heat. His skin turned tinder dry and began to crack. His eyes swelled until they threatened to burst. His heart smashed his ribs like a hammer on an anvil. His blood boiled in his veins and threatened to dry, choking his vessels with black dust.

His muscles turned to stone. His kidneys and his testes shriveled and began to disintegrate. His brain began to melt.

His hatred, intransigent, screamed at him. It fought in

every molecule of nucleic acid in his brain. It fought in every millimeter of his spinal column. It fought against every nerve which tried to carry a fatally false message to the dark crevices in the convolutions of the cerebrum that were Vanice Concuma's identity and will. It froze the sodium pump which enabled the impulses to be conducted. It sealed the synapses. And it tried to reverse the flood, to send messages from the brain and spine down the motor nerves to the limbs and organs.

The hatred that was stronger than anything else in Vanice Concuma would not let him despair, would not let him yield to his aching fear, would not let him feel his pain. It commanded him to live and to fight. It commanded him to build walls in his brain, walls that would keep away the fire and block off all the light. It built walls of cellular oblivion that isolated Concuma's identity and memory in heavenly darkness and coolness to gather their strength, to tolerate, prevail and retaliate.

Outward, bursting the walls, came a flood of defiance. It was not color, not heat. Nor was it their negation. It was simple, crude power. Like the birth of a star, it spread from its nucleus in a blooming rush of irresistible energy. It evaporated the light, destroyed the heat and dissipated the firebird on the same winds of time where it had claimed Shadow's dead mind was lost forever.

Nothing, absolutely nothing, could survive that burst of power. But the power could only kill, the power was only limited. When the firebird had gone, undestroyed, there was another to take its place.

It was a man. From deep inside his power cocoon, Vanice Concuma could feel his presence. He could not see him, physically. His hatred would not allow his sensory apparatus to return him to the grassy plain on the moon of the yellow planet. All future battles were to be fought from here, from within. This was a battle of identity, of destruction. Wherever the means to destroy were to be found, it was not in the external universe. It was inside Vanice Concuma. He was the weapon and his hatred was the trigger. He had only to learn how to fire it.

But he could feel the man. He visualized him—a masked,

cloaked figure. There was something behind him: a clock. The massive face of a clock, with curved hands clearly visible in lunatic motion, curled around and finally concave and all-enveloping the inner surface of a constricting sphere, with the numbers in a hopeless jumble. The warped hands indicated nowhen, not even anchored at any point on the inner surface of the sphere.

There was a spinning, cartwheeling hourglass too, sometimes bigger, sometimes smaller and sometimes the same thing as the spherical inside-out clock.

"Time is power!" said the masked man.

Hours flashed back and forth. Days flicked like occulting lights in random array. Centuries sedately fell apart into a jumble of unrelated tempora.

"The universe is being destroyed. Time is being drained, shattered, distorted," said the man in the mask.

Age smote Concuma like a dagger in the gut.

"You can't fight it with power," said the man in the mask. "Time *is* power."

Concuma was no longer conscious of the existence of his body. To all intents and purposes, he had none. It was not physical age attacking him; hatred would not let him feel his skin wrinkling and rotting, his arteries closing up and his nerves flaking.

All that was left of Concuma was his identity, his memory and his will. And, of course, there was his hatred, if that could be divorced from his identity. His memory grew and grew, became heavy and impossible to bear. His will became vaporous and began to lose its meaning. His identity became confused—tried to cope with the rush of time and could not. His hatred began to slacken.

He was losing.

*It's only a man,* he told himself. *It's not the clock I have to fight, but the man. Ignore the clock and concentrate on the man. Forget the clock. Forget the years and the centuries and the millennia. It's not time I have to defeat.*

And his bloated memory forced itself to forget.

His hatred gave him hands again—the left one strong and the right utterly useless. With the left hand he reached out and ripped away the mask from the face of his opponent.

The face behind the mask was his own.

The mask discarded, he stared into his own pale blue eyes and realized what they were. He looked at the other's throat. There was no wound. This Concuma still had a voice. He looked at the right arm, which was uninjured. With his tired, battered body, he had to fight a fresh, whole man who was himself.

"How can you win?" said Vanice Concuma. "There is nothing you can do. This is the end. I could not kill you before, but in your own body, with your identity, I must win."

In that moment, Concuma knew he was beaten. He saw his own death looking at him with his own eyes.

And he thought: *Find it now. Find the means to destroy. Find the secret now, because there is going to be no other chance. How can I fight myself and win when I am hurt and he is not? There is no course left but to destroy.*

With a last surge of power he sent the despairing cry for help into the universe, across the universes. A plea for help from anyone.

The Quadrilateral knew no answer.

The Blind Worm—or what had once been the Blind Worm—looked up at the disappearing stars and said to himself: *He has been trapped. The thing is confounding his mind. He is going to lose.* The cyclops experienced a sensation of lost hope.

But there was a voice. A small voice, with hardly the power to carry itself to him. It came from quite near, but it was very, very faint. Even so, Concuma recognized it.

It said: "Your enemy has betrayed himself. He had delivered himself into your hands. He has given you the chance to destroy him. Destroy his identity with something stronger. He is wearing your identity now, and you have something stronger. You have your hatred, which is more destructive than all the power in the universes."

Then there was silence. Concuma followed the signal back to its source, and searched, but it was no use. The ex-

141

penditure of power to carry that message had been too much for her. Zea was dead, finally, on the Ocean world where she had abandoned herself so long ago.

It was enough. Vanice Concuma knew his enemy. Whatever it was in truth, at this precise moment it was Vanice Concuma. It had thought to make itself stronger than the blond warrior by imitating him, save for his wounds. And, in doing so, it had betrayed itself. Because the one thing that Vanice Concuma hated more than anything else was himself. That was the strength of his hatred, the root which enabled it to suffuse him with its horror and decay. *He hated himself.* And so he hated everything he saw—even Zea, whom he loved. He could no more have ceased to hate than he could have ceased to be.

His left hand reached out for his unmasked enemy, and the finale of his long battle began. With careless ease he brushed away the two good arms which came up to stop him, and smashed his fist into the face of his alter ego.

He kicked and gouged and stabbed with his fists. It was a massacre. He felt bone crack, muscle tear. He felt hot blood drenching his hand, flesh sticking to his fingernails. He ripped open the rib cage of his opponent with his forefinger, breaking each rib just to the left of the sternum. Then, spread-eagle fashion, he opened the chest cavity.

When his hatred allowed the thing which had once been Vanice Concuma to know that he was still crouching in the silky green grass of the moon of the yellow planet, he realized that he was facing the dawn and displaying to it his own heart held in his left hand.

And yet the heart still beat within his breast. But slowly, very slowly. He was dying. He had done too much. His hatred had driven him beyond endurance. It had even robbed him of his identity. Belatedly, he was paying his debt.

As he died, he seemed to see tears in the blinding face of the sun, as though it were a weeping eye. He tried to blink the tears away from his own eyes, and achieved some success. But more tears hid the sky in a mask of red. He was crying blood.

## XXIV

THE WAN bluish luminescence that was the mind and voice of Sum illuminated the bowed body of Warwand.

"It's over," said the Quadrilateral.

The hood rose, and if there were eyes inside it they looked up. "Thank you," he said quietly to Vanice Concuma.

"Why have you come back?" asked the Quadrilateral.

"To help you."

"You owe me nothing. Our debt was canceled."

"You needed me. You needed Concuma and the black king, and I brought them to you. Without my help, you could never have found anyone to do what Concuma has done."

"Are you about to ask me for further rewards? I do not think that there is anything else I can give you. Why have you changed your form?"

"I gave up my old body because I came to hate the sight of it. I prefer my present appearance. I have changed a great deal since I completed the Quadrilateral. There are things connected with my old body and my former existence which I prefer to forget."

"I understand," said the Quadrilateral.

"If you owe anything for today, perhaps you owe it to Concuma."

"Concuma is dead."

Warwand sighed. "I was afraid so. When he sent that call for help—"

"The army of the dead!" exclaimed Sum.

Warwand stood up, half turning. "What's the matter?"

"They're still marching. They're still coming!"

Warwand was silent.

"The thing in the Gulf is destroyed," protested Sum. "There is nothing to animate them. Someone else has taken control. Someone else is in the war. We haven't finished yet. We can't stop them. There's nothing we can do. We're helpless!"

The sun came up and John Tamerlane knew that he had lost. His fire was dead, his army dissipated. High in the roof of the Wildland he rested, caring no more about what went on below. The army of the dead marched on unhindered. It was all over.

He lay on a carpet of trailing weed which bound the trees together and made a mat for the support of the mechanisms associated with the uppermost layer of photosynthesizing material.

Graycloak sat several yards away, sword still in hand, nursing burns and cuts on his face and shoulders.

"Concuma must have lost," said Tamerlane.

"He may be fighting still," replied Graycloak without paying any real attention.

"Then I can be master of the world, if he wins," said the black king.

"How is that?"

"The Wildland must die now. If Concuma kills the thing in the Gulf, then Earth is left without an owner."

"With the Wildland dead, is there an Earth to own?" asked the wild man.

"The cities. We can build again."

"A world for city men!" Graycloak sneered.

"Not so very long ago, I tried to bribe such a world from Sum. Or perhaps it was a very long time ago. I wanted that world—my world. A world of city men."

"You'd have needed the Wildland. For food, for clothing. Its death is our death."

"The plants need not die because the brain dies. The individuals—some of them at least—will be able to live on as individuals. They are vegetable in nature—they don't depend upon Sum for reproduction."

"We'll die," said Graycloak philosophically. "Don't worry about it—it might take a long time. Hell, I'm tired."

There was a pause.

"I don't know what to do or where to go now that it's

all over," said Tamerlane. "Home? The City of Sorrows? Where else is there? I feel so empty."

"You feel beaten, you mean. What does it matter? All the world's the same. It's crazy to stay curled up inside the walls of your dead city and dream. You're no city man, King. Why go *home?*" Graycloak made his last word into a curse.

"Beaten we are. *I* am. Whatever I hoped to gain, I've lost. Whatever Concuma is doing or has done, I've lost."

"What does it matter? Things always change. Try again with something else. The world won't end instantly. We've time while it dies."

"We didn't accept things yesterday. We fought for every inch of ground that we could. Are you telling me now that our fight didn't mean anything? That those inches weren't worth fighting for?"

"Where did it get us?"

The black king sat up and stared hard at the small man. "Graycloak," he said wearily, "I may be no real city man, but I won't ever become something like you. What are you but an animal living in the Wildland as a scavenger?"

Graycloak looked back bitterly, not daring to become angry. "I'm proud enough of my humanity to resent that," he said quietly.

"And wise enough not to fight for it," commented Tamerlane acidly.

"I don't want to be killed."

"Neither do the lizards."

The dead man entered the cavern of Sum's mind. His head was bald; his eyes were cracked and dry, wrinkled deep into their sockets. His mouth had rotted at the edges, leaving a double row of yellow teeth grinning insanely through the ragged gap.

His naked body was charred black. In his arms he carried a large piece of twisted metal, rolled into a ball at one end—a bundle of sheer edges knobbed with sharpened lumps. It resembled, in some ways, a morning star. The damage which it was capable of doing to the delicate luminescent structure which was Sum was obvious.

The guards of the thorn gate had apparently given way at last.

Warwand stepped aside. "It's too late," he said, and his beautiful melodic laugh echoed and echoed again until the chamber was filled with it, like the tinkling of a big bell.

Then the Quadrilateral struck, with all of its much-vaunted power.

"It's too late," yelled Warwand, and his voice rose in pitch as he repeated the phrase many times, until he was screaming it.

His curtains of power were torn away; stark power ripped deep into the darkness within his hood. His body was seized by invisible arms and lifted. With every atom of his will, with every vestige of his strength, he resisted.

There was power in his resistance—but far less power than could have held back the onslaught. He had thought himself a god, on a par with the Quadrilateral, yet here was the Quadrilateral smashing him to pieces.

"You cheated me," he gasped.

"Why?" The voice of the Quadrilateral sounded like pulsating thunder in his disintegrating brain.

"I got rid of the Dragon," he whispered into the eternity into which he fell. "I erased him from myself. I destroyed his cursed command to protect and preserve you. I destroyed his control over my every action, every thought, every process. I exterminated him from my identity."

"But why? Why have you tried to destroy me?"

"Because you cheated me! You gave me a universe *inside* my own mind. You made me a god. You made me live in my own mind. I *had* to get rid of Dragon from my world, because I hated him. But when I did—when I had—*there was nothing left!*

"Dragon made me. I am his. He is me. I wanted to be myself, to have an identity of my own, not some surrogate of a mad creator. I wanted to be *me*. I wanted to fight *for myself*. I wanted to *own* something. You made me destroy Dragon by showing him to me inside my own mind. You made me destroy all that there was of me. I'm not the Blind Worm anymore. I'm *nobody*.

"I wanted your universe. I wanted the universe I should

have had. I wanted to take it from you. *I*, Warwand, wanted to destroy you and the thing in the Gulf. I wanted it all. It wasn't enough for me to see him kill you. I wanted everything. But I failed, because you made me weak. You even cheated me there. I couldn't do anything.

"I killed him. But I was still the thing he made, wasn't I? Just like him, I tried to murder my creator. I should have guessed though. You wouldn't give me that much power. You made me weak. You cheated me."

He heard Sum reply: "It was no part of our bargain that I teach you to live with yourself. That was for you to do."

Then Warwand was gone, but not dead. The Quadrilateral obeyed its code. It would not kill.

The man with the morning star lay putrefying, mere feet from the bowl of glowing protoplasm which was the single-celled entity Sum.

The Quadrilateral did not try to understand. It was a hive mind and therefore it could not. It could not conceive of what it was to be an individual. But it wondered, it decided. By its own morality, it decided what ought to be done.


It was to Ylle that the black king went when he descended once more to the floor of the Wildland. It was there, if anywhere, that the remnants of his army would collect—there if anywhere that he would find people.

That is where he met the Blind Worm again.

Once again, he was the cyclops—an ugly, awkward figure standing quite still, his opercula moving gently as he sucked in air.

"I'm glad you're alive," said the Blind Worm.

Tamerlane nodded slowly. "You surprise me. I never thought I'd see you again."

"I never thought I'd be here again. No resentment?"

"Yes," said the black king. "But what does it matter now?"

"Concuma won. The army of the dead failed."

"How do you know?"

The Blind Worm laughed. It was a soft, oddly musical laugh that Tamerlane had come to know well. If the black king knew for the first time then that Warwand had been the Blind Worm, he did not show it.

"You have seen Sum?" asked Tamerlane.

"Yes, I saw him."

"I wonder how grateful he is for what we did for him. We, the humans."

The Blind Worm laughed again. "I might almost have believed that you have not changed."

"I've changed my ways. I've learned. But I haven't changed my self."

"Come with me," said the Blind Worm. "There is something I want to show you. Something you want to see."

Far away, the spire of Sum's mountain projected from the surface of the Wildland. From here, on top of the roof of the world, the Wildland looked like an ocean. It was easy to believe in the kinship of the enemies of long ago. It was easy to appreciate the immensity of both.

The mountain of wood was on fire. A long thin plume of smoke extended high into the atmosphere and thinned away into nothing. It was not very spectacular. At a distance, it seemed almost forlorn.

"What happened?" asked Tamerlane.

"Sum has gone. Into the Quadrilateral. The sentience and intelligence that was Sum has moved into the other hives. There are only two physical foci now."

"How could he do that? Sum *is* the Wildland."

"Only the intelligence has gone. The organism lives on. It is a mindless imbecile, wiped clean of any trace of self-awareness or thought. The organizer has gone, but the organization remains. The Wildland will survive for a while, probably disintegrate eventually into an association of symbiotes, then further into chaos. The structure will collapse, the waters will flow back into the seabeds. But plant life will continue. It will take hundreds of years. The world when you leave it will not be very different from the world as you found it."

The black king turned to stare into the single eye of the Blind Worm.

"Why?" he asked.

"It's a sacrifice," said the Blind Worm. "It's the Quadrilateral's way of evening the score, or tidying up the ethical loose ends. I am returned to where I started, but wiser. You have the opportunity to get what you want—the world is yours to work with.

"It's a great gift."

"It's not really a gift. A debt, perhaps. A moral obligation."

"I thought that Sum had cheated me, once," said Tamerlane quietly.

"So did I. So did Jose Dragon. So did Zea. Perhaps it did, by our standards. How can we judge it by those standards, though?"

John Tamerlane shook his head.

"I've won," he whispered to himself.

"And I have lost," said the Blind Worm. "Yet here we are, with the same world at our feet."

The Blind Worm looked at the bright sun.

"Shadows," he murmured, "in someone else's eye."

The black king, John Tamerlane, was already planning the future of the human race.

Brad Mantee, starcop on the galaxy's rim, was on a routine mission when everything started to go wrong. His perfect record with Star Control, the vast network of galactic dictatorship, slipped suddenly into oblivion as he found himself in hot pursuit of the madman who had stolen his ship and with it, the secret that could cost him his career—at the very least.

Unfortunately, Brad's best chance was through the madman's daughter, a girl from the one organization Star Control most detested. Their search led them ultimately to a primitive and uncharted planet where fiction became fact and dreams became flesh, but where also lurked a threat of universal slavery more total than man had ever known. . . .

**Turn this book over for
second complete novel**

**EMIL PETAJA**

has also written the following Ace novels:


LORD OF THE GREEN PLANET

SAGA OF LOST EARTHS

THE STAR MILL

THE STOLEN SUN

TRAMONTANE

DOOM OF THE GREEN PLANET

THE PRISM

# Emil Petaja
# SEED OF THE DREAMERS

AN ACE BOOK

Ace Publishing Corporation
1120 Avenue of the Americas
New York, N.Y. 10036

To

LESTER AND ETHEL ANDERSON

# PROLOGUE

The mind-link complete, Cell $88881^4$ gave the proper cerebral salutation to his superior, High Cell $7^2$, then downed vibration and awaited his instructions. He must not allow his impatience with time-honored formality to filter out; or, if it did, he must keep it at the absolute minimum.

*We of Yonder are one mind, when one mind suits.*\*

*Truth is truth. Our ancient cells wandered in darkness and bewilderment, pondering out their stark individualisms, finding their way miraculously to the stars of Yonder, until the ways of Touching and Blending were revealed. From that time we were One. There was no further need for emotion. Absolute logic was achieved and, with it, all the stars within our galaxy.*

*Truth is truth, Cell $88881^4$. Truth is that absolute logic not achieved—not quite. We make no pretense to perfection. We doubt if there is such a thing anywhere in the totality of time and space. Nor is the untidiness of emotion entirely absent from our cells. Youthful cells express it in their impatience to reach out and do things which are beyond their capabilities or in vulgar displays associated with the ceremonies of fission.*

*We loathe all emotion. We are contemptuous of it. We stifle it within ourselves and weed it from our star seedlings as soon as they have reached cerebral maturity.*

*Truth is truth. Now, Cell $88881^4$, we must discuss the matter of your single-cell voyage of star seeding this new galaxy. You are one of our top seeders and yet—*

\*"Yonder" is not, of course, the true logical name the mind-link race gives to its galaxy. Read on.

*I am* the top star-seeder, if I may say so!

You may not say so. Furthermore, refrain from using the pronoun "I." It is both archaic and an embarrassment to The Mind. Were it not for mind-link and the knowledge, the technology, the science, the value judgments, which mind-link provides you on your voyages to these far stars for purposes of seeding them with future life-tools for The Mind, you—an individual cell of The Mind—would be nothing.

Truth is truth. Cell 88881⁴ begs forgiveness of all the cells of The Mind which have contributed to our providing more life-tools for the further expansion and everlasting glory of The Mind.

Well said, Cell 88881⁴. May we now be refreshed with the method of procedure.

Truth is truth. We encase Cell 88881⁴ within a protective dome—

Well said. "We," inasmuch as Cell 88881⁴ could not do the casing, actually. Suitably housed for star flight, prenourished for the duration of the voyage. Proceed.

—provided with a sufficient quanity of life-stuff for the actual seeding, we embark. We land on the designated planet of the designated star. By mind-link with our technically oriented cells we ascertain which organisms actually extant on that planet have the best potential for survival and for cerebral domination of its other organisms. We select those life-forms and, using our life-stuff, we duplicate them. On occasion we are able to eliminate inimical biotics from their bodies before the exact duplication. The duplications are disseminated about the subject planet and Cell 88881⁴, who never actually leaves the protective dome, returns to The Mind, mission accomplished.

And in the fullness of time—The Mind can wait indefinitely—we return to that star to make use of our evolved tool. Our knowledge of its nature, of the totality of its being, makes The Mind its master. Master is not an exact term, of course. Being of The Mind and for The Mind is a privilege.

Truth is truth.

But remember, Cell 88881⁴, we are this time voyaging into a completely new galaxy, infinitely further than ever be-

fore. Mind-link has been fortified within Cell 88881⁴ and within all those cells associated with this utterly new project. There may be perils in this new galaxy, apart from the weakness of the link, which we have never before encountered. Caution must be a byword. There must be extreme caution and ingenuity.

And logic, Cell $7^2$—crystal clear logic which overshadows all other considerations. Trust m—

Ah-ah! The mind-link is ended. Logic be with you; and remember, Cell 88881⁴—

Yes, Cell $7^2$?

Never say "I."

His starcop night-run seemed routine enough. It was a bore, in fact, considering how weary he was already when the call came; he had been selected because his miniship was the only one of XDD-7 class there and ready. Brad had his own reasons for refusing to let some other cop take her, but it wasn't the usual finicky starship-starcop marriage.

*Oh, well, mine not to reason wy. Star Control said do, you did, with no excuses, no if's, and's, or but's.*

Slipping his ship into warp and then out, after swallowing two wake pills (the permissible efficiency limit), Brad viewed Sunnystar's raging night storm on the panel scope-vid with distaste. He flexed his wide shoulders. His lean handsomeness of feature (excepting a ragged, brown beard to hide the dimple in his chin he hated) twitched tight muscles around his dark, secretive eyes and wide but seldom-smiling mouth. There wasn't much to smile about for a solo, short-run cop at the thin end of nowhere. Sometimes when he took the trouble to trim his beard he surprised himself with what others must see when they looked at him: a tough, cynical, space-beat man, especially around the eyes and lips. He thought, *Old buddy, you're getting old, fast.*

*What the hell.* He shrugged. *You do your job, what else?*

Hunting for the beam-in light on the scope through an everlasting sandstorm, he shivered. There was a sinister, mindless madness about the way Sunnystar's perennial storms rearranged the landscape like some crazy exterior decorator. But it was just part of the planet's environment, like the snow peaks and the ancient volcanic canyons.

His eyes probed the latter for the wink of light that would guide him down to the landing area in livable shelter. Only

the deepest, most protected canyons were capable of sustaining life of any kind.

*Sunnystar.*

Brad shivered. Somebody had a sense of humor; one of the older medics once told him about that name. It seems that long ago, back on Terra, somebody had the idea that, since institutions devoted to the care and feeding of psychotics inspired unpleasant emotions from their very existences, the least people could do was to give them pleasant names to remove a little of the stigma. There were Happy Home, Friendly Acres, Tranquil Valley, Sunnystar. . . .

Sunnystar was no ordinary mental institution. When the first pioneers warped off their overpopulated seed-world three hundred and fifty years ago they confronted environments and situations to drive anybody crazy. They went crazy when they couldn't cope and there were places to put them.

But all that was gone. Man's incredible capacity to adjust over generations cut down the psychotic rate and kept him stubbornly and greedily plugging on and on.

They had been in Brad Mantee's bailiwick for the past nine years; they were at the fringe of the galaxy, where the pickings were lean indeed.

Why was there such an expensive mental hospital out here, why a complex buried at the bottom of the deepest canyon on Sunnystar, where the inmates and their warders lived like moles looking up at a narrow slit of dust-blackened sky?

There were reasons, although Brad and almost everybody else had nothing to say about it.

Man had reached the stars in a big way. But problems remained, the same kind of problems Earth had masochistically beat itself with, multiplied a millionfold: greed, war, violence. Space was a shambles impossible to police, too big and too complex. The push had moved on too fast.

The stars were up for grabs and, as usual, money was the key. The pioneers who died and went crazy found themselves shoved off their own homestead by financial manipulators or bandits who killed with no pretense of legal right. One alternative was to join the wolf packs or set up

10

your own robber baronage. The blood that had splattered the pages of Earth's history was sandbox play compared to the red tide of carnage the stars witnessed.

Aliens there were, many as bad or worse. It all added up to an inferno Dante never dreamed of.

Then Star Control had come with iron-fist rule. The habitable stars were thinly scattered; distances were so staggering, that out of sheer need, Star Control formed itself into a complex police machine which demanded instant obedience to its dicta, about which there was no possible protest. If it was fascist in nature, that was how it had to be to save the pieces. The galaxy had been in an intolerable situation. It was as simple as that. *You obeyed Star Control or you were out, with no place to go.*

Over the past hundred years of Star Control rule, the dictators of the stars themselves had taken on a fearful aspect. The pendulum had swung full right.

Starcop Brad Mantee was a cog in the great machine. It was no wonder his eyes took on an icy look.

Now those icy bits of flint glanced at his supine charge. Dr. Milton Lloyd was sedated and strapped in. The man had been already under restraint and sedated when Brad had picked him up at a top-secret science complex known as Project Yonder. At Project Yonder lived several hundred of the most important scientists and space engineers working on a means of penetrating another galaxy. What man had accomplished before was staggering; what he proposed to do now was unbelievable.

Dr. Milton Lloyd's frail, hunched form had remained in the same position since take-off. There was something pathetic about the way his wispy, white hair trailed down over his closed eyes. Brad had to remind himself of what Dr. Loyd had done.

*Why, for God's sake? Why would one of the sharpest minds in the galaxy crack—and kill?* That was exactly what Dr. Lloyd had done. His life with Project Yonder (as it indeed had been for decades, elsewhere) was coddled, serene and special. He had had beautifully faked surroundings, the best of food, the opportunity of working at his cerebral chores with an agreeable little army of his equals.

What made him create a situation which resulted in seventeen deaths?

Brad was only a cop, so naturally they gave him no details. Star Control was disinclined to permit questions or give answers. *Do your job and keep your irrelevant thoughts to yourself. The less one cog knows about the workings of the total machine the better.*

Brad's job was to remove Dr. Lloyd to Sunnystar, the super-secret planet at the jumping-off place where the addled Brains were housed. The patients were all important scientists, spies and other such people, whose hospitalization must never even be known by the general star population. Why? There still were outlaw groups here and there, there still were those within the star machine itself who were hungry for power. Addled or not, the Brains of Sunnystar might be of great value should a revolt against the restrictive clutch of Star Control ever occur.

It might. The pendulum must swing back sometime.

Sometimes Brad thought of Sunnystar as an *obliette* over the Bosphorus, where you dropped people who might rock the boat, men in iron masks. It was a galactic Chateau D'If.

The laser wink showed; the small starship landed.

The round landing pad was some miles from the hospital complex itself. A railed ramp wound further down into the deep canyon, into darkness where faint lights glimmered.

Brad yawned, wondering where the ground crew and hospital conveyances were. Peering, he caught sight of another ship at the far end of the pad and a figure moving through the dark waving a torch.

*Well, get going. Deposit your knocked-out cargo to Hospital Head Dr. Henderson, then shower, eat, and beddybye for ten hours. Hell, fifteen hours.*

Brad lifted out of his cup and hiked the old scientist up on his back. Dr. Lloyd was small but the dead weight was not light to Brad in his present condition. He moved out of the small cockpit and triggered the hatch and ladder. He eased the sleeping man carefully down the ladder and let

him slide down his legs onto the pad while he scowled a-round for help.

*No help.*

*Damn! What is this?*

The ramp winding down to the dim forebuilding lights was empty and dark. Above him the storm howled.

Above the roaring storm Brad heard a sharp cry. It was the figure with the torch, running toward him from that other miniship. It was a girl. *A girl! On ugly Sunnystar!*

A glance at that other ship made him start. It bore a civilian SS number. *Lord! Who in the galaxy could have possibly found his—her—way to this miserable outpost? What for?* It made so little sense that Brad had a sudden giddy notion that the feared revolution had indeed started.

He touched the laser blast on his belt and waited for her to reach him.

*That uniform she wore!* His ship's downbeam tinged it deep brown with a big, red heart on it where hearts are generally assumed to be.

"One of *them!*" Brad groaned. "Lord! How in the name of Apollo did one of *them* make it out here?"

The girl panted up to him, staring at Dr. Lloyd. "I knew it was him! I *knew!*"

"How did you know?" Brad grumbled. "And where in the hell are the attendants and the ambulance?"

Her anxious eyes were only for the little scientist, slumped down on Brad's boots.

"What did you do to him?" she wailed.

"Not a damn thing, Bleeding Heart. What was done was done before I got him, and for good reason." His irritation with her extended itself in the direction of the distant down-ramp glow. "Where are they? Dr. Henderson was notified hours ago, the sour old bastard!"

"I agree with that, anyway," the girl said. "He is a complete bastard, not to mention a tyrant. He runs Sunnystar like a military prison."

Brad frowned down at her trim tunicked shape. There was a hot gleam in her green eyes and her chin was up-tilted. She was pretty. *Feisty, too.* He experienced a wave

13

of acute physical hunger. Star Control didn't admit such hungers existed.

The girl's pretty face shone with defiance; there was challenge and something bordering on hate in the tightness of her lips and the hint of contempt for his uniform, if not for him.

"What in blazes are you doing on Sunnystar, Love Dove?"

"I've been waiting here three days. I knew my—I knew Dr. Lloyd would be here."

"How could you know that three days ago?"

"Never mind. I knew. Henderson gave me a cubicle in the receiving ward to sleep in, but I never got to so much as poke my nose into the main hospital."

"I'm not surprised, the way you bleeding hearts carry on."

She was crouching down, cradling Dr. Lloyd's head in her arms and stroking the hair out of his eyes. She flashed Brad a message of hate for all he stood for.

"Aren't you ashamed of yourself? A sick old man who has been squeezed dry and then thrown in the discard!"

"Lord—"

"Did you have to knock him out, you fiend?"

"I told you I didn't. The meds did, after he killed—balls of fire, what am I doing, explaining this to a nitwit like you? Where *are* they?"

He moved away from her toward the ramp. "Where are they, for—"

"They just might be hunting for me," she giggled. "I gave them the slip—made it look as if I'd got past the guards into the hospital wards."

Brad swore. "And now I'm supposed to pack Dr. Lloyd two miles down—" He turned while he talked. "Hey! What are you doing?"

She had a small med kit out; a hypo was already coming out of the old man's bare arm.

"Helping you," she said calmly. "Nullifying the drug. Now he can walk to the hospital on his own."

"Listen, you stupid little—"

"I know all about your precious rules. I'm a qualified nurse. Don't worry. Where can he escape to?"

14

There was nothing to do but to make it look as if Brad himself had administered the antidote. Since there were no attendants and no ambulance, there was a certain logic to it. But Dr. Henderson was a martinet and the breach would most certainly be reported to Brad's superiors.

"Damn you! Damn all you dogooder hearts!"

He brushed her off and lifted Dr. Lloyd on his feet. The scientist fell hard against him, gasping and gulping, but already he was snapping to. Brad felt a rush of sympathy for the man shuddering awake in his arms. His anger cooled a little. Whatever nitwit tendencies the girl had, she had courage along with it. *Coming here, braving Dr. Henderson and his handpicked dragons, taking it upon herself to bring Dr. Lloyd out of his drugged sleep.*

The scientist's eyes fluttered open. He took one look at Brad and his dark-blue uniform with the phosphorescent insignia, and he wrenched away. He gave a pitiful fling of his head to see where he was. When Brad tried to take hold of his arm to steady him, the old man gave him a wild backward shove.

"Leave him alone," the girl cried.

"He'll hurt himself," Brad told her. "I'm responsible. Can't you get that through your head?"

"Would you care?"

It was during this challenge that it happened. It was impossible, but it happened. Even while it happened, in a kind of time-stopping limbo, Brad refused to believe it.

Dr. Milton Lloyd's rest must have done him a world of good and the antidote did contain a shot of something like meratran. When Brad walked to him he hit the cop full in the face with a surprisingly aggressive blow. Brad staggered back and reached involuntarily for his laser blast.

*No! It can't be!*

It was.

Dr. Lloyd ran for the ship's ladder and when Brad desperately pointed the laser blast at him the girl jumped in front. She tumbled onto Brad, and stayed there, screaming, putting her body over the muzzle of his blaster.

Brad swore and twisted, overtaken by the gut-wrenching agony of having his perfect record with Star Control smashed

15

by a girl and a frail old man. The controlled fury of his starship's burn blew him back as the ship lifted, hovered briefly within a downthrusting ball of red lightning and then vanished into the unseen stars.

## 2

Brad considered beating her; it would help his ego. But it would not help the total situation. He started chewing her out with all the salty idioms at his command. It didn't help. She just stood there, taking it, wide-eyed, contrite but defiant.

"I didn't do it deliberately," she breathed when he was finished. "Please don't think that."

"Shut up."

"I couldn't let you *kill* him!"

"Why not?" Brad snarled. "He killed seventeen astro-testees."

"Are you sure?"

"I believe what I'm told. What's your excuse?"

"For one thing, Dr. Lloyd's my father."

Brad blinked. "Hell, I don't believe it. He's not even married."

"He *was*. My mother died. He was out on assignment when I was born; he didn't even know. Shuttled around from one star to another, always farther and farther away, he never did find out. I've never even seen him before—no recent picture, even."

"SC keeps the big ones under wraps." Brad studied her. He now looked at her as an unhappy girl trailing after her unknown father, not as a bleeding heart nuisance and an enemy of all he was sworn to uphold. "That's why you joined the hearts, to find your father?"

She nodded.

"In a way, yes. But I believe in them, too. All they want to do is help patch up some of the wounds your precious SC leaves behind. Star Control's too inhuman, don't you see that? It's too unfeeling, too grim."

"Got to be," Brad said. It was a rote lesson well learned. "You know how it was before: chaos, total and complete. SC's got to be tough. It's the only way to keep things in order. Can't you and your love doves see that?"

"We think the time has come for a change. Hadn't it ever occurred to you *why* great minds like Dr. Milton Lloyd snap off? They're driven too far and for all the wrong reasons. What's the point in all this pushing forward if there isn't any individual happiness at the end of it? It's like a horrible machine—on and on and on—for *what?*"

Brad shrugged and scowled up into the flailing storm high over their heads.

"Stop your babbling and let me think!"

She sighed. "I know; believe me, I do know. It was your job to bring Dr. Lloyd here and now he has escaped."

"In my ship! What if he gets picked up by one of the elusive outlaw packs we know are out there? What if he lets them con him into helping them start an all-out revolution? There are quite a few would-be Hitlers just waiting for the chance to mess things up. SC's all set for the next big jump."

"What are you going to do?"

He gave her a look.

"Commandeer your boat and go after Lloyd. What else can I do? Do you realize that this is the first time, the very first time! Nine years, the first time!"

"Sorry to spoil such a glorious record—"

"Shut up and help me ready your SS. Luckily it's one of our own early models." He gave a crisp look down the ramp toward the hospital. Hospital personnel were coming toward the pad. "Can't wait for permission. Halverson's such a stickler for going by the book. Can't waste time. Besides— hell, never mind! C'mon!"

He grabbed her arm.

There wasn't time before and during the lift for conversation. Brad grinned inwardly at the girl's wordless efficiency. *These hearts must have something besides currant jelly in their veins. Somehow they make themselves felt among the lonely stars and still manage to keep Star Control from cutting them up into little paper-doll pieces. How? A cockeyed combination of innocuousness and high purpose?*

Eventually Brad caught a feeble glimpse of their quarry in the vid; he let the wires in his nerves uncurl a little. His eyes began to droop.

"You need sleep," she said, as if it were an order.

"Can you handle it?"

"It's my ship, remember. I've been tailing after my daddy for half my life, it seems."

"But how in the—"

"Never mind. Sleep!"

"In a minute. You know, I didn't think SC ever permitted the top-level eggheads to get married. Frowns on close ties: total dedication to duty and all that."

"My father and mother were married secretly."

"Maybe they weren't married."

Her cheeks grew rosy. "Maybe not. That was twenty-four years ago and they loved each other dearly. My mother died when I was five and forever after my dream was to find my father and—" She broke off. "I suppose you think that's silly and stupid."

"Maybe not. I never had any parents to speak of. They were killed when I was two or three, don't know exactly. Anyway, SC training's about all the family I ever had."

"Sounds terribly lonely."

Brad shrugged.

"No close friends?"

"Well, yes, in a way. I—never mind."

She flashed him an odd smile.

"Secrets?"

"None of your business. Sure you can handle this? Keep him tagged on the bion-eye?"

"Sure I'm sure."

Brad rechecked the coordinates on the computer. Dr.

Lloyd obviously knew what he was doing; he would naturally move away from the SC webs of communication. That cut down his probable course by three-quarters. With two-thirds of the rest showing impossible features such as novas and galactic storm regions, the trajectory was further narrowed. She ought to be able to handle it, and she was almost as anxious as he was to find Dr. Lloyd.

He yawned.

"By the way, what's your name?"

"Harriet."

"Right. Goodnight, Harriet Lloyd."

"G'night, Brad."

He slept like a baby.


Time flung by while they trailed the elusive bleep. They talked; mostly they argued about the irreconcilable differences between Star Control and individual freedom of action and incentive.

"Tell me about the love doves," he suggested.

"Please don't use that expression."

"What then, bleeding hearts?"

She wrinkled her attractive nose. "We do have a respectable title."

"Never heard it." He added wickedly, "I heard a lot of juicy ones, though."

"I'm sure you did. That's because, try as hard as we do, we make trouble for SC locals sometimes."

"*Sometimes!* Stirring up prims, rekindling revolutions when we've just barely managed to bring things into line, giving vicious outlaws and predators the notion that they're misunderstood babies!"

"We don't do that—at least not deliberately."

"It comes out that way. Give 'em an inch and—hell! What is your title?"

"The Universal Foundation of Friendship."

"TUFF," Brad grinned. "Takes the place of the formal religions that got shoved in the ash can somewhere along the way."

Harriet nodded sadly. "The Foundation was started after the appalling Centauri massacre—"

19

"Let's not go back to ancient history. One of the chiefs flipped when his wife and children were—never mind. It's a wicked page all right, but it did slash through wholesale pandemonium and let 'em know SC was for sure." He gave a stormy squint into the thinly powdered blacks.

"Our main dynamic is reeducation." Her voice took on a gentle, persuasive note. "We are not *bleeding hearts*. We don't rush to the defense of convicted horrors; we do not interfere. We mostly just trail along behind your juggernauts doing our best to let bewildered prims and harassed farmers know that beyond their heavy work-load somebody cares about them. We're only trying to bring back some humanity to the human race."

Brad made a quizzical face and shrugged. After a long moment he said, "Tell me about you and your father. I mean, how did you manage to track him to Sunnystar? Didn't you realize how dangerous it was, dropping in on Henderson like that? Sunnystar's verboten to everybody but SC's with specific business out here."

She laughed. "I realize. It isn't the first chance like that I've taken of being scragged. For one thing, we hearts blare our ID's loud and heavy on the bionics readers. I use my sex quite mercilessly, too. Nobody's going to shoot down a poor defenseless female!"

"No? You don't know Dr. Henderson. You don't even know SC, apparently. Females of the species rate just what males get. You were damn-fool lucky, is what you were."

"Yes. I've been—lucky."

He gave her a narrow glance. "What do you mean by that? You mean you just *guessed* Dr. Lloyd was about to be hauled off to Sunnystar, days before the, uh, trouble at Project Yonder even happened?"

The girl stared bleakly into the fore-vid. When she gave an involuntary shiver Brad knew what she was sensing. There was an unutterable loneliness about trekking the star wastes, here more than anywhere man had ever dared, because it was so near the jumping-off place. Harriet Lloyd's presumptuous years of seeking her unknowing father among all those bright specks were something like Brad's own lonely years of driving on and on and on. *Well, at least she has*

*purpose to her insanity.* Brad wasn't sure there was any to his. Somebody had pushed a stud in his back and said, "Go, man!" Harriet had a goal. Suddenly, for an overwhelming minute, he wanted fiercely that she should make it.

"Well?" he prompted gently.

She gave her head a fast little shake, as if to put her ideas into their proper position.

"I don't know quite how to say this."

He shrugged. "Just say it; I won't bite."

She smiled. "How are you on ESP, that sort of thing?"

"We had the usual briefings and tests back at SC Training Academy. I've done some extracurricular reading on precognition, kinetics, stuff like that. It's pretty obvious that we're heading in that direction. The potentials are increasing: telepathy, for instance, only I haven't got any."

"I have," she said simply.

He whistled. "Congratulations." When the implications hit home he whistled again. "You mean, ESP is what has been pulling you to your father all these years?"

Harriet nodded.

"I—I think so. They say that within the DNAs of each of our individual cells we have microscopic replicas of all our parents and grandfathers and so on were: like red hair, buck teeth, whatever. This must include whatever ESP factors they possessed, too, which means a sort of preternatural overlapping. It's the explanation for a mother knowing it when her son dies violently parsecs away and even how an expectant father feels labor pains.

"When I was a child I was so lonely I wanted to die. I was placed in an orphanage after mother went. Sometimes I would look up at the stars and wonder which one was my father. That's the way I thought of it. One of those stars *was* my father; and, you know, sometimes *I knew which one was!*"

Brad pushed out a long slow breath of air.

"And that made you decide to come up here and find him when you grew up."

Harriet smiled crookedly. "Terribly sentimental, no? But

try to see. You were an orphan; you had nobody, only tough Star Control. But if there *had* been somebody—"

Brad gave a vigorous shrug. He didn't like this kind of talk; he never had. It worried at slammed doors in his mind. He didn't like the way Harriet was looking at him, either.

"See that fleck of a sun over there in quadrant G-88? He must be heading there. There's no place else on the charts; even that sun's not on the charts."

"They say desperate circumstances help," Harriet went on softly. "I mean, the telepathic contact is strongest between parents and sibs when death is imminent. It relates to survival, I guess. My father thought he was going to die after—what happened. He knew they were taking him to Sunnystar, and suddenly I knew. I was in warp and that's why—" She gave him a glazed, tight look. "These are desperate circumstances, too, aren't they? Father knows starships and astro-navigation after a lifetime in space. He invented some of the techniques. But he's sick; the lift the antidote gave him must be wearing off by now. He'll have to land on the first planet he finds, no matter what. I've got to get to him! I've got to! *Father!*"

"I've got to get him, too," Brad reminded her grimly.

She flashed him a wild tearful look.

There was defiance, even hatred, in that look.

Starcop Bradley Mantee was Control's unfeeling robot.

3

Their eyes remained glued to the reluctant bleep until it was swallowed up by a small, uncharted sun. Brad now took time to ask the computer about the star and directed snatch readers to inform him on its planets, if any. Inasmuch as the system was unexplored and uncharted, the bank had

little to offer. The reader gave it one small planet about the size of Earth. Indications were strong that the planet was still new and primitive.

"That's a break," Brad remarked. "Could have been a dozen suns and fifty planets to dig through."

"I don't like your use of the word *dig*." Harriet's face was a mask of worry. "Do you think he managed a landing? Look!"

The planet was deeply shrouded in wet, black clouds.

"It won't be easy for him or us. I do like just a hint in the scope to see I'm not setting down on an ice pick or—"

"Or on the Bad Witch of the North?"

He gave her an odd grin and started to say something, but then dropped it. For one thing, he was busy orbit-skimming the monotonous blanket that bundled the planet they must land on soon, whether it was good, bad or indifferent. There was no hope of locating a wayward ship under that; even the bionics reader, which could detect and advise of mind-life within a wide radius, had nothing useful to offer.

Dr. Lloyd could have crashed. Weak and slow of reflex as he was, the prospect of burning down to a safe landing would have to include several miracles. Brad didn't say anything to Harriet about this, or show it while he keyed the instruments toward their own precarious landfall.

Harriet knew that her father's chances were extremely bad, but she didn't show it. She snapped to and followed his wordless cues with over-bright eyes and set, dry lips.

They set down at an oblique angle, but on firm ground.

"My impulse right now," Harriet gulped, "is to just stay right here in the ship. We're safe here from witches and whatever; we've got everything we need for the nonce."

"Just what have we got to help us on a tropical prim planet like mother used to be a few million years ago? Let's find out."

Harriet showed him. There were the usual survival items, such as hand tools, capsulate food and portable shelters: the works, as far as basics were concerned. Harriet's green eyes flashed pride in TUFF for being so resourceful and efficient.

"What about weapons?" Brad grunted.

"Weapons?"

"Of course! I've got my l.b. but the ammo packs won't last long. Don't worry, I'm not going to kill anybody—not unless they try to kill us first. It does happen."

"Savages, wild beasts." Harriet gulped. "I *know*. I'm not a complete fool." She dragged out a laser rifle and an ancient side arm. "See?"

They were all but rusted from having lain in their holders for at least a year. There was little ammunition. Brad shrugged while he loaded his back pack and directed the loading of Harriet's. He squinted at the ring of fern trees beyond the clearing they'd landed in. The trees, like the rest of the small planet, were shrouded in fog, which gave the pteridophyte wall an inimical appearance, as if the forest was sure to harbor huge and horrible monsters.

"We're lucky at that, maybe Dr. Lloyd, too. At least the atmosphere's right and Lord knows there's plenty of water, oceans of it, probably. And with all that vegetation, we're sure to eat." He activated the door and ladder. "Shall we have a look?"

Harriet was staring hard at the instruments on the panel. "Brad."

"Yeah?"

"We have problems."

"Don't I—" He whirled. "What now?"

"No fuel."

"What in—"

"Oh, enough to lift us off, but remember what a long way we've got to go before we reach anywhere."

Brad checked, rechecked and grunted. "Just like a—" He shrugged and pulled her toward the hatch. "We better hunt up your daddy and my ship fast, and pray while we're hunting that my reserve's intact."

His first move outside was to check the spider legs and cups to make sure they were more firmly anchored than the lopsided angle of tilt indicated. Then there was the auto-shield to set up around the ship against animal invasion. He gave up the idea of sterilizing themselves completely against inimical local biotics; they had both had their biannual shots and that would have to do. The ship was

another matter, however; it must remain inviolate, protected from all manner of hazard, meteorological, biological or chemical.

When he had finished the routine SC precautions he moved to the edge of the fern forest where he found Harriet toying with a huge, tropical butterfly. The insect was electric blue in color; it fluttered around her gloved hands.

"Look, Brad!"

"I see it, I see it. Garish beggar."

"No, I mean—look closer! Around its head!"

"Ah. That kind of nimbus of greenish specks."

"Emerald halo," Harriet corrected.

"All right, so I'm not poetic. Even if I do read—" He switched quickly back to the phenomenon of the dainty band of coruscating flecks which the butterfly wore as a kind of mobile coronet. "They are odd at that. I wonder . . ."

"Me, too. Are they alive?"

"I don't think so. Could be, though. Some kind of symbiosis, I guess. C'mon, let's get going!"

Brad kept his ears and eyes alert as they moved into the ferny forest. It was too misty to see more than a few yards ahead of them and the fronds were thickening. Still, it was easy going after they reached the summit of the low rise. The ground was springy with moss and dead fronds; there was a pungent odor to the rotting vegetation, which was not too unpleasant. There were low places where the omnipresent damp became hidden pools which had to be watched for and skirted.

Brad kept Harriet behind him and pulled out his torch when the enormous green-blue plants hid an already gloomy, mauve sky. He wondered about animals and listened for evidence of them; if there were predators, the thicket would be a likely place to find them.

His prim-planet experience had taught him that *not* hearing their stealthy paddings and rustlings could be lethal; beasts and savages on the prowl don't telegraph their presences. They wait, watch and pounce.

"Where are they?" Harriet wondered, panting to keep pace with Brad's generous strides.

"They? You mean animals?"

"There was that butterfly, and I've glimpsed some others: dragonflies and like that."

"Insects come early in the game," Brad said. "I'd say there are fish here, or aquatic life of some kind. As to four-leggers, mammals and so on, maybe not. This is a very primitive planet. So far as sophisticated life-forms go, there probably aren't any, besides us. It's wild, virgin."

"Virgin," Harriet mused. "Virgo. That's my zodiac sign, did you know?"

"How could I? Don't tell me you believe in astrology!"

"Um—not exactly. I just like the idea of it. Since we're the first two thinking animals to set foot on it, mind if I christen this little planet Virgo?"

"Be my guest." Brad laughed. "There's plenty of water."

"Thanks. Sorry, Virgo; excuse us, please."

"What's all that about?"

"I'm apologizing to Virgo for desecrating her virginity by belching down on her in a great spurt of fire, and now for tramping through her beautiful virgin forests."

Brad grinned.

"You're funny."

"Thanks."

"Funny and sensitive. You think with your emotions, like all girls."

"You don't have any feelings, of course. Star Control knocked all your capacity for emotion and sensitivity to beauty out of you years ago. Right?"

"Right!"

They tramped on.

"Brad."

"Now what?"

"You're a fraud."

He shrugged.

"Yes, you are. I know something about you that you don't know I know."

"I doubt it."

"Yes, I do. You let it slip several times on the ship. You gave out with several literary references, from books *not* on SC's approved list!"

26

"I don't know what you mean." His mouth quirked a half-smile, while his eyebrows puckered a frown.

"Sure you do; I'm not so dumb. You, Starcop Bradley Mantee, are a *reader!*"

He stopped in mid-stride and turned.

"Starmen in outland areas read. It's handier than the micros, which are not always easy to come by."

"You're talking about technical stuff. I'm talking about fiction: beautiful ancient novels about gorgeous heroes and glamorous girls to be rescued, all those magnificent books in the dwindled libraries, which SC finally burned and disintegrated because they keep people dreaming fantastic dreams instead of doing their jobs."

"Like you said." Brad shrugged. "SC destroyed all the fiction books more than a century ago, what there was left. Nobody writes them anymore and might get in trouble if they tried. There's too much to do these days, too much hard-core reality to contend with, to sit around dreaming up phony situations on phony worlds."

Harriet laughed.

"You're talking right out of the SC bible, and yet you know as well as I do that some of those wonderful, ancient books still exist on far-out colonies—a very, very few, thanks to SC taboos and the natural processes of decay. It's my guess that you not only have read some forbidden books, but that you actually own some, that you find solace in them from the grimness and loneliness of—"

"Will you shut up? Please? You don't know what you're talking about!"

"All right, I'll shut up. But, if by some chance, another SC craft was to find your starship . . ."

Brad swore. He muttered something about her giving her ESP a rest—and her overblown soap-opera imagination.

He sloughed on, increasing his speed.

*If they should find my ship and that secret shelf. If they should . . .*

There were no traces of any path to follow. Certainly those flying insects with what Harriet had called emerald halos left no evidence of their meanderings save for the pupae nested under leafs of huge brilliant-flowered shrubs

27

and the neat nibble holes left by larvae. The rank floor of the forest, as far as they could see, had never experienced the tread of mammalian feet leaving irregular puddles in their wake.

Harriet made little sounds of awe and delight at the alien beauty of the wood. It was like a garden. Brad unclamped a cutting tool from his belt when the going got tough and slashed a way through.

He was annoyed with her guessing about the books. It was not only because they were forbidden. From childhood, Brad had been trained against emotionalism and flights of fantasy or whimsy. None of it was germane to the hard-headed job he had picked for himself very early. On a routine check-mission involving a planetary prospector, a loner, Brad had found the man dead by natural causes. The old man had been sitting up in his hermitage (in a self-made rocking chair) with a book in his lap when death came. He had been smiling.

It was a book with pictures in it: *Treasure Island*. It was about a kid and an old, one-legged pirate and a parrot shrieking, "Pieces of eight! Pieces of eight!"

Brad took the books along because they were so ancient and curious and because that was all there was. It was evident from the loner's well-used belongings that he had fancied himself some kind of adventurer, a seeker after fortune on strange island-worlds even more wonderful than the ones Robert Louis Stevenson had conjured up. He had not found any treasure, but there was an odd, contented smile on his face and a happy, unfulfilled dream frozen in his ancient eyes.

Brad took the books; somehow he forgot to turn them in. He had read *Treasure Island* and he was halfway through *Count of Monte Cristo*. He planned to "remember" them after he'd perused them all on his lonely treks; eventually they would be destroyed by SC's censorship force, like all the others.

There weren't many, about twenty altogether. They were ragged and dog-eared; there were pages missing in some. Brad had skillfully hidden them in one of the storage

bunkers of his ship, behind an oblong of metal that exactly matched the hull.

He scarcely knew what made him do it. He had read them over and over until some of those daring heroes were far more real to him than his superiors or even those few, scattered, starcop friends he had made over the years.

All he knew was that they helped.

*Oh, how they helped.*

Those long-dead dreamers of exciting, noble, adventurous dreams could never have guessed how much.

4

The pteridophyte became all but impenetrable. In a couple of instances Brad had to use his l.b. and some of their meager supply of ammunition to blast their way through.

Uncomplaining Harriet trundled along, keeping pace. Once she tried to match Brad's leap over a miasmic sump and didn't make it. Brad went back and reached down a hand to haul her out of the water. He grinned and carried her to a clearing where a spine of volcanic rock thrust back the jungle. He was surprised how light she was and how pleasant her nearness felt. It had been a long time since he'd been this close to any woman. Mostly his attachments had been casual, mechanical, and of brief duration. It was not their fault, always, nor his; it was the nature of his job. He was always here tonight and halfway to infinity tomorrow.

He'd purposely chilled his feelings for *them*.

Placing her gently on the black outcropping of rock, he told himself he'd better cool it with Harriet as well. There was no use starting something that could get them nothing but trouble. By the complexities of their lives and the exigences of space life under SC, they were, if not enemies,

certainly incompatible. *In those ancient novels a situation like this could have been contrived to come out sweet and rosy.*

*But not now, not for real. Not with SC calling all the shots.*

"May I have a drink?" Harriet asked after she had done what she could about mopping off her tunic and her face.

"I thought you just did."

"Please. You weren't much help back there; you should have helped me before, not after."

He tossed her a canteen and smiled by way of apology.

"Thanks. We might as well rest here and eat."

"Sure." He helped her remove her pack and dug out sealed tins of paste food for them both. It had been discovered a long time back that, while capsulates provided adequate nourishment for human survival, bulk was an important factor.

Because the paste food was virtually tasteless, Brad gave a wry look around them for some of the fruit trees he had noticed among the phantasmagoric blossoms. Harriet leaned back on her pack with a sigh while she nibbled solemnly.

"Shall we try some of those big yellow jobs?" He pointed.

"If you do the climbing. I've had it for now."

When Brad got back with an armful of the mangolike fruit, Harriet was fast asleep. Brad gave one of the fruits a fast standard test, which it more than passed. He ate three, wiped his beard off and then lay back on his cupped palms for a doze.

Training told him it would be imprudent for both of them to indulge in full sleep at the same time; so, weary through he was from their four-hour trek, he kept one eye open. He watched the cloud-muted sun sift through the lacey fern trees; it was slightly past its zenith. They'd have to find something better by way of defensible shelter before nightfall than this hump of basalt. They would need some place where their backs would be up against something solid at least. They hadn't seen anything yet that looked dangerous, but that wasn't any reason to assume nothing deadly existed. The area they had covered so far was very small; there could be something hungry waiting for them around the next bend.

Brad glanced at Harriet.

She was curled up like a child, vulnerable, not only to the alien environment and its perils, but to Brad. He stared at her with growing want; he wrenched his lusty look away and forced other thoughts.

"Brad."

She wakened him gently; her dark, lustrous hair brushed his cheek. He wrinkled his nose, yawned and then sat up fast, guilty and a bit sheepish.

"It's all right. I woke up when you tuned up."

"Tuned—I don't snore!"

"Don't you? All right, you don't snore. It was the wind in the branches."

He grunted and looked around the rock. All seemed peaceful, but the cloud-shy sun had descended beneath the level of the fringe of ferns at their back; nebulous shadows were elongating.

"Brad, I had this dream. It woke me, it was so strong."

"What dream?"

"Father, calling me."

"Your ESP again. But he doesn't know you exist, remember?"

"Maybe not. But all the same, he said—that way!"

Brad frowned. It was not the easiest way and not the way he had decided on. For one thing, there was a precipitous hill to climb some two hundred yards distant with night coming on.

He pointed that out. "Are you sure?"

She nodded vehemently. She was already on her feet, her long, luscious legs looming. She crouched and slipped on her pack, still nodding. "I'm sure. Trust me."

"Could be a psychic doppelgänger leading us astray," he grumbled. But when she leaped easily off the rock he strapped on his own, larger pack and moved after her without further demur.

When it became dark with tropical suddenness, halfway up the mountain, Brad decided that was as good a spot as any to pass the hours until sunrise. There were no animal trails, however dim; and, with a natural curve of solid rock

31

at their backs and a sheer drop in front of them, an undisturbed night seemed a reasonable assumption.

They slept.

The valley the sun presented them when they reached the summit and looked down the other side, was wide and long and verdantly inviting. Among the mammoth, blue-green ferns were lacey, silver-needled conifers and broad leaf trees with sturdy oaklike trunks and lofty patches of deep green branches like the pictures Brad had seen in the book about Robin Hood.

"Gorgeous!" Harriet clapped her hands in childish delight.

"Not bad. Still, there is one thing."

"What?"

"The evergreens and the oaks—maybe Virgo is a bit less primitive than we figured."

"What exactly does that mean?"

"For one thing, four-leggers: beasts, primitive man-types, maybe. Well, one thing, we might snag some game food. We could use it."

"You mean you would kill—"

"We're on that kind of world," Brad pointed out. "And we are meat eaters; at least I am."

"What about primitive man-types?"

Brad grinned. "No thanks. But *they* might not be quite so squeamish."

They moved down. The slope was gradualy and the going easy. When they reached the first of the oaklike trees Brad put his hand on the butt of his 1.b. and kept it there. When Harriet flung forward to embrace a vivid host of scarlet flowers he shouted her back.

"Can't I pick even one?"

"Better not. The fragrance they spill out's very heavy, might even be an hallucinatory drug. That's all I need: a turned-on female."

"Very well, spoilsport."

"Later."

"As you say, Officer. But I—*Brad, look!*"

He had already seen. He pulled her back behind a cover of ground brush and crouched there. Along a natural trail

like a dried creek bed moved a group of natives. They were tall, muscular blacks with ivory rings in their ears and with plumed headdresses. They carried primitive spears and some hauled along fur-bearing forest animals between them on poles.

"What are they?" Harriet breathed.

"Hunters, at least some of them. But more of them look like tribal warriors. Lord, it's as if I'd seen them before someplace!"

"Natives like them on another prim?"

Brad shook his head. "Never."

"Anyway, they haven't seen us yet."

"But the way you yelled out—" The shadows falling on them from behind said it better. "We've had it, baby; hang close to. We'll try the friendship bit before this." He put his hand on the blaster at his hip when he rose and turned.

The incredibly tall and incredibly familiar blacks behind them (the spears they held were most persuasive) ushered them to the front of the entourage, to the tallest of all, the one with many necklaces and a lacquered ebony feather-headdress.

"Greetings," Brad said, with a passable grin.

"Greetings." The Chief nodded. For some reason he appeared hopeful, and the others were gesticulating among themselves and pointing at them with evident satisfaction.

Peculiarly, Brad was not surprised that the Chief spoke a language he understood passably. It matched the mysterious familiarity of the whole situation. Harriet clung close; they waited.

"Whence come ye?" the Chief asked. "And why are your faces white?"

Brad's muscles unknotted and he was able to grin up at the seven-foot man, whose high plumes bobbed with a kind of amiable dignity.

"We are strangers. We come from over the mountains." He jerked his thumb back to indicate this.

The Chief's handsome, black face twisted.

"Ye lie. No strangers can cross the mountains where all things die. But no matter; ye are strangers, and no strangers

33

may live in the land of the Kukuanas. Prepare to die, O strangers!"

Harriet cried out and clung harder. Brad tried to pull out his blaster, but something deep in his mind said no. *I mustn't. I don't have a blaster. There are no l.bs.* The spears were beginning to move in on them; the blades were being removed from twists of vine the warriors had for belts.

"They're going to kill us," Harriet wailed. "That much I can believe. But who are they, Brad? *Who are they?*"

"Let's find out. Chief—"

"My name is Infadoos. But you knew that already?" The mahogany face studied Brad, as it seemed, with solemn hope.

"Infadoos! Of the Kukuanas! Beyond the Mountains of Sulimen, the mountains called Sheba's Breasts!"

The plumes bobbed. The white teeth showed in a wide grin.

"What is all this!" Harriet begged. "Brad!"

"I don't know, baby; how can I believe what is impossible? Maybe the fragrance of all those flowers *was* hallucinatory! But why are both of us seeing the same thing? This is out of *my* mind, not yours!"

"Brad—"

"Something in Chief Infadoos' eyes demands that I understand all of this; therefore, I do. Otherwise we'll get scragged."

"Scragged?" Harriet wailed.

Chief Infadoos held up a hand for the warriors to stay their weapons while he moved in and gave Harriet a penetrating stare. He seemed disappointed.

"Show teeth," he ordered.

Harriet obeyed.

"All there." Infadoos shook his head. "Not good. Take teeth out, please."

"Brad—"

"He thinks they are the take-out kind." He moved a little between the Chief and the girl. "Sorry, Infadoos."

"No good," The Chief shook his head vehemently. "Good must have hair growing on one side. Eyes are not right. One must come out, like teeth. Then you may not be killed." He made the signal for the warriors to go ahead.

34

"Wait! Listen, Infadoos! I know Good isn't the way you expected him to be. But I have other things to startle and astonish you. Watch!"

He whipped out the blaster, aimed it at a small rodent-like animal running out of the brush. Invisible fire leaped. The rodent leaped up in a blaze of blue-white fire.

The warriors yelled out in amazement and approval.

Infadoos showed his white teeth again.

"Truely, your magic tube is of the Word. You may live."

"Thanks, Infadoos. And my woman?"

The muscular ebony shoulders shrugged. "Since she is your chattel, she may live, too. Kukuana warriors can't waste their strength on slaves. But there are many things not of the Word besides her."

"I know. There were supposed to be four of us, right? Well, the other two died from exposure and dehydration, coming over the impassable mountains. You understand how that could happen, Infadoos?"

The Chief nodded.

"Of course. But this is not the True Word. We seek fulfillment of the True Word."

Brad's head was dizzy with unbelief, but there was nothing to do but to persuade Infadoos that they were truly of the Word. That much his mind was able to grasp.

"We are children of the stars."

"That is true, if you are of the Word. You, anyway, Master of the thunder that roars and slays from afar. Come! We will lead you to the place of the king. *Koom, koom!*"

Brad gasped, then grabbed bits out of his unconscious mind's stores. "Your King's name is Twala!"

"Of course. Only our king can guide you across all the further dangers which you will encounter on the path to the treasure chamber."

"Solomon's lost treasure!"

"Yea. According to the True Word we must help you. The way to the treasure is long; many will die. Yet time will be when Gagool will bid the white lords break the seals and take what they wish from the chests in the great caves. Others will be killed in horrible ways, but you will live. You will carry a purse of shining stones called diamonds out of

35

the black tunnels of death to Sitanda's Kraal and safety. It is written in the True Word."

He motioned his warriors and hunters to proceed. Harriet clutched his arm and held back.

"This is sheer idiocy," she said. "It's not happening!"

"Isn't it?" Brad grinned. "All right then. No harm in toddling along with them to have our chat with King Twala."

"No! Brad, let's run. *Run!*"

The high-plumed Chief turned, growling a warning to his warriors in a tribal dialect Brad could not understand.

"*Come!* Should you try to escape your destiny as written in the True Word you will be proven enemies and strangers, and must die."

"Who am I, Infadoos?" Brad yelled. "*Who?*"

"You must speak the name yourself, as it is written in the Word. Who are you, stranger from the stars?"

Brad gulped and moved forward with Harriet.

"I—am—Alan, Alan Quatermain."


5


The something in Brad's memory that told him who the black-plumed Chief was and who he must be to keep them from being slain (The rattle of the long spears, the flashing blades, the body smells, the small human detail, like Infadoos' skinny companion, Scragga, picking his nose and brushing a fly off his ear: all were too real not to believe.) told him to hold his bearded chin high and be the indomitable hero straight out of the ancient steel-engravings.

Brad *wanted* to be Alan on his way to the mines.

His brain and his insides thrilled with it. It was as if some small part of him always had been Alan Quatermain by empathizing with him and yearning for this adventure, for

the agonizing trek beyond the Mountains of Sulimen, for all of it, terrifying and glorious.

For an hour he reveled in it, tramping along behind the tall, black-plumed tribal chief and Scragga; he dizzy with the need for it. His life under Star Control had been bleak, circumspect, and soul-strangling. Now it was as if all his secret dreams were about to burst loose and carry him into wild, wondrous worlds of enchantment where every fragment of his mind and senses would savor, thrill and find complete fulfillment.

He forgot about Harriet. After all, she wasn't Captain Good with his false teeth and glass eye and half-shaven face. She was only a chattel. She was not of the True Word, and what was not of the True Word was nothing.

*It took two good days' traveling along Solomon's Great Road, which pursued its even course right into the heart of Kukuanaland. The country seemed to grow richer and richer. The kraals, with their wide surrounding belts of cultivation, more and more numerous . . .*

"Where's the Great Road?" Brad cried finally. "Where are the kraals, the cultivated farms?"

Infadoos turned. His mahogany face showed disappointment, his arm flung out in a gesture of dismay.

"We have spent many days seeking. It seems to me that all my life has been spent wandering with my warriors through these valleys, seeking the Word. We have done all that we could. We found ourselves with blades and spears and plumes. We hunted game for our food, according to the Word. Only with this day's sun has hope of fulfillment of the True Word come—with you, Alan Quatermain!"

Brad sighed. *And, much as I want to be Alan, I'm only a bastard brain-child of the True Word. Maybe Harriet and I are the illusions!*

Sense and strict training took over his brain.

"Infadoos." He licked his dry lips. "Where *did* you come from, before you began this search, I mean?"

Infadoos scowled. Then, because he couldn't understand what Brad was hinting at and refused to even try to understand it, he snapped the native equivalent of "shut up" and whirled front again.

They tramped on through the wide valley in grim silence. The weariness of seeking and not finding what must be found was in the faces of the warriors and hunters. It was as if they had been transplanted straight out of a book, and had no means of finding their way back into the book. Back into the True Word . . .

"Brad."

He took notice of Harriet panting alongside and slightly behind him, as befit a slave.

"What is it?"

"I don't understand any of this. They're like viz-pics I've seen of Africans who inhabited Earth a long time ago."

"Yes." He hesitated about telling her the impossible truth.

"How could they have got here? Do you suppose they're one of the lost colonies, or hiding from SC, who retrogressed?"

"I don't know; I don't think so."

"Why not?"

"I just don't." His jaw clamped shut with Infadoos' own torture in not finding the way back into the Word. The empathy, the memory-dream, the desire was very strong.

"Brad."

"All right!" he snapped out.

"I just noticed something funny."

"Funny!"

"Odd. Look at them, I mean, at their heads. I mean, around their heads—the same emerald halo—like the butterflies and every other form of life we've seen on Virgo."

Brad looked; it was true. Around the Chief's head and around the heads of every one of the hunters and warriors was the same coruscating nimbus of whirling flecks. He'd been so taken by the magic of things, he hadn't noticed.

"It's the one thing not of the Word!"

"What do you mean?" Harriet begged. "Tell me!"

While they trudged, Brad told her all about Alan Quatermain and King Solomon's Mines. "Don't you see? Chief Infadoos and his warriors are the group of Kukuanas who met Alan and his four companions after they'd crossed the impassable mountains called Sheba's Breasts. I managed to convince Infadoos that the others had died from the privations and horrors of the trek to keep him from killing us.

The Kukuanas of the True Word are very bloodthirsty. They kill for food, for fun, for almost anything. There was one particularly gruesome passage where their witch doctor has a passel of other tribals slaughtered ritually by the hundreds while Alan and his friends have to stand around and watch."

"And you like all this?" Harriet shuddered.

"I like the idea of being part of the True Word."

"But they are *real*, not book people at all."

"They're real; that's one thing I'm sure of."

"Brad, I thought of something else. How is it that we understand them? I don't think they're speaking English, are they?"

Brad gave a doubtful shrug. "I'm not sure, but since the True Word is English, as written by their creator, H. Rider Haggard, it's quite natural that we have to understand it. It's a device that writers have to use if their readers are going to understand the dialog. Somewhere along the line, *somebody* learns the lingo; otherwise no dialog, no conversation, no communication."

"Oh."

"Forget it. What I'm wondering now is: what about King Twala? What about the total Kukuana tribe? Do they exist, too, or is it only this group that got snatched out of the True Word?"

"From the bewildered look on the Chief's face when you asked about the nonexistent Great Road and the kraals—"

"Right. Somehow, I don't think we're ever going to have the pleasure of meeting King Twala, husband of a thousand wives, Chief and Lord Paramount of the Kukuanas, terror of his enemies, student of the Black Arts, leader of a hundred thousand warriors; Twala the One-eyed, the Black, the Terrible."

"All that? Pity." Harriet was suddenly looking at Brad with a critical, head-cocked intensity.

"What is it, Love Dove?"

"No emerald halo."

"You either." He grinned. "Guess we haven't earned ours yet."

6

"The road ends there."

Infadoos halted and spoke the words with solemn intensity. Brad knew why. They were straight out of the True Word. It seemed that it gave him comfort to speak words ordained for him to speak. At least that much of the True Word was left to him.

"We will proceed in that direction." He pointed.

Harriet tugged Brad's arm. "It's the wrong way!"

"What do you mean, wrong way? There's no Great Road. No semblance of path where he's pointing, or anyplace else."

"Father!" Harriet exclaimed. "It's not the way we ought to be heading to find the ship. The creek bed wasn't either, quite, but it was easier going and I thought—"

"All right, already. I'll tell him."

But Infadoos bridled up at the suggestion of trekking right rather than left. He showed physical agitation amounting to terror. The others did, too, when Brad thumbed Harriet's ESP way over the hills to their right.

"Not that way!" Infadoos snorted fiercely. "Bad witches that way!"

Some of the young warriors demonstrated how upset they were by drawing back their spears for hurling.

"They don't like the ship!" Harriet said.

"Why would they? Fire monster from out of the sky!" Brad turned to placate Infadoos and, through him, the blood-hungry young bucks. "You say the road ends there. Why does it end?"

Infadoos sighed and nodded in satisfaction.

"The mountains beyond are filled with caves and there is a great pit between them, where the wise men of old time used to go to get whatever it was they came to this

40

country for. That is where our kings are buried in the Place of Death."

"What was it they came for?" Brad asked, obedient to the True Word.

Infadoos chuckled.

"Nay, I know not. My lords who come from the stars should know."

Brad groped to remember the True Word.

"You are right, Infadoos. We of the stars know many things. I have heard, for instance, that the wise men of old came to get bright stones, pretty playthings, and yellow metal besides."

"My lord is wise. I am but a child and cannot talk with my lord on such things. My lord must speak with Gagool the Old, at the king's place, who is wise even as my lord."

"Delighted."

Infadoos scowled.

"Now he's mad again. Why?" Harriet whispered.

"I diverted from the Word. They're happier when the dialog's exactly right; it's their security blanket. Right now, I'm supposed to point up at those lofty, snowcapped mountains—"

"What lofty, snowcapped—"

"Shhh! I point and say, 'There are Solomon's mines.' My knowing the True Word makes him happy, and the others by osmosis."

"What about us coming from the stars? We did!"

"It's still in the True Word. Haggard, the creator of the True Word, had his natives call Alan's party 'children of the stars.' That *we did* is mere coincidence."

"It's all making my brains whirl like those halos."

"Me too. We'll just have to follow along until something helpful happens."

"If ever," Harriet murmured. "The wrong way!"

The slope they traveled (Infadoos remained stolid-faced and hopeful) was thickly wooded; when they at last attained an open flat halfway up the mountain, the sky took on the muddy, mauve look that told them night was about to leap down upon them.

Infadoos reluctantly gave the order to make camp. Fires

were built to cook the game and to guard against prowling jungle predators. Whether they existed in truth or not was of no importance; they menaced the tribesmen of Kukuanaland in the True Word and being jumped by a savage African lion was almost to be wished for, to add reason to their hunger for the Word. There were other hungers, big ones.

The game animals roasting on spits, the smell of wood smoke and their day's march, made Brad hungry as a timber wolf. He dug in, slashing a great hunk of haunch off, dripping suet and blood; he gnawed on it like Alan himself might have done. Harriet watched him, her nostrils twitching distaste; but when he slashed a hunk off for her, she accepted it, and nibbled at it, blinking away guilty tears.

After supper Brad tried to learn more about Infadoos and his warriors. He was mostly interested in where they had come from, exactly. Little information was forthcoming; but several fearful, covert glances in the direction Harriet thought Dr. Lloyd and his starship were located, had vague meaning. The best Brad could understand was that on that hidden shelf on his SS was Haggard's book, the True Word.

Then why did they shun and fear it? *King Solomon's Mines* was the very source of their being. It was their genesis, their alpha and omega, their sacred relic, their Bible. Why had they, as it occurred to Brad, moved and kept moving *away* from it?

Infadoos finally, with a little growl of warning, turned his back on Brad and the fires and began to snore. Brad located Harriet back along the fringe of forest, as far as she could get away from the slumbering warriors.

"I'm not asleep," she whispered without turning. "What did you find out?"

"Not much. What Infadoos doesn't understand makes him snappish. How can I discuss metaphysics and parapsychological phenomena with a primitive out of a nineteenth-century adventure novel?"

"What are we going to do?"

"Take off as soon as they're all asleep."

"Infadoos posted guards."

"I see 'em; I see 'em. They're drooping already. They

42

know from experience there ain't no wild beasties in this jungle. When they drop off and that middle fire burns down a bit more, we'll make our move."

"Brad—" Harriet turned; her green eyes mirrored the flickering flames a dozen yards away. "Are you sure? I mean about the animals? If something like this could happen . . . I'm sure I heard something a while ago."

"Like what?"

"Like a long undulating cry. It was oddly familiar!"

"It was in your head. Shut up and sleep. I'll wake you when the coast's clear."

It was not easy to thread among the long-limbed sleepers; twice Brad touched Harriet's arm for her to lie down and play possum when one of the guards stirred and yawned, on the verge of waking. When they had stepped delicately over the outermost of the sleeping warriors, Brad took Harriet's arm and ran for the trees.

Harriet blundered over a fallen branch. Brad caught her from falling but the crackling and her involuntary cry brought one of the guards to his feet. Born (or characterized) to sleep lightly and fear the night jungle, the black yowled alarm and brought others to the alert.

"Run!" Brad yelled. "Our only chance is to find a hole the spears can't reach in and pull the hole in after us."

They ran.

But the forest floor was slippery with leaves and the thickness of the underbrush made their progress difficult. They fled with torches at their back and spears whistling over their heads.

Brad heard Infadoos' voice bawl out with angry chagrin. "Come back! You are going against the Word! For this you shall die most horribly, and the woman who is your chattel shall die first, while you watch! It is she who has caused you to do this thing! She is a witch and all witches must die the death of the white-hot spear and the fire-tongued blade!"

They crashed on. There was no hope for stealth, nowhere to hide where these jungle-trained warriors could not ferret them out. Panicked, they plunged on; then, when

Brad heard rustlings and murmuring voices to both sides of them and then in front, as well, he knew there was no use. He might have given them the slip alone, but Harriet was sobbing for breath and spent.

"Easy." He stopped her. "I'll talk him out of it again. I'll think of something. We still have the rifle and our side arms."

But Infadoos remembered, and when the warriors dragged them triumphantly back into the fire circle the first thing he did was to unsling the rifle from Brad's shoulder and take the l.b. out of his belt. Harriet's small arm was inside her pack because its weight on her belt had bothered her, but he did not know how to get it out.

She screamed when the hands overwhelmed them and bound them to the wide trunk of a huge tree.

Scragga swaggered before them when the first dim light of misty dawn fingered the mountaintop behind them. He chuckled while he poked them with the point of his spear. Scragga was skinny, young and bandy-legged; it gave him pleasure to needle them, knowing they could not fight back.

After a while Infadoos came and whisked him back. The warriors made a semicircle behind him, dipping their spears into the fire to make them white hot.

"She—" Infadoos glared at Harriet, "She dies first. She is a witch and not True Word!"

"Of course she is of the Word! She's with me, isn't she? She is from the stars, from over the forbidden mountains!"

Infadoos grinned craftily.

"If she is True Word let her speak it."

Harriet stared up at the bobbing, black plume. She flung a wild look at Brad. "I—I can't. I don't know the Word!"

Brad twisted and strained to break his bindings but the effort only made them tighter.

"Infadoos, listen! I'm going to tell you something; it's not going to be easy for you to believe. I know the Word seems like it's everything. Well, it's not. There are other Words like yours, whole libraries full of them. Why not forget the Word, be your own man! Live to suit yourself instead of following after something you'll never find because it just doesn't exist!"

Infadoos gave back an uncomfortable growl.

"Try to understand!" Brad yelled. "You think you'll find Twala and the rest of your Kukuanas. Well, you won't. Let me tell you why. Because they aren't here. They just—"

The jolting slap that bloodied his teeth against his lips was triggered by boiling indignation. It was as though Brad had spat upon the True Cross. They felt that he must be stopped from such blasphemy, now and forever.

"The Word is All!" Infadoos shrieked. "Now I know that the woman is witch and that you are witch, too! All that you said before was lies. You are not Alan Quatermain; you are unword and worse. Die, witch! Die, unword!"

Chanting the exultant words of Gagool the Witchslayer, the ring of warriors removed their spears from the fire, white-hot now. Wildly eager, they swarmed to destroy those who had committed the sacrilege of denying the True Word.

7

The cry that froze the morning air and the crescent of smoking spears could not have come from a human throat. It was too savage and too special. Brad recognized it at once but not the reason for it. It spun a nerve-electrifying chill out of his loins that curled his toes; it made the hair of his head and his beard prickle. It came out of the depths of the deep forest, and with it came a muffled thunder that shook the huge tree they were tied to and the ground under it.

"That's it," Harriet gasped. "That's what I heard, and you didn't believe!"

"I still don't. But if it's who I *think*—"

"It's all getting to be too much, much too much!"

It sounded again, an exultant half-animal, half-human cry of perpetual, inevitable triumph. Besides animal and human there was in it something of a god, a jungle god.

"What new horror?" Harriet wailed.

"Wait—no! If it's what and who I think, impossible as— Harriet, yell! Scream! *Loud!* He's a sucker for ladies in distress!"

Her yell was quavering, weak and fearful of the screamer in the forest and the thunder as much as of Infadoos and his warriors.

"*Louder,* stupid! Don't you see? It's all done by True Word, and *his* True Word involves girls in deadly peril by the bushel. Scream! Yell! Make it sheer panic and terror like in his Word!" Brad demonstrated.

"You think I have to fake it?" Harriet sniffled.

She shrieked so that the brightening slate overhead became a blackboard with fingernails raked across it.

"That's my baby! Again, please."

Harriet obliged, and this time Brad yelled out manly expressions of needful assistance as remembered from the Word. Harriet's wild pleas for help were most calculated to draw his attention but his share in their mutual jeopardy was quite proper to the Word, as he guessed it; but he could be wrong. *Opar!* He must not be wrong. How often had he not heard that savage, full-throated boast hurled out between the stars in the lonely times when Zartan the untamable was his well-thumbed choice?

There was a hiatus, a trembling wait. The incredible admixture of fiction-made-fact paused, as if a first-act curtain had been rung down or a chapter ended.

Then—

"Kill them!" Infadoos bawled, the chords in his neck straining to break through his ebony skin. "Kill the witches!"

The god-creature in the woods held back his paean of triumph and warning; but the thunder of immense, world shaking hooves moved closer, shaking the trees.

The warriors were about to obey but the rumbling under their feet and the shuddery sound of a tide of flesh hurling upon them, was too much. It seemed that the she-witch had

46

shrieked for her jungle demons to come and help them, and that the demons had come.

When the gray tide of beasts crashed through on them, the Kukuana tribesmen yelled and panicked. Some few warriors turned and hurled their spears futilely at the trumpeting elephants, before they fled; others just fled. Infadoos bawled for them to stay and fight, but they would not. The demon herd was monstrous, a juggernaut of waving trunks and tusks. The captives had called them and now it was their turn to die, unless they could use those long legs to escape to the craggy heights where they hoped the demons could not climb.

Infadoos stood his ground. Scragga, perhaps from sheer terror stayed. After all, he was the Chief's son!

The elephant horde plowed full into the clearing, raising dust, trampling the morning fires and what gear the blacks had left behind.

When the Chief grabbed his knife and came at them, Brad read purpose in his contorted face. If he could manage to kill the witches, he believed the demons would vanish. Brad yelled, squirming violently to tear loose his bonds, his eyes trapped by the twisted fury of a face and upheld knife. Behind him Scragga drew his own all-purpose blade; his aim was Harriet.

Brad yelled.

"*Zartan!* Where are you! Help!"

Infadoos' blade was burning down to sever Brad's heart when the lead elephant rammed through the others and a bronzed giant of a man leaped from his position astride the great beast's neck. The giant's muscular arm caught Infadoos and his blade as in a curling whip, while at the same time his muscular leg rammed out at Scragga and sent him spinning.

"Thanks, Zartan," Brad said, while the forest giant set briskly about cutting them loose. "You are Zartan? Zartan the Stupendous?"

The handsome, savage face showed even white teeth; the immense shoulders shrugged indifferently.

"If you like." He watched Infadoos scramble away up the rocks where the hunters and warriors had vanished.

"Perhaps I should kill them so that they won't bother you again, Clayton."

Brad gulped.

"I—I'm not Clayton."

Zartan's dark brows knitted.

"No? Then why did I save you?" He whipped his look toward Harriet, who was rubbing her arms where the vines had cut. She was looking very lovely, in spite of her smudged and torn tunic. "I see. It was you who called me, in obedience to the Word. You, Jane."

Harriet stared, blinked and turned to Brad for her cue. Brad could only shrug. There was something honest, noble and frank about the animal-god-man that made it difficult if not impossible to lie. Brad noticed now that, like Infadoos and all his tribe, Zartan wore a nimbus of dancing specks around his head like a curious halo. Even the elephants had halos.

Zartan's grave, blue eyes remained appreciatively fixed on Harriet while he waited for a response.

"I know all about you, Zartan. I've read several of the books—I mean, I do know the Word." Her glance toward Brad was an appeal. "But I—I'm afraid I'm—not exactly Jane."

Brad experienced a twinge to notice that her flushed face and breathy rush of words suggested that she wouldn't mind being Jane at all, that under given circumstances she might adopt the role temporarily. Zartan's smile remained courteous to the point of reverence.

It widened suddenly.

"Of course not! You are Miriam. Your companion here saved you from the Arab slave-traders, and you escaped into the jungle only to be captured by these evil blacks!"

"No." Harriet made a helpless gesture. She could not lie to those honest, blue eyes in that heroic, brown face.

Zartan frowned.

"Corrie?"

"Sorry."

"Not Pan-a-lee!"

She shook her head. "Actually my name is Harriet Lloyd. My companion is Starman Bradley Mantee. We are hunting

for—for my father, Dr. Milton Lloyd. His—ah—airship crashed somewhere and we're trying to find him. Have you seen anything or heard anything that might help us?"

The tawny-maned head moved slowly back and forth. His lips tightened in disappointment. Like Infadoos, Zartan sought fulfillment of the True Word (a different True Word, but equally vital to his existence as the tribesmen's True Word was to them) and now, it seemed that the same kind of hope Infadoos had burned with had leaped in Zartan's muscular chest, compelling him to rush to their rescue. All this was very like his Word, but it was *not* Zartan's Word.

His fine brows knitted and he looked away from them.

Brad understood what went on inside that haloed head and sympathized. The why of all this was incredible and baffling, but they must take it at face value since it was here.

"You are unhappy because we are not True Word," he said.

"Yes."

"But we do understand about the True Word! A little, anyway. We understand that something inside of you insists that you keep moving on, hunting for full realization of the Word."

"Of course. Is that not true of yourselves, of everyone capable of thought? Are we not all seeking fulfillment of the Word?"

Brad nodded. Infadoos had said something very like that, but not as well. Brad remembered now that Zartan was actually of noble birth and possessed a brilliant mind to go with his magnificent body. Perhaps, then, he could understand that there were other True Words. Perhaps eventually, since true fulfillment was impossible, Zartan might do what to Infadoos was unthinkable, build a new, real life for himself on this wonderful world of brilliant vegetation and towering summits, forgetting the Word dreams he yearned for or allowing the Word to become a misty, Edenic memory forever beyond his attainment.

Brad would try, cautiously, because he didn't really know how it all happened or just how much more there was of this Word or other Words.

Zartan's massive chest heaved; eyes struck fire. His frown

49

was a fierce negation of everything Brad had said. For a cracking moment Brad thought the ape milk he had suckled in his forest babyhood was going to spill out in lethal action. But Lord Staygroke prevaled.

"I don't wish to hear any more of this nonsense," Zartan said curtly. "I must go. I must follow my destiny."

"Wait! Tell me this: Where did the Word start? Were you actually born and raised here in this jungle? If you were—"

"I must go." Zartan signaled his pachyderm mount to kneel so that he could leap lithely aboard. "Goodbye, Harriet Lloyd. Goodbye, Bradley Montee. I hope you find what you are looking for."

The dust of his abrupt departure left them coughing.

"I don't really know who he is," Harriet said. "I just said that. But I do vaguely remember hearing somebody like him mentioned, somebody out of the old books." She stared where Brad was staring, into the departing dust-clouds and the valley mists. "Who is he? I wanted to thank him."

Brad grinned.

"Wrong True Word, baby—no mask, no white horse."

8

Brad kept them moving in the direction Harriet's ESP said Dr. Lloyd and the starship were until exhaustion and hunger set in. He felt that they need not worry about Kukuana vengeance. What else they had to worry about besides the witch-killing blacks was impossible to speculate upon. They plopped down on a mossy bank at the foot of the mountain range they must cross if they were to follow

the voice in Harriet's mind; it was a pleasant flowery dell and a relief from Infadoos' seven-foot warriors and Zartan's elephant herd.

They ate.

While they rested Brad mulled things over, and after a while his thoughts spilled out in words.

"Asleep?"

"Not quite. What are you mumbling and scowling about?"

"Did you notice that even the elephants had halos?"

"So? The old religions had it that only man was privileged to wear one and become an angel; we've always been smug about such things. The dragonflies here on Virgo wear halos, why not elephants?"

"The dragonflies are indigenous. The elephants came out of the True Word, according to ERB."

"About that, I was very surprised. I mean, why animals, and such big, lumpy ones besides! I could understand cute little monkeys or—"

"Just what you said. Humans aren't really that special, although we like to think we are. I do have a theory about it, though."

"And?"

"These True Words spring out of books. Since Virgo is one hundred percent primitive, so far as we know at least, there are no books. So where did the books come from?"

"That's obvious: out of your ship, from that secret shelf of goodies you were supposed to hand over for destruction by the SC censors, but didn't."

Brad nodded.

"Right. That's the only place: my secret horde of books, or out of our minds."

"Out of *your* mind. I didn't read the books, remember?"

"Good enough, my mind or my books. I think from the books. Why? Because they were there, like they used to say about mountain climbing. There they were for the taking."

"Hidden in the wall."

Brad frowned. "Take a bit of finding. Maybe your father . . . By the way, was he a fiction reader, by any chance?"

"I wouldn't know."

"No, that's right. About that theory of mine . . . Suppose

somebody, some life-force we have never before run into, found the books; and they somehow, in some way we can't even dream about, nipped out characters purely at random. . . ."

"Elephants and native warriors and all?"

"Exactly. Including Gutenberg knows who or what else!"

"You ought to know," Harriet pointed out with a delicate yawn. "You know all the books."

"Practically word for word. But which characters did they snatch out and where are they?" He shrugged and lifted himself on both elbows. "As to where, whoever or whatever got brought into being, they're out there someplace bumbling around seeking the True Word."

"And not," Harriet murmured, "finding it."

The rising terrain was gentle at first, and the trees were thick. Some of the lacey verdure was jeweled with berry clusters and some of the trees hung with huge, yellow fruits. They ducked under cover when a late afternoon shower dropped suddenly and, since within a hundred yards or so the easy slope became naked cliff, Brad suggested that they find a dry, safe spot and spend the night there, leaving the alpine climb for the morrow when they would be fresh.

Harriet was willing. Brad picked an arc of cliff wall where nothing or nobody could sneak up on them from behind and where blue vines provided a partial screen in front.

Brad was just dozing off when he heard Harriet's sharp intake of breath and then the chanting of several voices. The voices were singing in rapid unison and the droll tune was familiar to him.

"What in—"

"Shhh!" Harriet begged. "They're coming into the glade down there. I've been watching them for five minutes. Aren't they cute?"

Brad crept forward to where the girl was peeking between the vines. Below them, in a kind of well-selected amphitheatre where tall trees formed a natural backdrop, came an odd trio dancing in lockstep from backstagish shrubs. They were dwarvish and had long beards which

they almost tripped over; they wore a kind of arboreal armor composed of wide leaves and huge upsidedown lilies for helmets. The graying dusk added to the solemn yet somehow gay drollery of their obviously designed-for-an-audience performance.

> ". . . who is longing for the rattle
> of a fascinating battle—
> and the guns that go
> BOOM!
> BOOM!"

Brad stifled a wild laugh.

"Who are they?" Harriet demanded, *sotto voce*.

"Don't you know?"

"No! Shhh. Don't frighten them away. I think they're skittish in spite of claiming to be such brave warriors."

"Three very fierce warriors are they, sons of Gama, who, like most sons, are masculine in sex. Fighting is their trade. But when it comes right down to a hand to hand battle they—"

"Quiet, Brad! Let *them* tell it!"

"And a good job, too."

The trio finished their rapid turn and then began to bow, looking crestfallen and bewildered when there was no response. They believed that there must be an audience out there someplace; it was in the True Word.

"That's our cue," Brad told Harriet. "Let's hear it for the sons of Gama!" He stood up and applauded vigorously. Harriet gave a perplexed moue, then joined when it was obvious from the exaggerated bowing and chortling that resulted on the stage that the trio was pleased.

"Encore!" Brad urged.

But his yell frightened them, and they went skipping back into the trees in a hurry.

It rained the next day. Brad wondered if this might be the beginning of Virgo's wet season and hoped not. While both starships were virtually weather-proof, a flood-size

downpour wouldn't help. Dr. Lloyd might still be hundreds of kilometers away, the going was all uphill and there was no shelter.

The rock underfoot was slippery with moss and lichen, and Brad's lead took them back and forth in wide sweeps where there were semblances of natural paths and handholds.

They were nowhere near the initial summit yet, with steeper heights to be scaled after that, when Brad found a cave. It was musty and dark within; a sinister charnel odor crept up from the volcanic fingers his torch revealed, yet the cave mouth was dry and that was all they asked at the moment. They wanted a dry place to rest and eat and wring themselves out.

In glum silence, they did what they could to make themselves comfortable. Harriet kept casting fearful glances behind them toward the plunging offshoots where the bad smells came from. Eventually she wondered aloud what was down there and how far down the network reached.

"It's obviously volcanic. Who knows?" Brad shrugged. "What gets me is that peculiar smell. Reminds me of a prim where—never mind."

"None of your masculine pussyfooting, please."

"Anyway, they were cannibals."

Brad took his torch and moved cautiously back toward the largest of the descending branches.

"Cannibals! And you're going down there!"

"Not far. I'll take a fast look. There's a sudden drop, looks like. I'll just flash the light down . . ."

"Here, take my laser gun. You ought to carry it anyway. I've never fired it at anything living since I got it."

"Thanks. Too bad the elephants made hash of the rifle. This hand gun's all we've got. You stay back there near the mouth and wait."

"I will not!"

"Suit yourself."

Their boots crunched hollowly on the rocky floor. Brad's torch caught the glitter of mica and flecks of precious mineral among the stalactites overhead.

"The mountain's probably honeycombed with these pas-

ages created by ancient lava flows, and bubble chambers like this one."

"Brad."

"Yes?"

"What *are* you looking for?"

"Not sure; I've got this funny hunch. As if—"

"—as if what, pray?"

"Like I've been here before; maybe it was all that ver-boten fiction reading. Like in one of those books there was an abyss where—"

"Speaking of abysses!" Harriet cried.

Directly in front of them yawned a huge irregular pit which Brad's torch could not find the bottom of. He felt the clutch of the girl's fingers on his arm as he moved the ring of light across the curved wall opposite and downward. His right thumb toyed involuntarily with the stud of the laser blast.

Whether the torchlight had anything to do with the scream was immaterial. It could have been that the screamer dared to loose her fear and forlorn terror because the flickering light gave hope where there was none, down in the stygian bowels of the mountain.

She screamed and screamed.

Then the scream was silenced.

"Where is she?" Harriet breathed.

"Someplace down there; there's a hole in that wall and a kind of broken path up. I caught a glimpse of something white moving. *There!*"

The swinging light caught a ghostly pastel blur of movement in their direction and shaggy shadows lumbering after. When the runner panted to within a few downward yards, Brad handed Harriet the torch and reached an arm down to pull her up.

Her child's face was a mask of fear, which changed to something naïvely like a smile when she saw Brad. She flung herself into his arms with a frenzied cry.

"You have come to save me from the Morlocks!"

"Morlocks?"

She pointed at the shaggy creatures who were still pursu-

ing her, shambling in a single file up the path by which she had escaped and squealing among themselves. They were less agile than the girl but seemed acclimated to the dark. In fact, when Harriet waved the torch their way they stopped and clung to the back wall as if the light seared their blank eyes.

"Keep the light on them," Brad told her. "I'll give them something else to think about."

He thumbed the 1.b. stud. Invisible light flung across the dropped. "Let's get out, before they find a way across!"

Harriet was already running ahead of Brad and the slim escapee, who clung to him like a confident limpet, all twining arms and wide, blissful eyes. They stopped for breath at the cave's mouth. He disengaged her from himself and held her at arm's length.

She was slim as a wand, even emaciated, as if she had lived on handfuls of fruits and edible grasses all of her sixteen or seventeen years. She had big glowing eyes, long wheat-blonde hair, and she was beautiful as a dryad out of a tree.

Staring openly, Brad found himself reacting to her adoration, though there was little libidinal passion in her wide smiles.

"You are from Time," she sighed. "You came to save Deena."

"Deena . . ." Brad smiled and shrugged. "Well, if it helps."

Harriet stood there, critical.

"Who's Deena? What are Morlocks?"

"They're from the books."

"I figured that much. Which books? Never mind, I wouldn't know about them anyway. Let's get out of here before those creeps down there make it across that hole you cut in the path."

The rain had diminished to the monotony of a drizzle. They took up the task of moving themselves upward in the direction of the first major plateau. Brad kept Deena between them for safety and perhaps because she seemed so helpless. She wasn't. She seemed quite capable of han-

dling herself in their climb. Her pink singlet, a brief affair, clung to her unfulfilled curves in revealing fashion; her sandals found niches and crannies before Brad found them, so that in the end she beat them up to the plateau.

They rested.

"Deena—" Harriet started.

Deena's eyelashes moved down coolly. She gave Harriet a shy look that expressed possible enmity, then turned and smiled beatifically at Brad.

"Well!"

"Don't worry," Brad grinned. "She's from a quixotic nineteenth-century idea of an umpteenth-century Earth where the Morlocks live underground and raise the surface dwellers for food. At the sound of a whistle Deena's people were brainwashed to come down to dinner: *they* were dinner." He nodded encouragingly to the girl curled up at his feet. "How did you get away?"

"There were others. There was this boy; I liked this boy. They escaped and I tried, too. But one of the Morlocks grabbed me and—" She shuddered. "I let him drag me along and then I pushed him over the edge and ran and ran. When I saw the light I knew it was you come in your machine to save me."

She sighed and rubbed her cheek against his arm like a kitten. Then she closed her eyes and slept, an exhausted child who doesn't quite believe that anything is *very* real.

Brad eased her gently off him and turned to Harriet.

"I'm this time traveler, you see. I blundered into her world on my time-bike and . . . well, I saved her from the Morlocks."

"And?" she said crisply.

"And nothing. I went back where I belonged."

"Good show." Harriet nodded emphatically and lay back.

Brad eyed the rise and fall of her full breasts with smiling satisfaction.

9

When Brad blinked open his eyes it was morning. Yesterday's rain clouds had spent themselves, and warm steam was rising up from the lichened rocks around them. Harriet was doing something to her hair and looking very charming about it. Deena was nowhere in sight.

Brad sprang up fast.

"Where is she?"

"She? You mean Deena?"

"Who else, stupid! What did you say to her?"

"Say? What would I say to a childish birdbrain who—oh, hell! I didn't lay a finger on her; when I woke up half an hour ago she was gone."

"Gone where?"

"Brad, you *are* silly! How do I know? Back to that birdbrain boy she said she liked. Anyway, you aren't who she thought you were. Maybe she figured that out during the night." She gave a sharp toss. "These book characters are all bent on one thing, following the True Word. You and I don't really match up. Your precious Deena's simply doing what her impulses insist on, like Zartan and Infadoos and the others."

Brad frowned, whipping fast looks around him with a view toward tracking down the dryad.

"She seemed so vulnerable."

"Maybe, maybe not. You're still under the spell of those big goo-goo eyes, Brad. May I suggest that we have something to eat and be on our way. Looks like we're going to have one of Virgo's rare sunshiny days. When that sun climbs up over that crag it's going to be a scorcher."

Brad gave the invisible goat path toward the mist-hung valley a heavy look and nodded.

It was noon by the time they reached the first patches of snow. A rivulet from those snows, tumbling icily along a ravine, had produced a kind of natural path along its bank which made their climb from the plateau somewhat easier. They rested there, ate, drank from the stream, and eventually turned their reluctant eyes up toward the glacial immensities they must yet surmount if they were ever to look over on the other side of the peaks. Hopefully, they would then confirm Harriet's insistence that somewhere beyond lay Brad's SS and Dr. Lloyd.

"Ready?" Brad asked.

They hadn't spoken much during the march. Brad rejected the idea that it was because he somehow blamed Harriet for Deena having deserted them during the night. It wasn't that he lusted after Deena, he told himself, but she was pretty and weak, where Harriet kept surprising him with her buoyancy, her resilience, her intuitive intelligence that kept him on his toes. Maybe it was all that reading: Brad was the all-man, would-be hero; Deena was the helpless, clinging female.

Harriet wasn't that way. She had trailed her father halfway across the galaxy, alone. It took brains and guts and a lot most of the book women didn't have. They were their heroes' ego-feeders. *Harriet is—*

*Well, she's damn special, and while she irritates the hell out of me every once in a while, she also—never mind. Later.*

When they took up their task again, across the snow-patched rise toward what promised to be a very difficult climb (they might never make it) into heavy, steep drifts, Brad produced a couple of staffs. When he handed Harriet hers and then tied her to him with nylon cord from their packs, he made an effort to indicate his admiration for her *sisu* by his concern for her safety. Harriet smiled tightly and nodded to indicate that she understood. Brad wasn't inarticulate, nor was he unresponsive to her feminine charms; but this wasn't the time or place. Why complicate it with

romance?

They breathed in the thinning atmosphere and, goggled against the reflected light, they climbed.

Toward evening, by which time they were completely flagged, the sun was gone and a rising wind tossed ragged shrouds of mist on them from above. They were hard put to see where they were poking their staffs or putting their boots. Insecure footing might send them both plunging down the glacial wall.

Now that the night fogs were rolling down on them with incredible speed, Brad doubted whether they would find their way back down the trail he'd picked out so cautiously for their ascent.

Since they could not go back, they must go forward and face the strangling wind where the oxygen was becoming so scarce it made them giddy. Every minute Brad expected Harriet to beg for a halt, and when she at last did he sagged back against the snow wall, pulling in the foggy air like a drowning man who has found a floating log.

They didn't talk; they couldn't. Brad worried food from his pack and handed Harriet some. They crouched there in the snarling wind, eating it and handfuls of snow.

When Brad got up and glanced tentatively windward, Harriet said, "Brad, I don't think I can make it any farther. I've got to sleep. I've got to! Sorry."

"I know. I was just looking for someplace a little better sheltered than this ledge. We'll dig out the sleeping bags this time. Can you make it just a bit farther, around that bend?"

"I'll try."

He helped her up; they sloughed slowly and painfully to the windy corner. Brad blinked hopefully around it. Not much could be seen through the driving fog, but he thought he glimpsed, with a start of unbelief, bits of glowing orange and red, off at an obtuse angle where a niche in the snow-heaped cliff-line made a kind of cave. *Bits of fire! As if somebody's built a fire there, for heat, for cooking food. Somebody who'd just left it!*

Brad's shout of joy was lost in the wind but Harriet saw it too, and when he hurried to the fire niche she loped along

60

gratefully. The fire was almost out, but those who had built it had left wood and a meaty game-carcass on a charred spit. The cut-in was boot trampled in a way indicating that there had been several in the party; the fact that the embers were still bright and that there were even a few persistent flickers of flame, indicated that they'd quitted the area only moments before.

Harriet fell into one of the seats they'd used while Brad hastened to build up the fire and reset the providential food on the forked sticks.

"Where are they?" Harriet wondered, warming her toes.

"Can't be far. Looks like they came over the peaks from the other side and—hey! Wow! Somebody forgot his flask!"

It was a leather affair like the ancient tosspots of Earth once carried wine in. Brad shook it. It was half-full, and when he uncorked and sniffed it, he guessed why. They who had built the fire and cooked the meat had drunk full well, so that one of them, having over-tippled, had dropped his flask in leaving.

Brad sipped delicately.

"Wow! One-hundred proof, at least. Must be some fast-fermenting plants here on Virgo, like Mexican maguey. What a party they must have. *Listen!* Did you hear that?"

From up the cliff came the wind-flung sound of jolly, drunken voices. They were deep, heroic, swashbuckling voices, sounding out their wild happiness in being to the unseen stars.

They were rakish, bawling, wine-happy voices, ranting demands of fate. They seemed to demand to know why they'd been snatched out of heroic dreams and made real where they didn't belong.

Brad made out some words:

"When the stars lie flint, the 'putes all set,
  When the lock is shut and the buzz says 'get,'
  When the red light dims and it's time to burn,
  When the Captain signals and we know we'll learn—

  "Sing, jets!
  Sing, stars!

61

"We're off to Mars!"

What brawling winds and distance snatched away, Brad's startled memory supplied.

"Who are they?" Harriet leaped to her feet.

"Quiet! Sing, Rysling! No, it's somebody else now. Shhhh ... Listen!"

Another raucous voice chipped in:

" 'Tis meet and well that an errant knight
  go boldly forth and devil the chances,
  for this is the morn for flinging of lances
  and to hell with the beauty who fears a fight!"

Before Brad could gulp down an astonished breath, a third voice flung out drunken balladry:

"And then came in to that hall of sin
    Into that Venurian Hell,
  A lusty girl who loved a good whirl,
    And her name was Checkecoo Belle!"

They were familiar to Brad; they heated the gnawing cold in his veins and eased the fear. They brought a lump to his throat. Often he had, out among the pitiless vacuums, sung out with them, sung out those very limericks and ballads. What would he have not given besides his right arm to have known those ancient dreamers of fierce dreams, who had fashioned such glorious characters, giving them not only meat on their bones but also the gutty love of action. Three creations of legend and high adventure were up on the high cliff; they were drunk, wild and ready for anything. Each from a different True Word, they had somehow met and teamed together, traveled together, got drunk together, and now they were flinging their songs to the howling night skies of Virgo!

Brad longed fiercely to follow his living book-heroes. He started to, forgetting his ship, Dr. Lloyd and even Harriet. Then, suddenly, the raucous voices retreated and were blown away on the wind and gone.

While they sipped the fortuitous brew and gnawed the heated haunch, Harriet asked who *they* were. Brad tried to tell her, but the lump in his throat wouldn't let him do a good job of it. She sighed and stopped asking.

They slipped down into their sleeping bags and slept.

## 10

While the howling storm had blown itself out by morning, the befuddling fogs were still with them. Brad picked each ascending step of their path with care. Every now and then a crevasse would yawn out before them, to be detoured with blind-man care; sometimes the merest poke of his staff would tear loose an icy drift and send it skittering into deep limbo with sickening speed.

They made no time at all, it seemed. Fearful of causing lethal landslides on the peaks, and to save breath where oxygen was so precious, they trekked in silence. The tearing effect on the nerves was as debilitating as was the stringent muscular effort. There was no sensible place to take a break, so they sloughed on and on, until finally Harriet literally fell in a heap from exhaustion.

Brad crouched and cradled her giddily in his arms. He had the whirling notion that they were going to die here. *That was the way it happened. You flung out into the stars; you did your job under SC's critical sensors; then you ended up crow bait casually on some odd bit of dirt somewhere or other. Nobody to give a damn. One speck of light on SC's god size computer board gone out briefly, before it would be replaced by another of equally indifferent value.*

"Anyway, we die together," Brad murmured, and kissed the snow from her eyelashes.

"Brad . . ."

63

They held onto each other as if waiting for a merciful end to neural torture. The world around them was all of one monotonous shade and texture, as if they floated within some gray sea of death. Their fingers and toes began to numb.

"Do you mind dying?" Brad asked thoughtfully.

Harriet shook her head slightly and smiled. "Not really, but I wish I could have said hello to my father. All that distance—we came so close . . ."

Brad brushed his beard across her cheek and winced. He thought about the heroic three of last night. Would they have let go like this? After all, *they* had come over the mountain. *It has to be possible!*

He forced his heart to pump blood into his arms so that he could fumble out half-frozen food from his pack and feed Harriet, then himself. It took a while, but the effort and the restoration of lost body-heat brought them back to the point of believing in life again.

He hiked Harriet back up on her feet and forced her to go on. Every movement was firey agony, every muscle screamed for mercy, but after all that was what life was. Death seemed too easy.

As if to make up for their misery, the last rays of sunset flamed out over the snowy summits in a burst of prismatic glory that stung their eyes to tears. Gaping and blinking at it in a welter of ancient beliefs in miracles, Brad saw figures.

There were seven or eight. They stood in a somber line against the flaming horizon.

Brad felt his neck hairs prickle. He didn't hear Harriet's gasp and her clutch at his arm took a full minute to register. He stared at the cowled figures, limned against the heavenly radiance and the highest peak of all, experiencing a sensation of transcendental rapture such as he never knew he had in him, especially after lingering on the lip of death a few hours ago and believing in nothing.

His knees sagged as the robed line moved gravely toward them.

"Providence!" Harriet cried.

"Funny, that's what she said."

"She?"

"Miss Brinkley."

"Who is—"

Brad gestured silence as the leader of the robed figures moved up to them. When he pushed back his peaked brown cowl they saw a lean, brown face and a high forehead with tilted lines of thin brow; it was a face like serrated parchment, a million small creases etched by age and ponderous philosophical thought. The sun behind him gleamed on his completely bald head, turning it into a shining, golden knob as if to illuminate what was so remarkable inside.

His narrow mouth smiled gravely at their astonishment. He seemed very pleased to see them, as did the other behind him.

He said, "My name is Tsung. I am from the Lamasery. Would you be so good as to present me to your friends, Mr. Conway?"

## 11

The sun on the snow, the faint whisper of wind tossing powdery rime across geometric angles, the Chinese monks smiling and nodding happily among themselves, and especially Tsung: all this seemed dream and shadow. It was sublime, but impossible to accept all in a minute.

It took Brad five minutes. What had happened before made it possible to believe.

"I'm not Robert Conway," Brad said bluntly. "Sorry."

The ascetic face clouded. "We had hoped—"

"I know. I rather wish I was, this time especially. My name is Brad Mantee, this is Harriet Lloyd. We're trying to find her father."

Tsung sighed. As if to accent his disappointment, the sun began to fade abruptly.

"Nevertheless, this is a rare moment. There is something

very special about you two, even though you are not of the
Word. I should have known it at once, of course. There
would have been more of you." He nodded gravely. "Our
mountains are always most beautiful after a violent storm.
I have not seen the sun so golden since . . ." He stroked
away his frown with long fingers that trembled a little.
"Well, so be it. Names do not matter, do they? You are not
of the Word, but you *know* the Word." He appeared most
anxious about it.

"Yes."

"Then you will permit me to guide you to the Lamasery.
It is not particularly far, but it is quite difficult."

"It'll be dark soon," Brad pointed out.

Tsung nodded. "You are right. Perhaps it would be best
to make camp in one of the recessed places we passed during
our day's journey. If you will follow, please."

"Glad to."

The monks improvised a litter for Harriet and the entourage returned to a sheltered spot and made camp. Harriet was too exhausted to question anything, but when
Brad had eaten and was bedded down, he found his brain
roiling with esoteric anagogics of all kinds. He had thoughts
of High Lamas and glorious hidden valleys where no one
ever grew old, where the spiritual and artistic wealth of a
world was cherished against the catalcysm sure to come—
a yearned-for haven. . . .

*But, is there? Is there a Lamasery?*

When they broke camp next morning he broached his
doubt to Tsung. After all, there had been no Great Road
for Infadoos, no fulfillment for Zartan and the others. They
had been taken out of the books but not all that went with
them. Neither the true backgrounds nor all the rest of the
characters they must encounter were there. They were hit-
and-miss selectees, it seemed.

"Of course there is a Valley of the Blue Star!" Tsung
smiled. "Of course there is a hidden Lamasery where the
High Lama awaits us! Shamure does exist! It *must!*"

"For your sake I hope so, Tsung. But tell me this: *When*
did you leave it? Yesterday? The day before? Last week?"

Tsung began to look worried. Brad hated seeing the

change that came over his ancient, yet somehow youthful face when mistrust and then realization began to dawn.

"It is true that I cannot remember exactly when we last saw Blue Star. But I know we did live there. It was beautiful, serene, all that the human heart longs for."

"Maybe too beautiful to be true?" Brad suggested gently.

"No! We must have faith!"

Tsung gestured for his followers to commence the day's journey. Brad looked at Harriet and shrugged. *Well, if that's how it must be . . .* Tsung was distinct from the others they had encountered. There were mystical worlds inside that knobby skull that transcended mundane law. Maybe Tsung's and his followers' belief in Shamure was so strong, that, in realizing his character out of the Word, the rest of it, all of it—the Valley of the Blue Star, Shamure, the incredibly old High Lama, the whole sublime fantasy—had perforce been realized, too.

*Might as well follow along and see. It's too wonderful an idea to miss, if . . .*

Eventually the stuff of dreams blew away in the nagging wind; sheer weariness made it necessary to face facts. Harriet jelled the mood of distemper when she pointed out to Brad timidly that they were wandering off in the wrong direction.

"We'll never find the ship, Brad."

"Looks like we'll never find anything, Tsung!"

The Chinese halted the march and turned.

"We've been tramping for hours. Can you give me one concrete hint about where we're going besides wandering around in aimless circles?"

"We must have faith."

"Sorry, but I've about run out. How about heading down the other side of the range where the girl says we'll find her father. He might be hurt, dying."

Tsung considered this.

"Very well. We will find this ship of yours. Then we will go to the Lamasery."

While they groped out an easy way down into the low, long valley of deep mists and forests on the other side of the glacial range, Brad moved up even with Tsung and

began to talk. He told him everything, all about Infadoos and the rest. He told Tsung about all the other True Words and his inescapable conclusions.

"And we are all such stuff as dreams are made on." Tsung took Brad's hand and made his fingers pinch his own flesh. "Does that seem real to you? Surely the blood flowing in my veins is as warm and valid as yours!"

"Sure. Sure, Tsung, you're alive, all of you. But the force or whatever that brought you to life wanted more than just blank entities. Somehow it blundered on my books and programmed your minds to match characters out of them, giving you all clear-cut personalities."

"And being out of books," Tsung murmured, "we are obliged to attempt as best we can to fulfill the destinies those ancient writers meant us to fulfill. An ingenious theory."

"If you've got a better one I'd sure like to hear it!"

Tsung wagged his head sadly.

"You have given me quite a jolt, Brad Mantee. But answer me this: if the persons you have encountered are book characters, what happens to them after the final chapter of the book? And if we are not to seek fulfillment of what seems to us to be the True Word, what are we to do to give sense and meaning to our lives?"

Brad grinned wryly.

"Just what we do under Star Control, muddle out your lives the best way you know how."

"Seeking what?"

Brad shrugged. "Whatever seems the right thing for you. We all have to keep plugging along doing the best we can."

"What you have told me, about an immense galaxy of inhabited stars, worlds my Word scarcely allows me to dream about, all scrupulously controlled by what you call Star Control—it sounds far more fantastic than anything I have told you."

"I'll bet it does at that."

"And far more difficult than following my True Word."

"Right. Open up those glorious pages and I'll climb right in with you. Wish I could. As a matter of fact, for a while there that's what I was trying to do!"

They moved in silence toward the patchwork snow, where

blades of grass began to prick through the hard, brown earth.

In an hour Brad felt Tsung's thin hand touch his arm.

"I am beginning to doubt the Word. I am forced to believe you. Trying to think back, I find my mind blocked by a wall; beyond that wall, memory becomes something quite different. It becomes wishful dream. But it is sad, is it not, my friend, to lose one's faith even in one's creator?"

"But you'll find new patterns to follow. Virgo's teeming with gorgeous potentials. You've lost one horizon, but you'll find others. You'll build fine exciting lives for yourselves here on this new world. It's all yours!"

"But is it?"

"What do you mean? Wait. Yeah, I get it. Something or some force pulled you up out of those books. It had a reason for what it did—"

"And its reason may have been purely selfish."

"Probably. That's the way intelligence feeds on itself—Super-intelligence even more so—it's out there someplace watching us right now, I'll bet. It's waiting to see what its puppets do next. When the time's right for it, it will show its hand and tell us all why and what we all do when there's no more True Word to follow!"

12

Skirting the forested areas, they moved fast now. They reached the starship before sunset, just where Harriet's intuition brought them. It lay on its side over charred and twisted trees, where it had tipped over during its landfall. Brad groaned as he ran downhill toward his ship. The metal teardrop's pads were dragged out and broken from the tipping over, yet the hull itself seemed to be intact.

The hatch was wide open; the ladder hung at a weird angle.

Harriet's frenzied worry brought her to the tilted rungs first.

"Easy. Better let me go in first. Don't know what we'll run into at this point." Brad moved Harriet firmly behind him and checked his l.b. Tsung and the others waited at a discreet distance, at the edge of the circle of blasted trees.

Brad climbed up, into the familiar cabin. The tightness of his rectus muscles and the tingling of a thousand wiry nerves, told him there was danger here. But his rapid flash of torchlight across the two chambers and into the engine room revealed nothing.

The ship was empty. Computers, engines, vids, and controls console had been neatly removed. It had been done so neatly that there was no evidence of the use of tools in the removal. It was as if a peculiarly sophisticated transmitter of matter had traced everything of mechanical, technological or personal interest and had whisked it away for a leisurely, scrupulous analysis.

Standing in the center of the emptied hull, staring, Brad heard Harriet's light footstep behind him.

"What could have done all this?" she whispered.

"Somebody with far more know-how than SC ever dreamed of. It's like they reached out across miles and scooped up everything invisibly with an incredibly neat scoop."

"Father too!"

"Right."

"How about your books?"

Brad pointed at an empty shelf where the controls cabin abutted the supplies chamber. "They got it all, everything. Slick as a whistle."

"Where, Brad! Where to?"

Brad shrugged. "Somewhere on the planet." He gave a long, low whistle as he crouched in an effort to find finger marks, smudges, tentacle trails or anything else to indicate a personal visitation. There was none.

Harriet shivered.

"It's—spooky. I mean, not a trace of them. They just located the ship somehow and took *everything*. Why?"

70

"They can't be locals; they're too clever by half, which means they come from someplace else. Someplace we've never been. Looks like while Project Yonder was getting ready for the next big jump Yonder was jumping our gun." He continued to examine the familiar, starkly hollow rooms. "Anyway they didn't touch my reserve fuel-supply." He took out three oblong tanks; it was ordinarily an awkward task, but in the emptiness, relatively simple. "This'll get us back to civilization in your ship, if—"

"If they let us! Brad, I've got the weirdest feeling we're being watched!"

"Probably, they wouldn't miss a bet like that. Their probes would quite naturally be keeping tabs on the ship, as one of the few artifacts on Virgo worth monitoring."

"Besides the book people."

"The book people are no trouble at this stage. They're still bewildered, still following the Word. Later on . . ." He was bending over the cup-seat before the missing controls, staring at an irregular, brownish blotch. "Well, let's get out of here."

But Harriet had seen it.

"Brad! It's blood, Father's blood! They killed him!"

Somewhat reluctantly, Tsung's men moved up to help Brad carry the three fuel tanks back into the forest where, by tacit agreement, they made camp. Since the unseen had removed everything else of possible interest from the starship there was no reason to suppose they or it would bother them yet. It would study them, Brad thought, monitor their actions, as it perhaps had been monitoring them all along, as far as they knew. In any case, running off in a panic and hiding would seem to be futile. The stripped ship had indicated power beyond anything SC had ever encountered before.

*You can't fight what you can't see.*

Brad built a fire, a big one. It was something to do and, while it served no useful purpose in the tropical warmth of the deep valley, it seemed to hold back the unseen terrors of the night. Three of them sat around it after Tsung's wide-faced, phlegmatic, under-drawn Tibetans had curled

71

up for sleep. The flames made shadows on their silent faces.

"It would seem," Tsung said, after a preliminary cough, "that our highly-sophisticated unknown has come to Virgo on an exploratory visit, and that his major interest lies in the investigation of intelligent life more or less equal to its own."

Brad nodded.

"Its use of my books was an experiment. Maybe it thought the characters in them were historical, that they represented the typical genius of—well, maybe not this planet, but others not distant. It wanted to see what we were like. What better way than to bring them to life and watch them and find out just what their life-pattern consists of."

"How?" Harriet demanded. "I mean, *how* could it do that: bring them to flesh-and-blood life?"

"How do I know? The fact that it could and did is what worries me; if it could do that it could do anything. And it's not about to let us take off and warn SC."

Harriet shivered closer to the fire.

"It killed Father!"

"Not necessarily," Brad said. "Dr. Lloyd could have bumped his head when the ship tipped over. He was probably out when the probes found him. Maybe they took him along and patched him up."

"You're just saying that! He could be dead!"

"Could be. I don't know. But why kill him? Their motive in coming here was investigational. He's their one live specimen. My guess is that in his present weak condition, mentally off the beam—"

"He is not! Or if he is, it's because Star Control pushed him so hard that—"

"Okay, okay. Whatever the reasons, whatever the exact state of his mind, Dr. Lloyd's not a prime specimen for their depth analysis. That's why they used my books."

Tsung's sighing breath had a wistful tremolo.

"I still find this very difficult to accept. That my mental being was once merely a series of clever words strung together in the pages of a fictional book written in the twentieth century for the amusement of the rabble. Am I really only that?"

"No!" Brad cried with emphasis. "It was a very fine book, a hopeful book for millions. You must rationalize the phenomenon. Wouldn't everyone rather be an exceptional character created by an unusually perceptive dreamer than a run-of-the-mill dullard running around like an idiot trying to make sense out of our lives?"

"But if I am restricted to the Word—"

"The answer to that, Tsung, is that you aren't. If you were restricted to what happened in the book, we'd never have met and I could never have convinced you of the truth. We wouldn't be sitting here discussing your quixotic mind-pattern like this! Don't you see? There's far more to this than meets the eye."

He stared thoughtfully at the prismatic halo around the lama's head, fired to gold by the leaping flames.

"Yes." Tsung clasped his thin fingers together as in devotion. "Whatever else I am, my body is real. My thought patterns, even my physical characteristics, were stamped out of that old book, but when will I become aware of my true capabilities?"

Brad picked up a snapped branch and threw it back into the fire.

"When we find whatever did all this."

"Or," Harriet added softly, "when it decides to find us."

13

Harriet woke Brad with much agitation.

"What? What?" He yawned and rolled his humerus bones into their shoulder sockets and gave his head a characteristic shake to clear off the clinging cobwebs.

"Tsung's gone!"

"Gone?" He blinked around him, at the dead fire, the

grassy patch and ring of the trees. When he caught sight of the lama bustling about with his stolid followers in the trees he turned to Harriet with a grouchy snarl. "What do you mean? Looks like they're fixing us breakfast. So you're complaining?"

He stretched his long, muscular body luxuriously and gestured her to the early group. The Mongolians had gathered a feast of fruits and berries. Even one of the game rodents roasted aromatically on a spit.

"Brad!" Harriet panted in a whisper. "There's something wrong. I can't explain it, but when I woke up I felt it, like a wave. They were pointing and whispering about us."

"You and your overactive ESP."

"No, honest, Brad—"

The beauty of the morning made Brad shake his head and wave away her qualms. He moved toward the sumptuous board hungrily and fell to. Tsung nodded welcome.

"Eat well," he urged. "We have a long journey before us."

"How about that, fresh meat!" Brad began wolfing down a succulent strip with drooling content. "How about you and your boys?"

"We have eaten," Tsung said. "In any case our religion forbids the eating of animal flesh."

"How about the killing of animal flesh?"

An expression of worry flitted across the lama's ascetic face. "Well—"

"Well what?" His hint of something odd did not prevent Brad's enjoyment of the unexpected feast.

"We do what we must."

Harriet said, "*Must*, Tsung? Why *must*?"

Tsung's lean, brown face became very bland and cautious. "You are meat-eaters; you need strength for what is to come."

Brad let his meat drop. Harriet was right; there was something wrong, something different. The whole atmosphere of the camp had changed. During the night something had happened. Something invisible had entered Tsung's mind and the others' minds and made demands. He wiped his mouth and faced the lama.

"Tsung, what is it? What happened last night?"

Tsung looked worried, but firm. The thing that had taken hold of him and the others, making them kill for food when killing was not of their Word, brooked no second choice. Brad read it in his liquid brown eyes. Tsung was, as always, politeness itself, but now a task had been programmed into his expanded mind. He must do it; he had no alternative.

Brad decided on a test to make sure.

"You and your men go any damn place you like. As for Harriet and me, we're going back to the other ship."

He stood up.

Tsung spread out his palms,

"I am sorry, Bradley Mantee, but you must come with us."

"Suppose we decide not to."

Tsung motioned to the men behind him; they moved in grimly. Brad saw now that they held weapons from Harriet's and his packs. They also had clubs and vine ropes. Their wide faces were suddenly no longer affable and easygoing; they were hard and tight.

"We are to guide you to a certain place as quickly as possible. You must come. If you don't come we must kill you."

"Kill!" Harriet cried. "That's against all your teachings! Totally against the Word!"

"Never mind the Word now. We have killed already to feed you, so that you will be in prime condition for your—interview. If you decide to fight us we must kill you both. There is no choice for either you or for us."

When they reached the lip of the wide, natural bowl of land where the dome rested, Brad gave a low whistle of approval. It was opaque and off-white, rather like an egg that had been sheered off on one end. There were no visible openings and, considering the teleportive efficiency with which his ship's accouterments had been removed, Brad thought it likely that there actually were no hatches or openings in the dome. What lurked within it had no need or desire to wander about alien environments subjecting

itself to alien perils. It simply stayed within the huge dome and sent out its invisible probes to garner bits of the environment (including intelligent bits) into itself for analysis and assessment.

"Efficient," he murmured. "Way beyond us."

"It looks so—inert," Harriet said, "so harmless."

"Under that white shell it's probably seething with all kinds of mental activity."

"What does it want?"

"Us. The books were an experiment; we're real. It wants to find out what we and our galactic race is all about."

"I just thought of something. Why didn't it snatch us here like it did the stuff in your ship and Father? Why make Tsung bring us, on foot?"

Brad shrugged. "Who knows? Maybe it does have limits. Maybe it just chose to do it that way, checking our reactions out. Whether we'd try to kill Tsung or—"

"We *couldn't!*"

"That's one thing it found out by playing it this way." Brad blinked downhill. "I have an idea emotional empathy is not among its primary motivations. In fact—"

"You must walk down to the place," Tsung interrupted, with his newly acquired, brittle firmness. "It is down there." He pointed to a spot some fifty feet from the dome which wore a faint violet haze over it. It was hard to see but it was there.

"What is it?" Harriet wondered in a whisper.

"The way in, I expect, a space-warp of some kind that bounces you inside the dome."

Harriet wailed, "I don't want to!"

Brad turned to Tsung. "How about the girl staying here with you? After all, she can't get away. I'll provide it with all the information it wants. Besides," he grinned, "I'm curious. I've been around, but baby, this is something!"

Tsung shook his bald head.

"No. Both."

"Couldn't you at least make the request?"

"There is no way. Go!"

They went.

Harriet's eyes were bright with excitement and fear. Brad

felt an electric jolt of intellectual pregnancy leap up from his insides and charge senses, nerves and muscles with its immense portent. He was about to learn much, including, probably, *why* the book people had been removed from their ancient pages and made real. *Not how, surely. The human brain is not capable of such knowledge. Other things. Other answers to nagging questions. Staggering answers to big, big questions. The creature within the dome must have unlocked science secrets which man would not begin to understand for a thousand years.*

He gripped Harriet's hand.

They stepped into the violet haze.

At this point even their escape, their probable elimination after the wanted information had been squeezed out of them, was secondary. Curiosity burned high.

Harriet's thoughts ended in a single focal drive.

"At least," she whispered, "I'll get to see my father."

If Brad was not so confident about it, he didn't say so. He nodded and held her hand tighter.

There was no sensation of any kind, no sound, no flash of light. Quite suddenly they were inside. There wasn't even the momentary irritation of a sudden viz-pic scene-change done for effect.

Brad stared around them into churning multi-colored mists that had striations and vague networks of odd, geometric patterns in an infinite maze.

"It reminds me of something," he said.

"Yes!" Harriet's audible heartbeat against him subsided somewhat as she found the dome was not a hotbed of hideous monsters with horrendous fangs. "The gelatinous threads that seem to hold the whole thing together! It's, it's like one of those huge demonstrative models of a single human cell!"

"That's it! Do you suppose it could be? I mean, if the environment where it came from was such that, instead of increasing the cells in number, one single cell increased in size and intelligence . . . the kind of intelligence that enabled it to create ambulatory servants or tools to do whatever needed to be done outside its—"

"*Bravo!*" a jolly voice broke in with a chuckle. "That is

not quite how it was, of course. Very different, in fact. But a good guess for a member of an inferior race."

"Thanks," Brad managed. "Thanks for the left-handed compliment." He peered all around him; there was nothing but the gentle movement of what seemed the protons and neutrons of a gigantic atom. "Where are you?"

"I am what you see. I thought you realized that much."

"You mean you're all of this? We're inside of *you?*"

The voice chuckled again. "Exactly. It is not necessary for more than one of us to make such a journey since we are connected by mind-link. But our purpose in permitting you to enter our shell was not to provide you with information but rather—"

"Wait! We aren't used to talking to a disembodied voice, even if it is sort of familiar. By the way, why is it familiar to me?"

"Start walking toward the throne and look around you." There was a new, pompous tone to this voice and a hint of regal thunder.

The throne was a long way down the high-ceilinged hallway and it was awesome. Suddenly Brad felt very, very small and his skin prickled as if it wasn't really skin at all.

"The Scarecrow!" Harriet exclaimed. "You're not Brad anymore! I can see your face *through* the patchwork cloth and the button eyes but—"

"You're a little girl in a pinafore," Brad grinned. "But who are these others walking alongside us?"

"Don't you know? This True Word I *do* remember. My mother—"

"I'm scared," sniffed the Lion, to Brad's immediate right.

"You're not the only one around here who's frightened," clanked the Metal Man, who had taken hold of Harriet's hand on the other side. "Well, after all we've gone through to get to the Emerald City—let's face up to it and let the Wizard know what we came for!"

The long emerald hall led them to the wide bottom steps of a golden throne. The dumpy little man with the ruby nose and puffed, red cheeks to go with it wore a high

conical hat over his white hair. The hat had very mysterious symbols on it.

When the little man stood up and glared at them with his shaggy, white eyebrows raised, the Lion fell flat on his face, whining and whimpering in terror.

The Wizard pointed his star-tipped wand at the Lion; the Lion vanished. He pointed his wand at the Metal Man, the Metal Man vanished, too.

"Now," he chuckled. "Now I presume you are comfortable, having been projected into one of the incredible milieus which your weird race indulges itself in?"

"It's not *quite* the way we usually do it."

"No? It was in the books."

"Sure, but those books aren't exactly a true representation of the way we normally function. In fact they—"

"Never mind! That's all we had to go on and I've made you comfortable by presenting myself before you in a manner which even an infant would find agreeable. We don't understand such incredible nonsense, of course, but since that is the way your minds work, we accept it for what it is worth." There was a testiness to his Frank Morgan voice which the Wizard's creator never intended. He had done what to The Mind behind all this was appalling and ridiculous, because the books were the only things it had to base its judgment upon. It was only now beginning to realize its error and that made the cell feel emotion; in this case, it was *anger*.

Brad began to understand. What would a super-intellectual non-emotional race imagine, finding those books and nothing else besides technical manuals? It must identify the books with their possessors; what was in the books must seem to be *what they were*.

The mind-link cell race had evolved strictly along lines of dead-serious science, much the way Star Control was now leading its galactic sheep. There was no nonsense, no delightful whimsey, no fantasy and no fiction of any kind. There were no artful dodgers of restrictive truths.

There was nothing but pure fact and cold logic.

This started a nodule of an idea budding in Brad's racing brain.

"Your irrational thought-patterns make any level of intellectual communication very difficult," the Wizard was saying. "I read within those erratic cesspools of confusion you call minds that your comfort requires a visual focus while you are communicating. You cannot mind-link as we do, so you may call me the Wizard."

"Not a bad fictional prototype at all," Brad murmured.

"What is this *fiction* concept?"

"You have nothing like it where you come from? No art of any kind?"

The Wizard waved his wand irritably.

"Why should we? What possible use are falsities in the expansion of The Mind?"

"Why, they make you happy; they comfort; they provide a sense of awe and wonder to the lonely individual who finds the universe unfriendly and—"

"Individual!" the Wizard cried. "That seems to be the key! Your race is made up of individuals, *lonely* individuals. We of course have no such problems. Mind-link joins the cells of all our galaxy and makes any single cell the equivalent of All. Truth is Truth. Logic is Everything."

"Sounds peachy-keen," Brad said, fully aware that such an adjective would further irritate the cell in its characterization as the Wizard.

"Please."

The Wizard seemed to be fumbling around their minds, trying to find something like what it normally was able to link itself with. It didn't seem to be doing well.

Harriet said, "My father! Where is my father?"

"You refer to the frail individual we found unconscious in the primitive starship?"

"Where is he?" Harriet cried. "What did you do to him?"

The Wizard eyed her curiously. The characterized chuckle came again. "Your agitation is interesting. Why? What if we had thrown away this debilitated member of your race? What difference? The cell has apparently served out its usefulness."

"He's my father!"

"We do not understand; from the vague meanings we read in your mind, we find the concept revolting, but then

80

you don't reproduce by fission. Your method is copulative, like other low life-forms."

"Our lowest life-forms reproduce by fission," Brad pointed out.

"Brad, please!" Harriet seemed unable to grasp the fact that an emotional appeal was wasted on the Wizard, because he *looked* so amiable. "Let me see my father! Please!"

"No. Later, perhaps." The Wizard put his finger to the side of his nose and twinkled his eyes at her. "I will tell you that he is well, at least as well as any body and mind of its race and age can be expected to be. We gave him new flesh where new flesh was needed; we could not give him a new mind, unfortunately."

"Will I be able to see him before—"

"Before we dispose of the only two members of your race capable of warning others of our advent? Perhaps. For the time being I have endured enough of your cluttered egos. You will go away now."

"But where? What—"

"No more questions, though by your questions you have revealed more about your race than you have by your absurd answers. I must be totally alone for mind-link with my peers. Your weight within me is a physical and mental drain, as is the assumption of this ridiculous characterization. Mind-link at this intra-galactic distance is particularly difficult and—never mind! Out! Out! Go play down the rabbit hole with Alice and the Red Queen!"

14

Tsung greeted them on the rise with a good deal of his Shamure warmth returned. Brad guessed why; it was exactly what the Wizard's irritability had revealed before they

81

were whisked back out. The cells communicated with one another by mind-link. Most likely the Wizard must consult with top level cells or perhaps with the totality of the race about what procedures were in order. Apparently, the mind-link race had never in its galactic history encountered anything quite like the human race. It would take very involved thought mechanisms to deal with all the new problems the cells faced in this galaxy, so far from any star they had ever touched before.

Mind-link at such a distance was extremely difficult. That was why the Wizard had dismissed them so rudely; it was why Tsung and the others were no longer captives. It was a drain on the cell to keep the Mongolians subjugated, just as it was a drain to have Brad and Harriet weighting down its physical body and confusing its mind with their emotional fantasies.

"They do have a weakness!" Brad told Harriet and the lama of the Word. "It's the thread that—"

"*Look!*" the girl cried out, point to the entrance place. "Hey—it looks like Dr. Lloyd!"

Standing below them in the purplish haze was a small hunched figure wearing the dark tunic of an AAA-level SC scientist. He was scratching the white wisps of hair on his head and looking bewildered.

"Him, too!" Brad muttered to himself. "For super-distance mind-link the cell had to rid itself of his weight, too, which means . . ."

He followed Harriet's run down to the place. She seized both the startled old man's hands and wept. The physicist wagged his head and sniffled, his vague eyes staring at her and welling up because hers were; his lips trembled.

"It's all right, my dear," he mumbled, allowing Harriet to lead him out of the violet haze before the Wizard snatched him back. "I'm all right now; I feel just fine."

Harriet wept against him for a moment, then led him gently uphill. Brad followed, emotional because he knew what this meeting meant to Harriet after so much, yet nagged by suspicions. *Is Dr. Lloyd really all right? Is he even Dr. Milton Lloyd?*

"By the way," the little man asked Harriet, "who are you?"

"I'm your daughter! You never knew it, but—"

"Of course, of course!" The wispy pate gave a trembling nod, then several more, bobbing in childishly anxious agreement. "Of course you are my daughter. How could I have forgotten?"

It was Tsung who suggested that they remove themselves as far and as quickly as possible from the dome. His brown-faced countrymen agreed with alacrity. Now that the thing controlling their minds was gone they reacted toward it with abhorrence, much like the abhorrence Infadoos and his warriors had displayed when Brad had tried to urge them in this direction. Evidently their programmed minds retained some fragment of memory of where their lives had actually begun, and since it didn't agree with the True Word it was detestable.

The people from the nonexistent Lamasery were sharper and of a far different stamp, yet they had had a taste of take-over. They didn't like it.

"Any ideas where to go?" Brad asked Tsung.

"There is a deep valley not distant from here; a high cliff overlooks it. The valley is so lush, so verdant and beautiful, that at first we thought it must indeed be our Valley of the Blue Star!"

"But no Lamasery."

"No, unfortunately. We were mistaken." Tsung sighed.

"Say, why not build one there?"

Tsung was dubious.

"Why not? You'll have to settle somewhere, sometime. You can't just keep on the move, seeking a will-o'-the-wisp that exists only in a book! Use your knowledge of the Word; build your Lamasery. Make Shamure real!"

The slanted eyes flashed bright.

"Will the creature who brought us to life allow such a thing?"

"Why not? I have an idea about why they did it, brought you to life. The Wizard gave us a couple of hints. My idea is that they go around seeding worlds for future use. Instead of putting androids or non-indigenous creatures on a given

planet, they use what they find there. In the case of Virgo all they found was my books. There's more to you than those book patterns, though. For one thing, flesh and blood —indigenous life-stuff, somehow. You *belong* here."

"And we are actually free agents who can use the Word or not use it, as we see fit. We may use it when it suits best, or parts of it, but discard it entirely when the time comes to do so. Our descendants will know only that much of the Word which we teach them."

"Right! This seeding's a long-range proposition. The cells want you to make your own lives, do your own things!"

"Perhaps. But in the fullness of time they will come back and make demands on us, as their creatures."

"So fight them then! Only now, build your world into something fine and wonderful. Show the kind of courage book heroes must! Defeat your would-be masters by using the very weapons they provided you with—the heroic hallmarks of the Words!"

Tsung smiled thinly.

"You make it sound easy."

"I know . . . Sorry. But you *are* heroes!"

"Provisional heroes," Tsung murmured, "unmotivated heroes, blundering through a world we were thrust onto full-blown, with no creators to write new Words." He gave Brad a long thoughtful glance. "What we need is a leader to bind us together, to make us truly men, men of viable and honest purpose."

15

A two-day trek brought them to Tsung's beautiful valley, which they named Shamure. The lama's eyes welled up as his trembling hand pointed high up to a break in the

precipitous headland where, in the evening mists, the shadows raised a haunting vision of towering architecture, the illusion of Shamure Lamasery itself. It had been the most bitter discouragement their wandeirngs had brought them. Brad pointed out that the deep valley was thick with trees for lumber, trees which must be felled if they were to cultivate fields in this fertile Eden. By means of vine ropes and muscle, logs could be hauled up to the high ledge and Shamure could be made real. Modest at first, it would grow larger and more noble, until it would at last become an inspiration to all the heroes of Virgo. It would take work, drudging toil, but it would give them something to do that was fine, something to dream on. If they were masterminded from another galaxy by the cells, they could at least show their masters what was in them. There is dignity even in slavery if the slaves refuse to cringe.

There were shallow caves at the foot of the high cliff, where they made camp. The next morning, Brad and Tsung began to make plans for a permanent settlement, where other book people would be invited to come and live, sharing the benefits of a stable community.

Harriet looked up from feeding her father, spooning a kind of wild-rice porridge into his mouth. Dr. Lloyd showed no inclination to do anything himself. His hands remained limp at his sides; his eyes crinkled up pleasantly at whatever was said to him, good or bad. He did whatever he was told to do, poorly, but he did it.

Harriet's smile was bleak as she pricked up her ears to their mounting eagerness and excitement.

"Listen to you two! Have you forgotten the thing in the dome? Any time he chooses to, the Wizard will clamp down his controls and there goes all your fancy plans into a cocked hat."

"He hasn't so much as brushed my mind since we were forced to bring you to the dome." Tsung's eyes flashed.

"How do you know?"

"I know. I am trained to understand the subtleties of the mind, the so-called metaphysical forces and cosmic vibrations, more than most men. Therefore, I know there has been no intrusion." He turned hopefully to Brad. "Perhaps

this cell was instructed by mind-link to remove himself from Virgo; perhaps the Wizard has returned to his home!"

Brad shook his head.

"I doubt it, and Harriet is probably right. The cell is keeping an eye on us."

"I'm sure he has no monitoring eye or ear on me, nor on my group," Tsung insisted. "In fact, since we have been making firm plans for lives of our own, related to the Word but not *of* the Word nor subject to its domination, I find the entirety of my mind soul fired with increasing vigor." He smiled. "This is in spite of my great age. We of Shamure do not age as rapidly as others." His eyes gleamed like black diamonds. "You have pointed the way," he told Brad. "You have taught us more than you know."

"Such as?"

"That if we rebel mentally, if we reject domination by the Word *as well as* by the cell itself, this dome dweller will find it increasingly difficult to control us at all. Eventually control will be impossible. All of the implications of the Word and areas of instinctive knowledge I have not yet plumbed tell me that this is true! If we reject mind domination it cannot happen, and I hereby reject it!"

Brad whistled while he stared hard at Tsung's transfigured face. He stood up, turned and moved rapidly toward the wood.

"Brad!" Harriet called. "Where are you going?"

"Hunting."

Since Tsung's people had resumed their taboo of killing for food, Brad's solitary expedition into the forest in search of small game was altogether logical. Harriet had her mindless father to fret about, whom she cared for as if she were his mother and he her backward child. Tsung and his apostles were happily occupied in the initial stages of building a new Shamure. With the crude but utilitarian bow slung over his shoulder and half a dozen imperfect arrows poked into his wide belt, Brad went across the greensward with springing steps.

He was going hunting, but not for small game. What he had learned from the Wizard had been percolating for two days and nights inside his mind, and what Tsung had

just told him fanned a weak ember of hope into a small flame. His ideas were only half formed, yet it seemed to him that somewhere among all those magnificent heroes must be one whose Word had the answer, one whose creator had endowed him with the perspicacity and cunning to defeat the Wizard. *Only one!* They were all brave to the point of *idiocy*, all intense as they could be about the urgency of battling any foe they met, loaded to the gills with high adventure and high purpose.

*But that isn't enough!*

The Wizard, the cell of the mind-link race, was an adversary far more powerful than any which their artful creators had hurled them against.

Striding under the random tapestry of thick foliage, Brad reviewed the books taken from his secret shelf. *Let me see . . . There was* him, *and* them, *and* him. The problem was in knowing which characters the Wizard had picked. Surely not all had struck its fancy. The selection seemed random, perhaps even desperate. The alien's logical nature had been outraged by emotion and lusty animism, yet it had gritted its nonexistent teeth and kept trying. Its job was to produce creatures like those which the strange galaxy harbored. That the books were fiction was an accident.

Brad grinned.

*It's something to have led the galactic intruder down the garden path!*

He stopped grinning and put his full attention on the task of determining which, if any, of the book people could help him defeat the Wizard. *Hard fists and naked swords are all very nice but they won't do it. Not even a little bit.*

Ticking off this book, eliminating that hero, Brad was left wallowing in dreamer Bunyan's Sea of Despond. *None of them will do, not a single one.*

*Single.*

*Combination? Several heroes, each using his or her special Word-given talent?*

His mind beating was interrupted by song.

> "Who doth ambition shun,
> And loves to live i' the sun,

Seeking the food he eats,
And pleas'd with what he gets.
Come hither, come hither, come hither!"

Brad's breath caught; he froze. Then, drawn by the happy sound of male voices singing one of his fondest lyrics, he moved through the oaks until he came to a glade where wood smoke sifted up from a fire where an animal like a hind roasted over a spit.

" 'Act II. Scene I—The Forest of Arden.' " Brad gulped. " 'Enter DUKE Senior, Amiens, and other Lords, in the dress of Foresters . . .' "

A lad in a medieval doublet and hose put by his lute. The Duke said, "Now, my co-mates and brothers in exile, Hath not old custom made this life more sweet than that of painted pomp? Are not these woods more free from peril than the envious court? I have asked you these things oft, here around our bountiful fire, in this our newfound home. And is not your answer a gladsome 'Aye! Here we are content!' Speak it again, I pray thee, gentle comrades of Arden!"

They spoke the words obediently, but Brad thought much of the spirit had gone out of them from repetition. There were undercurrents of bewilderment and with some the words came grudgingly.

"Melancholy Jaques, come!" the Duke protested. "You were silent and your eyes turned away! What have you to say?"

"What can I say but this, my Lord: All the world's a stage, And all the men and women merely players; They have their exits and their entrances; And one man in his time plays many parts . . ."

Brad stood still, breathless, while the majestic words rolled out; they came not from an actor this time, but a reality, thanks to the devices of a mind that had no idea what it was doing.

The Word rolled on to the end of Jaques' primary speech. There was a heavy silence around the fire. Brad only moved when a hand reached out from behind an oak trunk and shook his arm. He jumped back.

The noble in forest-green smiled.

"Jove, Jove, who have we here? A man for the greenwood life, I'll be bound! But what are you doing, lurking out here like a wolf? Come, bowman, join our beloved Duke and his comrades in exile! It shall be my pleasure to introduce you to each one, all nobly born, I assure you."

Brad stared at the man in the homespun doublet and cloak and the jaunty, feathered cap, who had a graying beard.

"I—I know them all."

"Dost, indeed? Then you must be Orlando, banished as well by the foul usurper, Frederick! Welcome. Trice welcome to the Forest of Arden! But where is your aged servant, the excellent Adam?

"Still locked in the Word, I expect."

The look he received was critical. "Methinks thou doth jest, in a manner that likes me not. But come, stranger! Tarry not on the fringes of our greenwood bounty like John-O-Dreams!"

His arm went companionably around his shoulder and he led him to the fire.

Amiens was singing again, plucking the strings of his lute. Now his song accentuated the hidden sadness of their banishment, and what Brad read on their faces was the typical, unspoken confusion of men who had been snatched preemptively from the Word, who found the world about them awry and different than it ought to be. Their banishment was from somewhere quite different than medieval France.

"Blow, blow, thou winter wind,
Thou art not so unkind
As man's ingratitude;
Thy tooth is not so keen,
Because thou are not seen—"

"Hold! Hold thy doleful verses, young Amiens, pray! See what I have found in the forest and brought to you, Duke: Orlando, son of Sir Rowland de Bois, and no other! Welcome the lad hither and thou, Jaques, as well. He is your own flesh, is he not?"

Jaques stroked his beard and gave his long, sad face a

cock. But the Duke rose and took Brad's hand warmly.

"Welcome, Orlando! We have awaited your coming as it was named in the Word, discussing it amongst ourselves and pondering the when of it. We love this day, for it is only second to that other great day yet to come, when my brother Frederick, hearing how that every day men of great worth have resorted to this forest, will address a mighty force here on foot with the purpose of taking me—"

"I must tell it, Sire!" Jaques cried. "Remember the Word!"

"Aye, tell it, then."

Jaques stood up and gave his cloak a wide theatrical sweep.

"—purposely to take his brother here, and put him to the sword: And to the skirts of this wild wood he came; Where, meeting with an old religious man who—by the way, Orlando, if you are he, did you perchance see such a wonderously wise, old religious mystic in your journey? One who could work such a miracle as to convert the Duke's brother from his wicked course?"

"As a matter of fact," Brad said, "I do know such a man. But I doubt if Frederick will ever meet him."

"Why not? It is True Word that he must meet him! What is this religious ancient's name?"

"Tsung. High Lama of Shamure."

"What heathen nonsense is this?"

There were murmurs of discomfort and a falling away from Brad, as if he had committed some grave crime. Brad sighed, remembering how it had been the same with Infadoos, Zartan and all the others. Since they were creatures born from the Word, it would be pulling teeth to wrench them away from what to them was greater than gospel. Yet he was sure that he must *blend* the Words, use bits of this one and that. He had to convince the Duke and his followers of the truth and remove them from the domination of the Word as he had removed Tsung and, through him, Tsung's men.

He needed all the help he could get. Tsung and those who walked with him, fired by the new, glorious dream of building their own Shamure on the high cliff, would all fight the Wizard. But Brad needed more. He could not pos-

sibly cover the wide area which the book people had roamed by himself, to recruit more fighters. Here was a noble handful who could help, *if* he could persuade them of the need.

*I must be careful, though, stick to the script as much as possible, artfully lead them onto new paths, give them new motivations which seemed to be only variations of the Word. For all their nobility of face and form, for all the splendid lines their creator had given them to speak, they're rather naïve, actually. Their day in the Word had been a simple one, a day of swash and sword. It's no good bringing in super-galactic menaces to confuse them more than they are already.*

*Careful . . .*

"Listen, my excellent comrades," Brad began slowly, trying as hard as he could to keep both the idiom and the sense of his words acceptable to them. "The false Duke, your brother, has enlisted the aid of a foul demon. This demon dwells within a wondrous castle in the shape of half an egg. Before any of you here can be restored to the lands and holdings which are rightfully yours this demon must be destroyed!"

"But the religious mystic!" the Duke protested. "You have seen this man! Can he not perform his duty in the Word and convert my brother Frederick? Can he not"—he winced over the alien ideas—"Can he not exorcise this foul demon?"

"Demons! Heathen mystics!" Jaques snorted. "What Wordless nonsense is this!"

" 'There are more things in heaven and earth,' good Jaques," Brad quoted evenly, " 'than are dreamt of in your philosphy.' "

The Duke scowled across the fire as he began to pace. "Truly, this doth sound like Word, 'though it be not. How say you, Orlando?"

"This is not my brother Orlando," Jaques said with sour emphasis.

"Art certain of this?"

"Do I not know my own younger brother!"

The Duke wagged his bearded head, screwing up his benevolent face into a ponderous knot.

"If I am not Orlando, which indeed I am not," Brad said softly, "then you must admit that there are other Words, and there is the possibility of variations in the True Word."

The Duke worried his peppery beard. "I have seen things here in the forest which I do not truly deem to be of the Word. We wait and wait but the Word proves itself not."

"Aye, good Duke," trebled Amiens. "For an example, where are the wild winds my songs tell us of? Where are the snows? We live here in the forest we discovered after our—our banishment and we love it dearly. Yet I, who see it with an artist's sharp eyes, would not call it True Word!"

Brad was gratified at the solemn nods and significant murmurs which followed. He was making progress.

"But *demons!*" Jaques exclaimed scornfully. "This is too much!"

"You must believe it when you see the Egg Castle for yourself," Brad said. "But before that happens, we must recruit all the help we can find in this fair land, to battle the fiend. Each one of you must help in the recruiting; and there is no time to waste! Who knows when the fearful monster in the Egg Castle will decide to strike?"

16

It was several days later when he stumbled weak-legged and hungry back into the camp. Harriet ran to meet him. Brad put his arm around her with a grin, as much to hold himself up as anything else.

"Where were you?" she begged. "We've been worried to death about you."

"I—I've been hunting, like I said. Never mind. What's been going on? Any sign of the Wizard?"

Harriet shook her head, leading him to a seat by the evening fire, where Dr. Lloyd was mumbling over a wild-rice cake and smiling inanely. He wagged his pate and his gnawed cake at Brad.

"Naughty, naughty!"

Brad gave the physicist a sour glance; but when Harriet touched his arm, he revised it into a fast little smile and a flick of the hunched shoulder in passing. Since he was very tired, he wasn't quite able to falsify old grievances such as the deaths of the astronauts at Project Yonder, nor the theft and crash of his SS. *And something else? Something not quite kosher behind those vague, lackluster eyes?*

Harriet hurried to bring Brad food.

"What's he mean, 'naughty, naughty'?"

"Just how much you worried us. He's heard me talking about you all these days you were gone. I'm afraid I did quite a lot of it; I was so scared, Brad! Where—"

He brushed off her questions, eyeing her father over the rim of his wooden trencher, held up close the better to wolf his food.

"Are you sure that's it?"

"What do you mean?"

"Nothing. No questions, don't ask me any questions just now."

"You're tired to the bone, aren't you? What you need is sleep; we can talk tomorrow." She moved back into the shadow. "I'll plump up your bough bed. I—I gave Father your sleeping bag. Okay?"

Brad nodded absently.

"Where's Tsung?"

"I don't know," Harriet called. "He and the others have been busy as beavers. Wait'll you see how much they've got done. Tsung's been sleeping with his men down in the huts near their work. Come, your bed's all ready, Master!"

Brad finished eating and crawled on all fours to the rear of the cave. He was so weary from three days without sleep that he ignored her silent figure entirely, until, just before the curtain of sleep rolled down, he felt her hand on his forehead. It was cool and pleasant when he took hold of it and drew it across his lips.

"Brad, please tell me—"

"No questions, baby. Tomorrow."

The next day seemed to come the next minute. It was as though Harriet had never left him when she shook him gently but urgently. In any case he'd been too beat to do anything about it if she had stayed.

"Brad, something's wrong!"

His quick glance around showed him everything that was in their camp, with added housewifely touches Harriet had provided during his absense. There was the morning cooking fire, the skyline of misty forest and Dr. Lloyd still senilely munching, as if he had never stopped, sopping his cake in bark tea.

"Your father!"

"Brad! How can you say—no! It's Tsung! Look!"

The lama's tall figure, cowled against the driving mist, was moving with swift purpose toward the cave. Behind him came the others. Their wide, blunt faces appeared grimly inimical as they followed Tsung up the path in a serpentine line. They carried machetes and clubs, as they had once before.

Brad moved down to meet them.

"Not again, Tsung!"

The parchment brown face attempted a smile.

"I'm afraid so."

"You mean the Wizard's got hold of your mind again? I thought you decided that if you wouldn't let him control you, he couldn't."

"I was wrong." Tsung's face was a dry mask but somewhere in his slanted eyes was an apology. "The Mind is too vast. It has me, I'm afraid. One part of me abhors it, but the part which controls my physical movements is helpless. To this extent I was right." He gestured toward his men. "In any case, my poor countrymen are completely taken over. As you see, they are quite capable of killing you both if you do not do what The Mind tells us you must do."

"Both? What about him?" Brad nodded at Dr. Lloyd.

"He is—"

"Already controlled?" Brad finished brusquely.

Tsung nodded.

"I thought so. Whatever mind the accident left him with, it's the Wizard's tool. He plays idiot, but he's really watching every move we make, reporting. He's their bug."

Tsung sighed. Harriet started to run to her father. The sudden change in him, the penetration of his eyes and the firming of his facial expression, stopped her with a cry.

"It doesn't matter any more, Harriet," Brad told her. "Don't you see? Dr. Lloyd didn't really survive the ship crash. That's a skillful patch-up of his body, but nothing else. I don't quite know how I guessed it but I did. You wouldn't, of course; you wanted what you'd come so far to find too badly." He turned to Tsung. "Well? Now what, the dome?"

Tsung nodded.


Again Tsung and his followers were left on the bowl's rim to await the Wizard's pleasure. Brad thought, while he and Harriet were moving hand in hand to the place of the violet haze, that this move expressed sublime confidence in The Mind's power over its creatures. Was it overconfidence, perhaps? Brad was far from ready to rely on such tenuous threads of hope. There were too many unformed ideas churning in his head, too many wild emotional torrents caused by too much exposure to too many heroes out of too many Words.

Dr. Lloyd's mind contact had told the Wizard all about Tsung and his high resolves. The Wizard, by re-controlling Tsung and his less spiritual followers, had convinced himself that the book creatures were incapable of true resistance. Brad had other hopes, but they were thin and nebulous. He was in a sweat.


They were inside the cell again, facing Dorothy's jolly, little Wizard.

"Well, Dorothy? Well, Scarecrow?"

The scorn the alien had borrowed from the character it had assumed was lively but spurious. The mind behind it had virtually no emotion, and that was the basis of Brad's

faint hope. What The Mind could not understand or tolerate was still the best weapon against it.

"You can drop the charade, Wizard," Brad said.

The figure on the throne put its finger to its nose and chuckled.

"You say drop the charade, suggesting that we call you by your correct names, yet you call *me* Wizard! Is that not a contradiction? Shall we not show some semblance of uniformity, logic?"

"You didn't show much logic about the way you grabbed people out of my books. Why didn't you at least follow through with one group, say Dickens, Dumas, or Shakespeare?"

The Wizard frowned. He gave his wand an airy wave.

"These creatures were casual experiments. We had nothing but the books to go on, so we took a few from each. There is a logic to our method which you have no way of knowing. When we seed a selective planet we take care not to draw too many primitives from one particular tribe or area. They must not become too intelligent too fast; divergence does the trick. Then we can shape them to suit ourselves."

"But you don't shape them. You leave them to their own evolutionary devices until they've ripened to your uses, right?"

The Wizard's eyes twinkled.

"But this is marvelous! You do have a brain in that preposterous body! When I say we shape them I mean, of course, that we extrapolate their potential through a hundred generations and choose those which will have the raw life-force treatment and which will not. It's all a matter of selection. As you say, we *do* bring them into being, using our raw life-force and the raw materials of the seed planet, carefully choosing those creatures which—"

He chortled cheerfully, quite as if he actually were spelling out ABC's to a little girl from Kansas and a straw-headed scarecrow. To The Mind, Brad and Harriet's level of intelligence seemed only slightly higher.

This was its logical thought.

*Because of their emotion-sensitive minds.* And yet, Brad told himself for the hundredth time, *The Mind, having long*

*ago dropped emotion in favor of pure logic, had no way of knowing that these very quixotic sensitivites of human nature contained worlds of potential power of which they knew nothing.*

*Have not humans, good or bad, swayed millions by pure emotion?* It was within such combined forces that Brad's hope was anchored.

But it was not enough.

True, there were other areas to consider, mystical areas, such as Tsung and his lamas exemplified. The Christs and the Buddhas of ancient Earth had not worked their world-shaking power merely by emotionalism. There was more; it was something elusive, nameless, cosmic. These metaphysical areas within nature and the stars were tapped *through emotion*. Certainly not through logic, for they were not logical.

It was true that Brad's galaxy, under Star Control, had lost most of this ancient mysticism and white magic. *But here on Virgo it lives again within the hearts and souls of the Word people.* The great dreamers who had created the Words and the followers of the Words had believed in wonder. They had had to believe in wonder, else they could never have fashioned such sublime dream-seeds as now walked the small planet.

Their creatures lived, by the Wizard's casual error.

Brad felt hope flame through him.

The Wizard must have felt it, too.

"Of course, before we remove ourselves from this planet we shall eliminate them all. Mistakes like this do happen; not often, but they do happen."

Harriet wailed, "Not all of them! They can't hurt you! How can they?"

"They are mistakes; mistakes must be expunged. I'm sure that your Star Control feels the same way."

"Yes!" Harriet blurted. "They have no more conscience than you do about destroying races of primitives who happen to disagree with SC about what is progress and what isn't." She shook Brad's arm. "Don't you see now what you've been working for all your life? Don't you see? What SC is moving toward, as fast as it can is—*him!*" She flung an accusing finger at the Wizard.

"Is this the time for love-dove polemics, when a worldful of heroes is about to be snuffed out by alien invader?"

"I couldn't help it," Harriet choked. "These things pop out. I guess this will show you how wrong you were!"

"How wrong I was! I'm to blame for every misjudgment SC ever made, of course—personally!"

"I didn't mean that," Harriet said. "But I had to point out how much Star Control is just like this—this—"

"Say anything you wish my dear," the Wizard chuckled. "To us it is a compliment. This ranting and raving between you indicates how incredibly primitive you are. Lack of unified behavior and all the seething emotionalism it engenders points up how ridiculously simple it will be for The Mind to take you all over, when the time comes." The chubby figure bowed blandly. "Thank you, my dear. Thank you for telling us all about your Star Control and its fumbling attempts to bring order out of intellectual chaos. It is just such bits of information which The Mind uses in its grand sweep across the stars. Thank you, Dorothy!"

"Thank you," Brad iterated glumly, "Dorothy!"

"Brad, I'm sorry!"

"Forget it." He turned to the Wizard. "You mentioned something about life-force? Something you carry with you in your cell and combine with raw materials from the planet to be seeded. Would you mind relieving my curiosity by telling me just exactly what form this—"

"Sorry, Scarecrow, there is no time. Our task was to draw out a bit more knowledge about what lies beyond this small star on the doorstep of your galaxy. We have, I think, gleaned quite enough, as much from your behavior as from any precise information you have given us. In any case, the energy drain has been far more than we have ever expended before; we must return to Yonder at once. But first," the Wizard waved his wand significantly, "we must clean up the mess, expunge our grievous errors." Unlike yourselves, we are a tidy race; we never leave debris and pollution behind us on the worlds we visit."

"You mean kill us!"

"Exactly; I prefer expunge. There is no residuum for the next visitor here to mull over."

98

Harriet clutched Brad's arm.

"Brad! What can we do?"

The Wizard answered her with a chuckle.

"Nothing, nothing at all. Goodbye, Dorothy. Goodbye, Scarecrow."

## 17

*Delay. Delay tactics.* That was the fine edge of Brad's hope. *Our hope and all those wonderful book-people out there—bemused yet rich with high courage and sense of adventure. Yes, we're emotional. Emotion is the breath of our lives: joy in living, reckless laughter in the face of peril, love, burning hate. The book people are all the hopes and dreams those put-upon ancients had hoped and dreamed. All the fine sense of wonder, the awe, the fantastic glory. The revelings in conscious, sensate existence!*

*Die? How can they die! Burn the books if you must, destroy their shells, but the dreams will arise again from the ashes!*

Brad watched the Wizard shimmer and fade.

"Wait!"

His urgency brough the Wizard back.

The chubby little face grimaced.

"There is no time; the link is already weak from so much energy expended. We must waste considerably more when we expunge you two and the mistakes."

"Sorry about that. But—won't you let me die with just a fragment of my curiosity satisfied? I mean, we of Star Control never dreamed of a race as—as evolved as The Mind! Just a couple of very small answers—*please?*"

The Wizard wagged and teetered. Never had the cell encountered anything quite so passionate. It was stimulating

and, in a way, refreshing. *So different from the usual animal types. This absurd little scarecrow of a* soi-disant *intellectual being is so very anxious. Bare inches from the effort which will sweep him and the other blunders into oblivion, what can it matter? In its own way, the whole experiment, mistakes and all, has provided The Mind with new fields of thought. Next time . . .*

"Very well. Two questions. No more. Hurry!"

Brad took a deep breath.

"The life-stuff you bring to your seed-planets, what is it?"

The Wizard chuckled.

"No you don't, Scarecrow. It would take me days to even attempt to explain it. Suffice to say that it is a miracle of our chemical genius; we grow it artifically from the genetic building-blocks from which all life evolves."

"Chemical! Artificial! Yet I'd swear that Zartan and Infadoos and the Duke—and above all, Tsung—are not merely tools!" Brad took another prodigious breath, then let it out in a low long whistle of discovery. "It's what you take from the planet itself, the raw materials *and something else besides*, that makes the difference! I think I understand about the raw materials. They're what each individual planet will ultimately use itself in its natural evolutionary processes in the development of thinkers and builders. But there's got to be something else! What? What? *What?*"

"It varies," the Wizard chuckled, putting his finger to his nose craftily. "This star is, we think, unique. There was already a kind of important life here, a microscopic kind of life that did more than just permit us to stamp out book people like cardboard, something that actually *involved* itself with our experiments . . ."

"The emerald halos!" Brad yelled. "Harriet! Don't you see? The book people aren't rubber stamps! Virgo's microscopic symbiotes were just itching for full-blown intelligent life to come along. Tsung was so right; his mystic's intuition told him that the planet itself had provided the real essence of his thinking being. The halos! Before they'd only had low-level life. The Mind provided them with much more and—hurry, Harriet, hurry! *Tell Tsung! Tell the Duke!*"

Harriet stared openmouthed, then she nodded.

"You mean—what brought me to Father."

"Yes, use every bit of ESP you've got in that cute little mind of yours and say, '*Now*, heroes! now!'"

They were in the place again, but the purplish mist was gone. The cell in the dome had withdrawn the last bit of its mind energy in its urgent need to depart from Virgo.

That they stood there alive was a miracle, a major miracle. But it was not quite as overwhelming as the miracle Brad saw when he was able to turn and blink up at the rim of the low hill.

*They* were up there, as many of them as Brad and the Duke and the Duke's men had been able to find in three days, and as many more as those recruited had been able to add to their numbers since.

They made a gorgeous splash of color and motion and excitement on the bright horizon, living shadows from so many of Earth's most picturesque eras: sword wielders, spearmen, spacemen with awkward, primitive ray-guns, splendid savages, plumed gallants, Mississippi urchins with bare feet, droll little dance-hoppers, Infadoos and his warriors, Zartan with his pachyderms trumpeting in the distance, Deena and her refound friends, and the three swashbucklers of the drunken camp.

In the center, holding their single-minded attention and directing their emotion-charged thought down on the dome, was Tsung.

"What are they doing?" Harriet cried.

"Focusing all their mind and soul power on the cell, stopping it from going back, breaking the mind-link. Come on!"

He grabbed hold of her hand and ran toward the flamboyant crowd atop the rise.

"You!" Harriet panted. "You located them when you were off 'hunting' and prepared them for this!"

"With an assist from Dukes and lute players, and especially from Tsung."

"But you didn't tell Tsung anything about this! I'd have heard you and so would my—"

"That's why I couldn't. Luckily Tsung understood *without*

me having to tell him. Our lama's a canny one, all right; that mystic's intuition of his made the barest hint a revelation. When the Duke and all the others showed up he knew what they were there for; he was only waiting for my signal, which *you* gave him just in time. So you see, darling," Brad said, "we all did our bit."

They soon reached Tsung, who, like all the others, continued to be grimly preoccupied with the destruction of the dome.

"Look, Brad!"

"I'm looking," Brad whispered. "We're out of it, of course. It's their emerald halos, their symbiotes; the microscopic hangers-on and helpers don't want to lose the miracle The Mind's blundering gave them. See how they're gathering in one seething, bright cloud over the heroes' heads! They're in this thing, too!"

"But will it work? Will it be enough?"

"Think positive, like the ancient dreamers who started all this. They've got to do it. The mind-link was weak to begin with; overuse of the cell's permissable supply of energy weakened it further; and now—"

He stared down at the dome. Although it had once seemed so inert, so imperturbable, so smug, it glowed with white, atomic fires. It glowed and pulsed, as the living thing within it flailed its being against the walls of its shell in a vain effort to lift and soar across the stars without the necessary link with The Mind.

It fought; it seethed; it expended every iota of its self-contained energy.

"It's cracking open!" Harriet cried. "Like an eggshell!"

Thus, without the whole Mind to help it, the cell spilled out in a wave of gaseous putrefaction and died.

The exultant yell that roared up into the bright stars above Virgo had many voices, jubilant, heroic voices, shouting defiance to Fate itself. These were impossible creatures, born out of dreams, and if *that* could happen, then no Mind, however logical and vast, could subdue or destroy them.

Tsung alone was silent. Reverently silent, he shed tears of happiness, his lips trembling prayers to his gods.

"Now," Harriet murmured, "I suppose we must go back."

"Back to Star Control and all that? Yes, I suppose we must. It's our obvious duty to go back and warn SC of what lies out Yonder."

"Brad, I was thinking . . ."

"Don't tell me, let me guess. You were thinking that I know all these splendid chaps and gals—from the Words and that you'd like to get to know some of them, too, before we refuel your ship and take off."

"In a way. Also—"

"Sure, I'm way ahead of you." Brad brushed a kiss across her nearest ear. "You were thinking that it would be nice of us to help Tsung, who after all saved our lives, to finish building Shamure— Maybe add our own touches, make it a sort of shrine of inspiration for all the heroes."

"And for us, too." Harriet blinked at the whirling bits of green fire that were returning to their individual halos around each heroic head, even the elephant's heads. "I was wondering, Brad. Do you really think you and I will ever rate happy little armies of symbiotes like those?"

Brad grinned.

"Shall we stick around and find out?"

**ANDRE NORTON novels available**

from Ace Books include:

| | |
|---|---|
| 05160 — 50¢ | THE BEAST MASTER |
| 09265 — 50¢ | CATSEYE |
| 12310 — 40¢ | THE CROSSROADS OF TIME |
| 13990 — 50¢ | DAYBREAK—2250 A.D. |
| 35420 — 40¢ | HUON OF THE HORN |
| 41550 — 40¢ | JUDGMENT ON JANUS |
| 49235 — 50¢ | LORD OF THUNDER |
| 47160 — 45¢ | THE LAST PLANET |
| 54100 — 50¢ | MOON OF THREE RINGS |
| 57750 — 40¢ | NIGHT OF MASKS |
| 63410 — 60¢ | OPERATION TIME SEARCH |
| 63820 — 40¢ | ORDEAL IN OTHERWHERE |
| 66830 — 40¢ | PLAGUE SHIP |
| 69680 — 50¢ | QUEST CROSSTIME |
| 74980 — 40¢ | SARGASSO OF SPACE |
| 75990 — 50¢ | SHADOW HAWK |
| 76800 — 40¢ | THE SIOUX SPACEMAN |
| 78430 — 45¢ | THE STARS ARE OURS |
| 78010 — 45¢ | STAR BORN |
| 78070 — 45¢ | STAR GATE |
| 14230 — 45¢ | THE DEFIANT AGENTS |
| 27225 — 40¢ | GALACTIC DERELICT |
| 81250 — 40¢ | THE TIME TRADERS |
| 43670 — 45¢ | KEY OUT OF TIME |
| 78130 — 50¢ | STAR GUARD |
| 78190 — 50¢ | STAR HUNTER & VOODOO PLANET |
| 78740 — 40¢ | STORM OVER WARLOCK |
| 86320 — 50¢ | VICTORY ON JANUS |
| 92550 — 50¢ | THE X FACTOR |